GONE UNNOTICED

(A Kate Reid Novel)

By Robin Mahle

Published by HARP House Publishing
August, 2015 (1st edition)

Mahle, Robin
Gone Unnoticed

ISBN- 978-0-9966830-0-5 (trade back)
ISBN-10: 0996683003 (trade back)

Cover design: LLPix Photography, www.llpix.com Laura Wright LaRoche

Editor: Hercules Editing and Consulting Services www.bzhercules.com

ONE

The door began to buckle under the weight of the master key, a heavy metal battering ram intended to tear it from its hinges. The thieves were somewhere inside, behind that door, inside the shop's storage area. Kate was positioned next to her partner, gun drawn and donning full tactical gear—black flak jacket, and a bulky helmet that hindered her vision. A horse wearing blinders sprang to mind. Another thud from the key sent wooden splinters flying and the door finally gave way.

Will Caison was the muscle behind the key and he lowered the metal cylinder to the ground and drew his weapon. The two stepped over the threshold, walking around the fallen door.

A flip of the light switch at Kate's hands—nothing. "Power's been cut," she whispered.

The noonday light disbursed through the storefront window and cast enough grey light along the back corridor to guide them.

Will raised a hand at the sound of hushed voices arising in the distance. He looked to Kate and pointed a black-gloved finger in that direction. Cautious steps came from each as they moved forward, prepared for a confrontation.

Kate's breath hung inside her helmet, and the acrylic shield fogged momentarily before clearing again. The weight of her gear, a hefty addition to her slight frame, made stealthy movements all the more difficult. That familiar claustrophobic feeling settled over her and she became short of breath. This was the third time operating inside the gear and it hadn't gotten any easier. Her partner appeared to move with ease and Kate was determined to keep up.

Will raised his hand again, signaling a cease in their movements. He turned to the right and peered inside a darkened room; an office or perhaps a second, smaller storage area. Again, he pointed his finger in that direction and took the lead.

Their covert movements, however, did little to disguise their arrival. Gunfire erupted, lighting up the dim room and illuminating the occupants as they scattered to shield themselves from the onslaught.

"Take cover!" Will found shelter behind a masonry column.

Out of the corner of her eye, Kate caught sight of movement. Raising her weapon, she took aim at one of the suspects, but it was too late. A laser landed on her chest and triggered the light embedded in her jacket. She died a simulated death.

The fluorescent lights above lit up instantly and the training exercise was over.

Will raised his face shield. "I got hit too." He pointed to the flashing red light on his vest.

A voice boomed over the loudspeaker, "Reset!"

Kate pulled off her helmet. "Goddamn it!"

"Can't win 'em all. Better luck next time." The actor hired to portray one of the criminals approached and patted Kate on the back before leaving the room.

The inclination to punch the guy square in the jaw briefly consumed her, but the moment passed, and it was hardly the actor's fault. She'd failed the test and it wasn't the first time.

Kate's academic scores were near the top of her class, but if she didn't pass this segment of her training, there wasn't much point in going any further. It had been ten weeks since she'd entered the FBI training program at Quantico and she had only reached the halfway mark.

The place called Hogan's Alley, an advanced training facility that offered these types of drills to not only FBI trainees, but DEA trainees and other law enforcement, was a fictitious replica of Main Street, America. Kate carried her helmet beneath her arm and stepped off the curb onto one of the streets in this fabricated town. Today's training scenario involved the robbing of the town's bank where the suspects fled and hunkered down inside the sundries shop that now needed a new door. And so far, Kate had failed the three exercises in which she'd taken part, each time ending with the flashing light on her chest telling her that she'd just died. Good thing it was only make-believe.

"You'll get 'em next time." An agent whose job it was to help train the NATs, or new agents-in-training, approached Kate and offered words of encouragement.

She smiled in response and, while the words were appreciated, they just made her feel worse. And it was only a matter of time before her mentor and friend, Supervisory Special Agent Nick Scarborough, would reach out to offer consolation. He followed her training closely and had been a welcomed sounding board for her, but his help could only do so much. The success or failure at the Academy rested solely on her shoulders. And she'd begun to question her abilities.

Will pulled the straps off of his vest as he caught up to Kate, who was still standing in the street. "You want to grab some lunch before heading to class?" He looked out among the passersby, hands at his waist, but did not look her in the eyes, instead joining in her surveillance.

"Sure." An unenthusiastic reply that alluded to her current "woe is me" mood.

The functioning deli, only a block away and still inside Hogan's Alley, was where many trainees stopped for a quick bite before moving on to other aspects of their training.

"Can I have a Reuben, please?" Kate stood at the counter, perusing the deli's limited offerings. "And a diet Coke."

"I'll take a ham and Swiss on sourdough and a Coke," Will said.

A small table against the front window offered a view of the makeshift town and was the desired location from which to enjoy the likely unhealthy, but delicious-looking sandwich. She stared out among the many purposeful people heading in all directions and the idea came upon her. Was this all within her reach? Even her firearms training was above par, but her reaction times during the tactical drills were appalling. She'd expected that to have been the easy part. There'd been enough times when her life had *actually* been in danger and she'd figured a way out. This should have been a breeze, but it was her nerves, frayed over these incidents, that still clouded her judgment and prevented the successful completion of the scenarios.

Will pulled out his chair and brought Kate's attention back to the moment. She turned to see him place his tray on the table. "Kate. Come on. You know they're not going to kick you out for this alone. Hell, I think you've probably got the best academic scores out of all of us. Don't let it get to you, okay?"

He was young, twenty-seven. Younger than Kate, although not by much. Her thirtieth had come and gone with little fanfare. That was shortly before the move to Virginia and the new life she'd hoped to start—was waiting to start. Will had come right out of the military, having served in Iraq, and now his only goal was to work in the FBI's Counterterrorism Unit. His tour in the still war-torn country was likely the reason for his success in Hogan's Alley.

Most of her classmates had advanced degrees, were in previous law enforcement, or had served in the military. So here comes Kate Reid; the girl who escaped, the woman who misfortune seemed to follow. They all suspected she got into the program because of her friendship with the veteran Agent Scarborough—and because of previous media attention. She went through the same rigorous screening process they had, but that didn't seem to hold much water, so far as she could tell. And while they did sympathize to a degree with her past, that sympathy had begun to wane after she'd failed her first two case exercises. Now with number three having been woefully unsuccessful, she could almost hear the "I told you sos."

Consequently as she looked into the eyes of this eager, younger man, who was undeniably handsome – although those types of assessments meant little to her at this point in time – she wondered if she would be able to survive this as she had so many other challenges in her life. "I don't know, Will. It shouldn't be this hard. It isn't for you."

"It's supposed to be this hard. That's why only the best make it through. You know the old saying 'if it was easy...' And give yourself some credit here. You're kicking my ass in the classroom and, frankly, you can hold your own on the target range too. So, don't be too quick to dismiss your abilities. It'll happen, it'll click for you."

"I guess I'll find out soon enough." The Rueben was piled high with corned beef, but Kate managed a bite of it anyway. They didn't have much time before they had to be back in the classroom and so she didn't bother to continue with the circular discussion of her skills. Time would tell.

» » »

Kate dropped her keys onto the small foyer table as she walked inside the home she'd been renting since her arrival in Virginia nearly four months ago. Nick had helped her to find this house in Woodbridge. It was a short distance to the base and he lived only ten minutes away. She figured that was the real reason why he steered her to this place. Someone was always trying to look out for her, but Kate suspected he wanted to be close out of guilt. Nick had nothing to do with Marshall's death, but she knew he felt responsible and had taken it upon himself to look after her, just as Marshall would have.

She'd reached the point in her training where she'd been allowed home on the weekends and was glad Saturday had arrived. Most of the day was spent on base—they still had to train, even on Saturdays, but Kate needed to sleep in her own bed tonight, away from the questions her roommate would hurl at her regarding Hogan's Alley. During the week, she slept in a dormitory on campus. Jocelyn Munoz was her roommate and Kate liked her, but still felt inferior to her due to the woman's background. She was around Kate's age, thirtyish, and had come from the New York City Police Department. She had worked in white-collar crimes and wanted to do the same for the Bureau. Kate made an effort to get to know her better, but Jocelyn had a family—a husband and two young kids. And so any free time they'd had would find Jocelyn on the train back home to New York to be with her family.

Kate pushed off her tennis shoes and dropped her handbag onto the table before walking in sock feet towards the kitchen. It was late, too late to eat dinner, and she certainly didn't have the energy to cook. Cooking was never her strong suit anyway and since she lived alone, she never saw much point in cooking for one.

The refrigerator door rattled when Kate pulled on its handle. Too many bottles, mostly white wine, but a leftover beer or two shifted inside as well. An opened bottle of chardonnay waited for her inside. Hardly a single glass remained, but pouring what was left, she then opened a new bottle and filled it the rest of the way.

A large sip of the chilled buttery goodness washed down her pallet and the flavor soothed her nerves. Now she could settle in for the night and retreated to her bedroom to pull on her sweats and try to relax before heading off to bed. She returned to the living room, where her wine waited on the side table next to the couch. A brief glance at her cell phone that rested next to it told her she'd missed a call from her dutiful friend, Nick. "Sorry, Nick. I'll call you back tomorrow," she said before returning it to the table.

Some time had passed, although she was unsure exactly how much, but Kate was ready to turn in. A deep breath filled her lungs as she pushed herself up and a momentary vision of a younger, more naïve Katie Reid surfaced in her mind's eye. She was standing in a parking lot, explaining to Marshall, then only known to her as Detective Avery, that she was interested in cold case research. It felt like a lifetime ago, but it was instantly recalled as if it had happened yesterday and for seemingly no apparent reason. It was a common occurrence, welcomed at first, until awareness set in and she remembered he was gone. The faint smile quickly faded from her lips when a knock sounded on her front door.

"Kate, it's Nick," the muffled voice strained through the door.

She closed her eyes, annoyed by the disruption, but half-expecting he would show up. She shuffled to the door, turned the deadbolt, and pulled it open. "Nick? What a surprise." She stepped aside.

"Come on now." Nick began to walk in. "I knew you weren't going to answer your phone and so I figured I'd just stop by."

Kate extended her hand towards the living room. "Have a seat. Can I get you a drink? Water, a beer?"

Nick hoisted his pants and dropped onto the couch. "No thanks. I can see you're ready for bed and so I won't stay long." On her return, he continued, "Why didn't you answer?"

But before she had a chance to reply, he simply raised his hand. "Forget it. I know why, however, I can tell you that if you had, I wouldn't be here now when you so clearly do not want me to be."

"It's not that. It's just—are you here to tell me everything's going to be fine? Don't bother, okay? I'm all right. I'll manage." She tipped the wine glass to her lips.

"I have no doubt about that, but I'm actually here on another matter and if you'd have answered your phone, you would have known that."

Now he was just trying to make her feel bad. "Sorry, Nick. I was just tired and didn't feel up to chatting. What is it?"

"I talked to Agent Hawes about your test scores."

Supervisory Special Agent Hawes was one of her instructors and, while that wasn't the unsettling part, what seemed to be coming, she feared, was a move to pull her from the program. "What's going on? Is this because of what happened today?"

"Look, I'm not gonna lie to you, your operational training is critical. That being said, as you're only halfway through the program, they are still holding out hope, as am I, that you will find your footing. What's important here is the real reason why I needed to talk to you."

"And that is?" She took another drink.

"I'm going to be conducting some training—a presentation—at the BAU facility and I'd like you take part."

The Behavioral Analysis Unit was headquartered on the base and often conducted training for those new agents whose goal it was to eventually work in that discipline. And it was Kate's ultimate goal.

"Of course. I wouldn't hesitate, so why the urgent need to speak to me about it tonight?"

"Because we're going to present a case that you are already extremely familiar with."

There was that disconcerting feeling again. "And that would be?"

"Hendrickson." Nick took pause. "Kate, that case was immensely important. From its beginnings when you were young, and then what happened twenty-plus years later; well, it's perfect for analysis. And, as we have a first-hand account, your knowledge is invaluable."

A sudden flash of Hendrickson's burnt face appeared in her mind. "I see." She began nodding. "No. You're right. It's a good idea. I'd like to be involved." Part of that was true, but she still dealt with the memory of Hendrickson and, while she handled it as well as could be expected, there were times when the flashbacks would get the better of her. But if Nick wanted her to do this, he must have believed it to be a good idea.

"Are you sure? It would win you a lot of points, enough that could possibly make up for any shortcomings and, as you know, the time's come to pick your field offices. You could pretty much write your own ticket here."

At this point in her training, Nick was right. The trainees could select their top five field offices for assignment. She already knew that the D.C. office was where she wanted to go. Nick wanted her there too—with him.

"Yes. I think it would be a good idea," she replied.

Nick had no real idea what Hendrickson had done to her. If he had, the question might not have come up at all. Marshall was the only one who ever knew the whole story. Even her parents hadn't known some of the finer points of the monster's depravity. But she had faced those demons down, hadn't she, peering into the charred remains of the room in which the monster had held her captive as a child. And Nick stood by her while she did. But Hendrickson was gone and she was the one who took him down. Marshall might have fired the shot, but it was Kate who killed Hendrickson—killed the idea of him.

Nick didn't know everything and maybe it was better that way. It would only turn him into another Marshall—a man who felt compelled to protect her from the world. And what good did that do him?

"I know it's a lot to ask. I get that, believe me, but I promise you, the director of the Academy will take notice and this will help with the completion of your training." Nick rose from the couch. "I'd better let you get to bed. You look damn exhausted."

"I am." Kate followed, showing Nick to the door. "So how's Georgia been? I haven't seen her in a while. Is she out of town working a case?" Kate was fond of Georgia and glad that she and Nick were managing to make things work. It seemed to her at first that they were too much alike, both preferring to work on their careers rather than their relationships. But after the Highway Hunter trial, they seemed to be making time for each other.

As she pulled the door open and stood to the side, Nick turned to face her.

He held her gaze. "She's doing well and, yes, she's been away all this week. I'm hoping to see her next week, though." He paused again. "You're sure you're okay with this? Be honest with me."

A smile appeared on her face. He didn't yet know her well enough to appreciate that she had become an expert in false assurances. "Yes. I'm okay."

"Good. Presentation's on Monday morning at ten o'clock. Why don't you meet me in the lecture hall around eight and we'll go over everything. I'll email you the files tomorrow, just so we're on the same page."

A light breeze drifted through the opened door and Kate suddenly became very aware that she was dressed in only a sweatshirt and no pants. Redness settled in her cheeks as she discovered she'd been without pants the entire time. *Oh my God.* She closed her eyes.

"Did you just realize you aren't wearing any pants?" Nick said as he cast his eyes down at her slender legs, which appeared like toothpicks jutting from a giant gray Popsicle.

"Uh, yeah. I guess I'm more tired than I thought."

Nick leaned in and kissed her on the cheek. "Good night, Kate. Get some rest."

"Good night." She closed the door and shook her head all the way back to the couch. "Good grief." Whatever wine had remained in her glass was now gone and she returned it to the kitchen.

Kate walked back to the side table lamp and leaned over to pull its chain. Beneath the lamp was a photo of Marshall and her at her parents' home in Rio Dell. Kate did as always and raised the frame to her lips and, on the image of Marshall, kissed him goodnight.

Exhaustion weighed heavily on her body and she shuffled along on the dark wood floor down the hall. Upon entering her bedroom this time, she'd noticed the window was open, which was unusual because she swore she'd closed it before leaving for work today and hadn't even noticed it when she got changed earlier. Appalled by her own negligence, she walked towards the large window. In the light of day, it offered a beautiful view of the huge hickory trees in her backyard just beyond the lush bluegrass lawn that was a bitch to mow, but looked stunning when it was freshly cut.

When she'd arrived a few months ago, the weather was only beginning to warm and she took to planting flowers in a bed that'd she'd constructed adjacent to the small covered deck out back. She'd gotten the landlady's permission, of course. Mrs. Mitchell was a very kind woman and whenever Kate needed anything done around the house, she'd get her son to stop by and fix it immediately. So, Kate wanted to repay her by planting the beautiful flowers.

And as she stood at the opened window, the scent of those same flowers drifted in with the breeze. It was the lilacs she could smell right now. Their blooms would fall soon enough, so she inhaled the fragrance as deeply as she could before finally closing the window.

As she engaged the lock, her eyes were drawn to the far end of the yard, near one of the trees. She blinked and looked again, waiting. It was a flash of something—a glimmer. Her eyes struggled to focus on the shadowed tree, but whatever it was had vanished.

Kate crawled under the covers and turned off the light on the nightstand. Unable to close her eyes just yet, she stared off into the darkened room. The sounds the house made, a refrigerator that constantly dropped ice, the toilet in the main bathroom that ran – something she'd forgotten to tell Mrs.

Mitchell about – and an attic that seemed to creak and shift along with the settling soils. These were all sounds to which she was only beginning to adjust. This life she'd come to know was so far removed from all that she'd known in San Diego.

The beach and the smell of the sea air—Kate missed it all so much. But slowly, she was getting used to the new place, the new town, and the new job. She had refused to spend the money she'd made off the sale of Marshall's apartment, and so this place was a bit of a stretch, considering she was only an FBI trainee. But that money wasn't hers, even though he'd left it to her, and she didn't feel right spending it. It would make his parting too real, too final. She'd watched his casket sink into the ground that day, but admitting he was gone was something she rarely did.

Instead, to make ends meet, she passed on her morning coffee at the local coffee shop, opted to take lunch on most days, when she didn't have operations training, and refused to upgrade her car, although she suspected it was sorely needed.

Her thoughts were beginning to slow and she closed her eyes and began drifting off. As she succumbed to the weight of sleep, a final thought pierced her mind and it would instead haunt her dreams.

My little Katie.

TWO

The apartment Madlena Jankovic shared with her father and younger sister was far from appealing, but was still nicer than the place they called home back in Serbia. The family had entered the country through means that were considered against the law, but it was easier to get in than most people would think. The Jankovic family hadn't wanted to be illegal immigrants in America; they wanted jobs—good jobs. War and a crippling economy made living in that part of the world much worse than what they now faced as illegals.

Her father had been a plumber at home and now had gone from place to place, working for cash, and it was okay, but it didn't allow for many luxuries for the family. Her sister attended high school, and Madlena had only recently begun to find other means of earning an income. She tried being a nanny, but without references, no one would hire her. Working in a laundromat for a while wasn't bad, but it had closed down. Now Madlena was faced with few options. The money her father earned wasn't enough to make ends meet.

With little in the way of education, not having finished the American equivalent of high school, Madlena decided, just for the interim, to perhaps look at a less desirable alternative. One that would pay for a great many things and would ease the burden placed on her father.

She was pretty—very pretty by most anyone's standards. Slender figure, ample breasts, and a well-rounded backside. Her full lips and pale skin were breathtaking against the backdrop of her black hair. It would be easy money, she thought.

Some of the friends she'd made since coming to America last year had done it, so why couldn't she? They'd managed to get nice apartments and drove decent cars. Right now, Madlena had neither of those things. So maybe she would try it. Just to see what it was like.

That was a month ago and, today, Madlena, although she'd since been "taken under the wing" of a not-so-nice man, owned a full block in one of the seedier sides of town. Sharing her profits wasn't all bad, and she still took home a fair sum of money. And while her father questioned it at first, she made up some story, and when the money started coming in, well, he soon forgot about whatever it was she was doing to earn it.

Her sister was wearing nicer clothes to school and they could actually afford to go out to eat once in a while. Madlena couldn't look herself in the mirror sometimes, but what did that matter? She was helping her family.

It was a Saturday night and those were always her busiest nights, so she packed her small shoulder bag with clothing and shoes and headed out for the evening. "I'm going out with my friends, Tata. I'll see you tomorrow."

Her father sat in his reclining chair and waved goodbye without his eyes leaving the television. "Goodnight, my sweet."

Madlena didn't let her family see her dressed for work, not ever. So she carried her bag and walked in tennis shoes to the end of the block where the not-so-nice man would pick her up and take her back to his place to change.

"You'd better get going. It's getting late," the man said from the comfort of his living room sofa.

Madlena walked out in her red stilettos and much-too-short, form-fitted dress that left little to the imagination. "Okay, I'm leaving now. I'll text you where to come pick me up at the end of my shift." She closed the door behind her and got to work.

The air was muggy and Madlena cursed the humidity as it wreaked havoc on her hair. She reached her small section of this neglected part of town and put a smile on her face at every male passerby, many of whom looked as though they couldn't afford her anyway. But some of her services catered to such clientele if they were willing to walk around the corner and into the alleyway. She'd only charge ten bucks for a quick blowjob. She wondered if this was the American dream as she wrapped her lips around whoever handed her a Hamilton.

The streets were busy and traffic seemed heavier than normal. Maybe it was due to summer? People getting out more. Whatever it was, Madlena hoped it would bring more money. And it looked as though she'd spotted her next possible clients.

Two men inside a Lincoln Navigator looked very promising indeed. Madlena licked her lips and rubbed them together to freshen up the shine as she strutted towards the SUV that had pulled alongside the curb. The passenger window rolled down and a man, perhaps in his mid to late forties, leered as she approached.

Leaning in to give them full view of her young and perky cleavage, she asked, "You want to party?" Her thick accent could be difficult to understand, but it appeared these men knew exactly what she'd said.

"How much?" the passenger asked.

Madlena looked at both of the men. The other was plump with a receding hairline, not particularly attractive. "For both? One hundred."

"For the night?" he asked again.

She narrowed her brow and shook her head. "For an hour."

He turned to his partner, who gave a nod. "Get in."

Madlena stepped inside the SUV and closed the door. "There's a hotel around the corner that is friendly to our sort of arrangements." She clicked on her seatbelt.

"Oh, we won't be going to any hotel." The passenger pulled out a gun and pointed it directly at her eyes.

» » »

Not a seat was available in the lecture hall where Agent Nick Scarborough stood on a small stage behind the podium. A large screen came to life behind him with the words "Profile of a Killer" in yellow bold letters on a black background, a transparent image of the FBI emblem just visible beneath.

Kate remained out of view to the left of the stage. She'd asked for a moment to herself before the presentation was to begin. Nick spotted her and made his way over.

"Hey." He smiled. "You all right? You ready to go?"

She hadn't mentioned anything to Nick about what had happened the other night after he left her house; the words that haunted her mind. They'd gone over the slides and gone over the presentation in great detail this morning so that she would not be caught off guard. And, in fact, she'd spent most of Sunday preparing for this, testing her strength.

If he noted anything unusual in her demeanor, he'd insist she wasn't ready and she didn't want him to be right. Kate was ready and she had to face this head on. It was an opportunity to help ensure she would achieve her goals and that could not be squandered because of unpleasant memories. She would not let Hendrickson take this from her.

"I'm good. Where do you want me?" she asked, casting a wandering eye towards the stage. It was better to avoid his stare just now.

"At the table next to the podium. That is, if you don't mind?"

"Sure," she replied.

"And you can handle a question or two, should they come up?"

"Yes. Don't worry, I'll be fine."

"Okay, then, come on and follow me." Nick placed his arm around Kate's shoulder and led her to the table. "You can put your things under here." He pointed to the small storage area beneath the podium.

"Sounds good. Do you need me to run the slideshow?"

"Nope." Nick pointed to an area with what appeared to be lighting equipment at the back of the hall just above the seating. "They've got me covered. You'll do great and, Kate, I know this won't be easy, so if it gets to be too much, just nod your head and I'll work in a break."

"Okay, thank you." Kate looked out onto the students who were getting settled in for the presentation. She spotted her partner, Will, in the front row. He gave her a nod and she returned a smile.

"Thank you all for coming to this special presentation we've put together. I know many of you are interested in becoming a part of the BAU and this case will be featured among the categories that you'll be learning a lot about. Profiling and the behavioral sciences are our specialties. Now, as most of you know, there are four units inside the BAU.

They, of course, include violent crimes against adults and children, in addition to counterterrorism and white-collar crimes, among other interests. Today, I'll be presenting a case that is a crossover of sorts.

"I worked on this particular investigation and, during that time, I had the pleasure of meeting Ms. Kate Reid." Nick extended his hand to introduce Kate. "She became an integral part of the investigation and, as you may or may not know, she was also a victim of the now-deceased perpetrator, Joseph Hendrickson." He paused for a moment to examine Kate's reaction. A reassuring nod from her, and Nick continued, "Ms. Reid, who, as a result of her involvement in another investigation several months ago, decided that she'd found her passion and wanted to train to be a Special Agent, just as you all are. And she's agreed to put her first-hand knowledge of the Hendrickson investigation to use in an effort to help us all learn from her." Nick turned to Kate once again. "Ms. Reid, you can't know how much we appreciate you being here today. And allowing us to pick your brain so that we might learn from you is perhaps the most generous gift you could offer. Thank you for joining us." Nick began to applaud and prompted the same from the audience.

The image on the screen behind Nick changed and was now a picture of Hendrickson. He was dead on the floor of the cellar where he'd held a knife at Kate's throat while Marshall and Nick initiated a firestorm that brought him to the ground. Kate had been prepared. Nick sent her all the photos he'd planned to use as well as the case files – everything from the original investigation when she was a child, to the discovery that the Chief had been keeping Hendrickson safe for all those years.

It had been a long time since she'd recalled all of it. During one point in the presentation, they showed a picture of Sam's car and the forensics they'd used to analyze it. If she'd had the distance and the perspective, she would've understood the need for this learning tool, but the memory was still too close and too real. And it was hard as hell for Kate to get through.

"And so as we begin to understand the inner workings into the mind of a serial killer, we can find patterns. We can discover the killer's habits, modes, and methods. It is through these techniques that we form a profile of the unknown subject. And in this particular case, it was the help of Ms. Reid, her insistence on, at times, disregarding her own safety, that we were able to track down this man. However, I would not recommend that any of you disregard your own safety as the formidable Kate Reid did."

A few chuckles spread among the audience. Even Kate smiled.

"Instead, learn to employ these techniques, utilize every tool you have at your disposal, and hopefully, you will have a successful outcome."

Applause quickly erupted.

"They're applauding for you," Nick said as he looked at Kate.

She stood up, her legs feeling weak both from having sat down for too long and from nerves. The students applauded even louder and someone in the group whistled. Kate searched for the one from whom the noise erupted and found it was Will. A fractured smile emerged momentarily in acknowledgement, then quickly faded.

The students settled down and began collecting their belongings. The presentation was over and she'd made it through.

Will approached the stage where Kate remained standing. "You did great." He nudged her arm with his elbow. "I'll catch up with you later?"

"Sure. And thanks."

Nick shut off the overhead screen. "I'm so proud of you. Marshall would have been proud too."

"You did all the work. I just sat here, really."

"No. You did more than that, so don't pretend you didn't."

A woman began to approach from the far side of the room.

"Hey. What're you doing here? I thought you weren't coming in until tomorrow?" Nick said.

Special Agent Georgia Myers stepped onto the stage. "I took an earlier flight. I wanted to catch your presentation. It was fantastic. Kate. You did an awesome job."

"Thank you, Agent Myers. I'm glad you were here, but you know, I'm sure we could've used your expertise."

"You're damn right. You should've said you were coming," Nick replied.

"Oh stop. I would've come in early either way. I just like watching you in action."

Kate suddenly began to feel like a third wheel with these two who hadn't seen each other in more than a week. "Listen, I'd better get going. I've got a lot of studying to do tonight. Thanks for everything, Nick. I appreciate the opportunity."

"Thank you, Kate. Have a good evening and we'll talk soon." Nick watched her leave, then turned to Georgia. "You hungry? Want to grab some dinner? I'm starving."

» » »

A place called the Globe and Laurel operated in Stafford, VA, just a few miles south from the National Museum of the Marine Corp. and very near the base. The owner, a retired Marine, had operated the restaurant since 1969, although it had been relocated a few times. It was Nick's favorite place, even if he never had much time to visit it. Now that Georgia was here, he wanted to make time.

"Just a Sam Adams for me," Nick said to the waiter. "What do you want, babe?"

"I'll have the house white, thanks."

"I'll be right back with your drinks." The waiter smiled.

Nick watched the man walk away and then turned to Georgia. "So, how'd you think Kate did today?"

"I'll tell you, all things considered, she did a hell of a job keeping it together. I'm not sure I would've asked her to do something like that, Nick."

"I know. I was hesitant." He began wringing his hands and looked away from Georgia's disapproving gaze. Perhaps he had felt guiltier than he was letting on. "But you know, with her background, she'll be able to move right into the BAU and her help today pretty much guaranteed it. She's struggling with the ops training and needed something to boost her standings."

"And so having her recall events that almost took her life was the way to do that?"

The waiter returned with their drinks. "Are you ready to order?"

The two recited their desired entrees and once again were left alone.

"Maybe you're right," he continued. "I guess I wanted her to put perspective into it. You know, look at it from a learning standpoint. I thought if I could just get her to detach from it, she'd be better off. Now and in the future."

"First of all, that's never going to happen and you know that. No one could possibly separate themselves from something like that. For Christ's sake, she lost her best friend and she was kidnapped. We can't all be like you, Nick. We can't all isolate ourselves from the world the way you can," Georgia replied.

"Hey, that's not fair."

"I'm sorry, no, that wasn't fair, and I didn't mean… I know what you went through with the Highway Hunter case. It's no easier for you than it is for me or anyone else, for that matter. I just don't want you pushing her, you know? She's completely alone right now, except for you, and she'd follow you to the ends of the earth, whether it was good for her or not."

"You think I'm taking advantage of her?" Nick asked in a tone he rarely used with Georgia. A tone that suggested he was looking for a fight.

"No. All I'm saying is be careful. You're all she's got right now."

"Well, you're friends with her too."

"Of course I am, but not the way you two are. You got history. You both have been through a lot of stuff together. I can't compete with that." Georgia glanced away for a moment.

Nick noted the gesture with caution. He was drifting into unchartered territory. Georgia was a strong woman, not inclined to fits of jealousy. "You don't need to worry about Kate and me. You know that, right?"

"I know that."

He wasn't convinced. "Let's just start this evening over, all right?" Nick raised his chilled pint glass. "Welcome home."

» » »

Kate closed the laptop and placed it on the small desk adjacent to her bed. She was back in the dorm room and her roommate was still in their shared bathroom, preparing to turn in for the night. It was getting late and she'd studied enough. The day still weighed heavily on her and she could feel the tension in her neck and tried to rub it away. If only she could rub away the images in her head. Although Nick's presentation hadn't included any photos of Sam, it had included a few pictures of Marshall. He was, after all, instrumental in the case too. And maybe that was the real problem. There were pictures all over her house of Marshall, but here, in the dorm, there was only one. But now everyone had seen him exhibited on the projector screen. Nick had shown a picture of him, taken during one of the news conferences after Hendrickson was killed. Marshall looked so strong, so handsome. None of those people knew him and, to them, he was nothing more than another cop who was killed in the line of duty while apprehending the Highway Hunter. Displaying him to the students, though, reopened the wounds that were still raw and only held together by a few thin strands of tissues that had formed simply with time.

She'd been able to move on as best as anyone could, but being reminded of that time, well, it was hard. As much as she wanted to become an agent, there were days during this training that she'd questioned her motives. She'd uprooted her entire life, empty though it had been, to come here and train under the premise that one day, she'd get to work with Nick and hunt down killers and those that brought pain into this world. Kate began to recall a conversation she'd had with Marshall when she questioned her purpose once before.

"What did you say this was? A violet?"

"A Redwood Violet."

"That's what you are. You're able to bloom in the darkness and shadows, just like this flower."

Somehow, Marshall always knew just what to say and she wished he could be here now to offer up his wisdom. But then, she wouldn't be here at all if he was.

Her phone jolted to life. Kate retrieved it to see that it had been a text notification.

"I plan on kicking your butt tomorrow on the driving course. LOL"

It was from Will and was a welcomed break from her present state of mind. She appreciated his friendship and stood to learn a lot from him. She still felt so very out of place, doing something that had once seemed out of reach, and his reminder that there was still humor to be found even during the difficult training was embraced.

"Yeah, ok, buddy. We'll see. Good night," she replied.

Kate pushed up from the bed and turned to her closet. She needed to secure her weapon before turning in. A small metal case waited inside the closet and she removed the clip and ensured the chamber was clear.

Jocelyn returned from the facilities, wiping her face with a towel. "You heading off to sleep?"

"Yep. I'll go get washed up. Good night."

"Good night, Kate."

» » »

"Are you ready, Reid?" the instructor asked as he latched his passenger seat belt in the older model Chevy Tahoe they used for the safe driver training.

Kate figured this was her opportunity to really unleash and have some much-needed fun. The tires had special bars and wheels attached to prevent rollovers and so it was very safe overall, intending to teach maneuverability. She spotted Will standing outside of the building, near the track, where simulators had been installed to allow them practice before getting into the real thing. He had his arms folded and stood at attention.

She gave him a wink as if to challenge him. A moment later, the tires screeched and Kate spun out onto the track. Her hands gripped the steering wheel firmly as it vibrated under her palms. She let out a sound that resembled a squeal as she sped towards the open lot.

The instructor laughed. "Okay, now, as soon as I tell you, pull hard to the right." A moment passed. "Now!"

Kate yanked the wheel to the right and the SUV raised slightly, skidding on two wheels, but still balanced on the bars as she spun it into a circle.

"Straighten the wheel! Straighten the wheel!" the instructor yelled.

Smoke billowed from the tires and the stench of burned rubber filled the cabin. Kate did as she was told and pulled out of the spin.

"Apply the brakes!"

She slammed on the brakes and came to a stop, lurching forward in the process. Her breath was heavy and she immediately turned to the instructor. "That was awesome. Can we do that again?"

"Afraid not. We gotta get everyone in here today. Great job, though, Kate. Well done. Now, let's head back."

Adrenaline still surged inside her and Kate felt nothing short of euphoric. She was beginning to understand why racecar drivers loved their job. It was exhilarating. She pulled up to the front of the building where her classmates waited for their turns. Kate stepped out. Her legs felt wobbly, but she steadied herself and removed her helmet.

Kate ran her fingers through her brunette hair, which had grown long again because Marshall liked it best that way. "Wow. You guys are in for a treat. That was amazing."

"Looks like you did all right." Will winked at her.

"I'll take that." The instructor took the helmet from Kate. "Who's next?"

She stepped inside the building to remove the coverall that had protected her clothing underneath. The door opened soon after, letting in a bright light that made her squint, and until her eyes adjusted, Kate hadn't realized it was Nick who was walking towards her. "Hey. What're you doing here?"

"Oh, just checking things out. Looks you had fun on the course."

"You could say that. What's going on?" She smoothed her hair a final time and straightened her t-shirt, which displayed the big black letters F.B.I.

"I was wondering if you wanted to help me with something."

She'd seen that look on his face before. "Yeah? What's that?"

"I got a case that I thought you might want in on." Nick pulled up a metal folding chair and swiveled it around, sitting down on it backwards.

Kate raised a brow. "A case? Like a real case? But, I don't even know which field office I'll be operating out of yet." She suspected it would be D.C. and, after the presentation, felt more confident of that choice, however, word had not officially been handed down. "How would I be allowed to work on a case while I'm in training?" She pulled up a chair next to him and rested her elbows on her thighs. "Somehow, I think you're trying to do me a favor here."

"No, not exactly." His eyes told a different story than his lips. "It's just that your help yesterday—it didn't go unnoticed. And, in fact, some of the higher-ups at the Academy watched the lecture."

"Okay. I'm still not certain where you're going with this."

"Your training is obviously important. And you've excelled academically and in all other aspects with the exception of the tactical drills. After some discussions with your trainers, they've agreed that it could benefit you to apply your training to a real life investigation."

Kat sat upright and studied Nick's face. "Are you trying to get them to circumvent my dismal operational scores by showing them that I can do well in other areas, areas other than tactical field work?"

"No. I don't know—maybe. I just don't want them to discount your other skills. Look, not all of us end up in the field, arresting people or resolving hostage situations. Most of us work behind the scenes, analyzing intelligence, data, and things like that."

"All of those people went through this same training and passed," she replied.

"You're right. They did. But not all of them fought off abductors and helped to track down killers before Day One at the Academy."

She wasn't so sure about that. Many were in law enforcement already.

Nick leaned over to make his point clear. "They're willing to overlook this one minuscule detail of your training by allowing me an opportunity to get you involved in real case work, proving that your skills lie elsewhere. Your goal is to work with me, right?"

Kate nodded, although it was difficult for her to swallow the idea that her instructors believed operational training was a minuscule part of her overall preparation. Nick was putting a pretty good spin on the situation.

"You know how many of us actually get out in the field?"

"You mean, besides you?" she quipped.

"We study and research. Kate, that's *your* wheelhouse."

He was right. That was where she felt most comfortable. But the idea of somehow skirting the system when the same opportunity wouldn't have been offered to any of her cohorts – it just wasn't sitting right.

"You know I want more than anything to do casework. That's why I'm here. And so, yeah, I want to work with you, but I don't want to be given special treatment. You know better than anyone around here what I've been through and I don't need any more eyes shifting in my direction suggesting I have an unfair advantage. Can you help me get past this part? Can you help me overcome my deficiencies in the ops training?"

Nick grunted. "How did I know you wouldn't want any special treatment? If you want me to help, yeah, I can help you with some drills. I think maybe you could use someone to talk to as well. I don't mean just me. I mean someone who can help you move on. You're not an island, Kate, and no one expects you to be." He slapped his thighs and returned to his feet. "So, you want to know what this case is?"

"I do." Kate rose to meet him and placed her hands on her hips. "What is it?"

THREE

It wasn't the first time Kate had been inside the FBI D.C. field office, or the WFO, as they called it; she'd visited Scarborough there plenty of times, but it was the first time she had entered under the grounds of assisting on an investigation. They'd reached an understanding that this case would take a back seat to her training and was only intended as supplemental; a testament to her existing skillset. That was fine by Kate, and the idea of working on something real, rather than the mock cases she worked on at the Academy, was invigorating and exactly what she needed to get out of the funk she'd been heading towards. Once again, Nick had come through for her and, once again, she felt that familiar feeling of being "taken care of." Not to mention the twinge of guilt. If her classmates believed Nick was responsible for getting her into the Academy, how would they feel about this latest development? She'd been so sure of her own confidence, but perhaps she wasn't as strong as everyone told her.

But for today, she was meeting with Agent Scarborough to discuss a case that had recently been turned over by Metro Police. Nick hadn't gone into much detail during their conversation, only indicating the need to be present for a nine a.m. briefing. And so here she was, walking into the lobby of the eight-story stone building on the corner of G Street and 4th.

"I have a meeting with Agent Scarborough. I'm Agent-in-training Kate Reid."

The man behind the security desk motioned for Kate to place her gun and other belongings into the tray and walk through the metal detector. Another guard on the other side of the security station pointed her in the direction of the interior lobby where she could wait.

Kate retrieved her belongings and proceeded to the reception area and again indicated a pending meeting with the agent. This time, the woman pressed a button on the phone system and waited for a moment.

"I have NAT Kate Reid here to see you." The woman glanced over Kate while she waited for a reply. "Thank you." Placing the phone back down, she said, "He'll be down in just a moment. Why don't you have a seat?" A row of chairs were pressed against a wall a few feet away, and the woman pointed in that general direction.

"Thank you." She had arrived in her required FBI trainee gear; blue polo shirt with the FBI emblem over the left breast and khakis pants. Carrying a side arm was a requirement when she was on duty, even in training.

The elevator doors opened in the distance and Nick emerged. "Right on time, as usual." He approached and extended his hand.

Kate smiled and smoothed her shirt. "Thank you."

"Well, come on. I got some people I want to introduce you to."

On the fifth floor, Nick led Kate to a large room that housed several desks with computers lined up in rows all facing the front. Large monitors were mounted on the wall. It reminded Kate of a type of communications room, perhaps where task forces would meet and exchange information. It was similar to the classrooms at Quantico.

About ten men and women were stationed in various places around the room. Some were on the computers, others huddled in conversation and, as Nick entered, all seemed to focus on the room's newest occupants.

"Some of you may already be aware, but we have an FBI recruit in our midst. This is Kate Reid and she'll be helping out on this investigation as part of her training."

Kate attempted to make eye contact and convey a brief nod to each one in the room before following Nick to the far end where a seat awaited her.

"Let's go ahead and get started." He clicked a remote and the wall monitor came to life. "This is the group we are attempting to track down." He opened a webpage called "European Beauties." Women posed on beds, in the bath, or some other such provocative location. Nick turned towards the lead investigator with the local police. "Some of you have already met Detective Roger Moreno with Metro PD. Detective, why don't you fill them in?"

He pushed up off the back wall and walked along the far side where Nick was standing. "Thank you, Agent Scarborough." He began clicking through a series of webpages with images of more women. "The Metro police have been working on an investigation into suspected drop houses. Complaints have come into the department from neighbors who say they've seen women coming and going from these homes. The women don't appear to be coherent, likely drugged, according to the complaints. We've found two of them; both had been cleared out by the time we arrived. However, video equipment and a few flash drives were found. On the flash drives, we discovered images of women much like you see on that website, some much more graphic in detail. And what led us to this website was a simple banner that had been created and the file saved to be uploaded to the web page. Given the name of the website, we are inclined to believe these women are mostly of eastern European decent. We believe they are likely victims of sex trafficking."

Moreno continued, "Late last week, Metro Police issued a search warrant for this man, James Henry Corbett." An image of the man appeared on the screen. "The forty-five-year-old former high school counselor is believed to be the ringleader or, at the very least, high up on the command chain, for this group and is suspected of kidnapping these young women. An IP address from one of the websites we discovered originated from a home that was listed under Corbett's name. However, we've been unable to locate him. His last known address, according to the school district who had previously employed him, was vacated some time ago. We contacted the FBI on the discovery that this case appears to be a widespread operation covering many different locations both within and possibly outside the United States. I've had some communications with our brothers in Richmond regarding the discovery of similar drop houses. However, they have also come up empty-handed. The Metro Police and Richmond PD are now asking for the FBI's help in finding those involved in this ring as well as ensuring the women, whose numbers we are as of yet unsure, are recovered safely."

An agent in the second row raised his hand. "What leads you to believe this is sex trafficking? Have you had any reported missing persons cases that could be tied to this?"

"The websites were our first indication. The predatory nature of them alone suggests trafficking. And, the drop houses were located in densely populated immigrant communities, mostly of eastern European decent, much like the women you see presented on this website. We believe most of these young women probably have no legal identification, no jobs. These types of victims can disappear without anyone noticing. Their families are often fearful of reporting them missing because they too are probably illegal."

Kate examined the images of the women on the screen. They were exotic and very young. If these girls were being plucked off the streets, no one saying a word, how were they supposed to find them?

"Thank you, detective. We'll begin coordinating with your teams and have our people get started on shutting these websites down. You all know what to do, so let's get going," Nick said.

» » »

Two days into the investigation, and Kate had been tasked with reviewing the files of women who had gone missing in the D.C. area that fit the criteria. There were very few that came up as possible immigrants. Only three so far were of the particular lineage they sought and of those who had been reported, two were from families who appeared to be in the country illegally. She wasn't surprised they'd disregarded their own consequences for coming forward. No parent would put themselves above his or her own child.

On second thought... Kate turned away from the computer screen and rubbed her eyes. She considered for a moment that there were decisions her parents made that she still could not forgive. Decisions that shaped who she was today.

Returning to her work, Kate pushed back the memories of the past. How easy it was to recall them. They were still so close to the surface.

A welcomed distraction from her present thoughts came by way of a text from her friend and classmate, Will. *"Want me to bring some dinner? We can study together."*

Time had slipped from her periphery and although hunger was making its presence known, she hesitated to reply. Food sounded like a great idea, but she wasn't sure if she should tell him about working this case with Nick. The extra help she was getting to win points with the instructors wasn't fair to the others. Just for once, Kate wanted to be recognized for her own hard work, not for riding on the coattails of Nick Scarborough, although she was doing little to prevent the stigma from taking hold.

"Come on. Whadya say?" He sent another message.

"Sure. Sounds good."

"Great. I'll bring something up from the cafeteria. I'll be over in 30."

Kate closed the case file and walked into the bathroom to splash some water on her face. Jocelyn had already gone down for dinner and she'd declined her request to come along, something that would surely raise an eyebrow on her return, seeing Will in their room.

Not long after she tried to make her appearance somewhat more palatable, a knock sounded on her door. Kate peered through the peephole. She opened her door to the vast halls and the smiling face of Will Caison holding out an entire pie. "Come on in. They let you take a whole pizza?"

Will set the pie down on her desk, then headed straight for the small refrigerator next to the closet. "You got any beer?"

She tugged on her oversized shirt and laughed. "Here on campus? No. Besides, are you here to study, or have a party?"

"Why not both?" He looked inside the refrigerator at the insufficient contents. "Jeez, you don't have anything in here." He closed it again. "Where's Munoz?"

"She went down for dinner already," Kate replied. Will was the type of guy to always call people by their last names and so Kate's roommate became Munoz and she was Reid, although she noticed lately that he'd begun referring to her as Kate more often than not.

"Anyway," she began, retrieving a couple of paper plates for the pizza. "Thanks for picking up the food. I hadn't realized how hungry I was."

"We all gotta eat and I thought we could bounce some questions off each other in preparation for the assessment on Friday."

Kate set the plates on the desk and grabbed her laptop. Will had already opened the sodas he'd found inside the fridge and served up the pizza.

"Thanks. Okay." She fired up her laptop and logged into the FBI server. "So, let's take a look at the case studies first. That'll probably be the main focus."

As she typed away on her laptop, she noticed Will staring at her and cocked her head. "What?"

"Nothing. It's just. Well, I thought you might say something."

"Say something? About what?"

"About the case you're working on with Agent Scarborough and Metro Police."

Kate folded her arms in her lap and gave Will her full attention. "How did you know about that?"

"I heard rumblings from some of our classmates. I guess someone overheard Scarborough talking with Hawes."

SSA Hawes was the operations instructor and Kate hadn't realized anyone else had been privy to the conversation. Nick probably hadn't either.

"Why didn't you say something?" Will asked.

"Because you all already think I'm only here because of Agent Scarborough. I guess I didn't want to add fuel to the fire." Kate raised the can of soda to her lips.

"Hey, don't lump me into your generalizations. I don't believe you're here solely based on your relationship with Scarborough. I think it's you who's feeling guilty about it. Look, if he wanted me to help on a case, I'd be shouting it from the rooftops. And don't tell me there aren't other cadets here that don't have connections because I sure as hell guarantee you, there are."

"Okay, I get it." Kate was feeling both offended by his tone and embarrassed by her own assumptions. She'd been so wrapped up in what everyone else was thinking about her and had discounted her own abilities. "I'll be honest with you, Agent Scarborough is trying to keep me from getting kicked out of the program. Assisting him on this case is part of that."

"Kicked out? Why?" Will was a man who cared little of what others thought about him, as was evidenced by his reply and the ingestion of nearly the entire slice of pizza in one bite.

"Because I'm having trouble with the field exercises. And as much as I don't want to admit it, this extra work is intended to help pull me out of the hole I dug for myself."

"So they're not going to require you to pass the ops training?"

"No, I'll still have to pass, but Agent Scarborough is going to be spending some time with me on that too and try to work out what the problem is. So that combined with the additional workload is supposed to win me points. I don't know, Scarborough thinks I need to talk to someone about—before. That maybe my reaction times aren't what they should be because of what's happened in the past. I'm not entirely sure he's wrong."

"I'm sorry, Kate. I didn't know." Will's expression softened. "I gotta tell you, though, I've been around plenty of soldiers who have PTSD. It does have varying degrees of severity, and I'm not convinced that's what's happening with you. But, what do I know?"

She considered his question. He didn't know. He only knew what was printed in the papers or what was shown on TV, not what she actually went through. Kate didn't hold it against him, though. "It's okay. I don't know what it is, to be honest. All I know is that I want to work in the BAU and if Agent Scarborough can pull some strings, I shouldn't feel bad about that, should I?"

"Sounds like you already made up your mind about it." Will grabbed another slice. "Let's just get back to studying. Forget I said anything."

Jocelyn returned from the cafeteria and, when she opened the door, the two were startled by the noise.

"Hey, you're back," Kate said.

"Am I interrupting something?" Jocelyn stepped inside and closed the door behind her. "What's up, Caison?"

"Just studying. You want to join us?" Will pushed aside some of his things to make room.

"Actually, that'd be great. If you're sure I'm not interrupting." She looked at Kate for confirmation.

Kate had grown to like Jocelyn. She was easy-going, helpful, and always managed to see the positive side of just about any situation, which, considering her background, was a pretty impressive quality. So rather than become embarrassed by what her roommate was clearly trying to imply, she simply shrugged it off. "Sit down." Kate patted the seat of the chair next to her.

Studying until the wee hours was nothing new for trainees, and it was only when Kate caught a glimpse of black skies from the window of the dorm room that she realized the hour had become late. "Anybody know what time it is?" Rather than wait for an answer, Kate grabbed her phone. "It's almost midnight. I don't know about you two, but I've got to get some sleep."

Jocelyn raised her arms and expelled a pent-up yawn. "Yeah, it's time to quit for the night." She stood up and closed her notebook. "Good night, Caison."

Will seemed to pick up on the fact that this was her way of telling him to leave. "Right, okay. Yeah, I guess I'll see you guys tomorrow." He shoved his laptop into his bag. "Thanks for studying with me." He was looking at Kate, although Jocelyn answered.

"No problem."

"Thanks for the food and the help. I'll see you tomorrow." Kate walked to the door and held it open.

A quick nod and he was gone.

"You know he's got a thing for you, right?" Jocelyn said, pulling her hair back into a bun.

"Oh, I don't think so." She paused for a moment. "Wouldn't matter anyway. That's not something I'm interested in."

"I know, but he might not." Jocelyn slid under the light covers of her twin bed. "You might want to nip that in the bud."

Kate crawled into her own bed, grunting a reply. "Good night."

FOUR

In an unassuming house nestled in the suburbs of Baltimore, James Corbett waited for word from the higher-ups, specifically, the man who he had come to know only as the Arranger. No names. That was part of the deal. He understood the nature of the business and didn't question it. Not when the money was pouring in freely.

Still, he knew that the FBI was looking for him and had already been to his previous home. They'd tracked him down by his internet service provider. It was then he switched to a proxy server that disguised his IP address, but it had been too late. They knew about the websites and had already shut them down. Not that it mattered much. It was merely a hiccup and several more websites were already in their place. But he was keeping a low profile nonetheless. What he hadn't wanted was for his boss to consider him too much of a risk.

So as he waited for the call, he knew he would have to offer the Arranger some assurances to pass along to those in charge. Corbett and his team had gotten sloppy and amends would have to be made.

The call was coming in. "Yeah," Corbett said. "Understood. I'll be there."

And that was it. He was to meet someone at a predetermined location and pick up the next set of assets. That was what they were called—assets. The women they found.

Usually prostitutes; sometimes young women working at a local dive bar or strip club. They were scoped out, ensuring little to no family and no documentation. That was key. Without documentation, it was nearly impossible to track them down.

"It's happening tonight. I need you there by eight p.m." Corbett barked the order over his cell phone.

"I got it. I'll be there." Stan Kovac was Corbett's second in command. He handled the transportation and distribution of the assets.

Corbett ended the call and returned to his laptop. The SD card from his camera slid into the drive and he began uploading the pictures of some of the latest acquisitions. They were beautiful and young. Most hardly spoke a word of English, which was fine by him. He took his time with each of them, photographing every inch of their firm bodies. As he opened the files, he stared at the images. His own private porn site and he'd had the privilege of breaking them in already. It was the best way to instill fear and let them know who was in charge. Heat began to rise in his groin as he looked at their ruby red lips and soft skin. He continued to leer at them while he serviced his growing need for release.

» » »

Kate was the last to arrive to class this morning. She quietly lowered her laptop bag to the floor and slid into her chair next to Will.

"Pushing it a little, aren't you?" he asked.

"It was a late night." She retrieved her tablet and placed it on her desk.

"That's what happens when you're pulling double duty."

"Looks like we can get started now," the instructor said as he surveyed the room. He turned to the interactive screen and began to write the words "Forensic Evidence."

This was what she'd been waiting for. Kate had some knowledge on this subject after having worked in evidence collection for more than a year and the graduate program at UCSD, although that had been cut short.

As the instructor began, Kate noticed a marked shift in Will's body language. He was sitting further away and his books rested so far at the edge of table, they just might fall off. His legs jutted out the side, almost into the aisle. His wasn't a particularly tall man, only slightly above average, but that still meant he surpassed Kate and her five-foot-six-inch frame. She wondered if Jocelyn had been right. It had been some time since she'd seen that look in a man's eyes, but Will had it the other night while they were studying. It hadn't been her intention to give him the impression she was ready to start some kind of relationship. Not to mention the fact that they were colleagues, trainees, and that would only make matters more complicated.

Kate was not here to meet a man. She was not here to do anything other than become an agent.

"We're going to review the following information for tomorrow's assessment," the instructor began. "First, you'll need to understand how ViCAP works and what its uses are, as well as CODIS and, finally, you'll be given the parameters of an actual case file and will need to understand the use of these programs, including NGI, and how these databases impact the agent's ability to see to a successful prosecution."

This was something she could wrap her arms around with ease. She'd had the experience and knowledge of such programs and it filled her with a renewed confidence. Maybe she had earned her spot here after all.

It was this confidence that made the time pass with record speed. She'd breezed through the subjects and was ready for more when the instructor started to wrap up the session.

"That's it for today. You're all free to go." He shut down the video and began to pack up his files.

"I'll see you later." Will moved quickly to leave.

"Reid, can I have a word with you?" the instructor asked.

Kate grabbed her bag and walked to the front of the classroom. Most of the other recruits had already left. "Yes, sir?"

"I'm sure you are aware that I spoke with Agent Scarborough."

"Yes, sir."

"There's a chance that if you are able to be of value in the case he and Metro Police are working on, and we can arrange for extracurricular training with regards to the tactical teams, we might find an agreeable resolution. We both agree that there are extenuating circumstances here and it would be a shame for you not to see a satisfactory completion of the training as a result. That being said, you will need to make up for every hour that you miss and bear in mind that it should be kept to an absolute minimum in any event."

"Thank you, sir. I've already been working closely with Agent Scarborough on the issue and have discussed how we might approach the problem. I appreciate your assistance and I'll be the first one to tell you that I intend to pass that segment of the training." Kate paused for a moment. "Is there anything else, sir?"

"No. You may leave."

» » »

The paper target was moving towards her as her instructor approached. Kate removed her safety glasses and pulled the headphones from her head.

"Nicely done, Reid." He pulled the target down to examine it and then turned to Kate. "Remind me not to piss you off."

Six shots, three in the center, two in the head, and one just outside the X.

"Thank you, sir." The partial grin on her face was hard to conceal, but she tried anyway.

The firearm was returned to her holster and, as the day's temperature reached its peak, she was ready to find some relief and head back to the main part of campus.

Will jogged to catch up with her. "Hey, you have lunch yet?"

"No. You want to go grab something?" Maybe he'd reconsidered his earlier brush off.

"My treat." Will walked alongside her now. "McDonalds?"

"How about we just head to the cafeteria?" Her shoulder raised as it carried the weight of her duffle bag.

» » »

Nick had put a call in to Kate, but it went straight to voicemail. The plan had been to have her to come down this evening and work with Agent Dwight Jameson on reviewing the new details they'd received from Metro.

"You're back?" Georgia stepped into the doorway of Nick's office.

"I am. And I see you are too?" Nick smiled at the welcomed sight. "How long you here for?"

"Gotta fly out Monday morning, so it looks like I'm yours for three days." She walked inside and glanced at the paperwork on his desk.

"I've got some things I need to jump on right away. You mind if I call you later and we can go out and grab some dinner?"

"Sure. Actually, why don't you come over tonight? I'll cook." Georgia stood at the front of his desk, waiting for a reply.

"That'd be great. I'll give you a call later."

She nodded and turned to walk out of his office.

"Hey," Nick began. "Thanks for checking in on me." He watched her continue on and admired her from the back.

Before she left his view, a call came in on his cell phone and he was disappointed by the disruption, but on glancing at the caller ID, he realized he needed to take the call. "Kate. Thanks for getting back to me."

"Sorry for missing you earlier. How's it going?" she asked.

"Can you come in later? Do you have time?"

"Yeah. I just finished with firearms training and so I'm free for the rest of the day. I was grabbing a late lunch with Caison, but we're just about finished, so I can head up now if you'd like."

"Great. See you in a few."

It seemed like only minutes had passed when Kate appeared at his door.

"Afternoon," she said.

"Shit." Nick turned his wrist to check the time. "You got here quick. I completely lost track of time. Come in, please."

Kate dropped into the chair. "So, what do you need me to do?"

Nick started rifling through the papers on his desk. He picked up the file Detective Moreno handed over as well as two others. "I'd like to find out what these three women have in common, besides the obvious ethnicity. Can you review these ASAP and get me something, anything we can cross-reference?"

"Of course. I can get on this right away." She stood up and turned to leave.

"Hold up. How'd everything go today?"

"Great. The firearms instructor said he wouldn't ever want to piss me off."

Nick chuckled. "No, I don't think he would. Let me know when you're finished. I'll catch up with you later."

"Thank you, Agent Scarborough."

Kate pulled up a chair at one of the empty desks in the bullpen. She could have gone home to do what Nick asked, but she preferred to be around the other agents. It make her feel like she was a part of something.

She booted up the computer and logged into the FBI server. However, the files would need to be scanned in and so Kate headed towards the printer room. On her way there, she ran into Agent Jameson.

"Hi, Kate, nice to see you." He stood a full head and shoulders above her and was built like a brick chimneystack, square and thick.

"Agent Jameson, good to see you too."

Jameson and Scarborough had been the last ones to see Marshall alive. She didn't often run into him, but he sometimes worked closely with Nick and this was one of those times. It seemed there were reminders of her past everywhere.

"I understand Scarborough gave you the profiles of the reported missing victims?"

"He did. I was just getting ready to scan them in so I can start working on them."

"Good. I'm glad to be working with you again."

"Thank you, Agent Jameson. Same goes for me."

"Call me Dwight. I think we've known each other long enough to go by first names. I'll see you later, Kate."

There were half a dozen printers and a few scanners inside the room. It might have been easier if she'd just taken a picture of each page and uploaded them, but she needed to be sure that the quality of the documents remained intact and couldn't risk one single word being misread because the image was shoddy.

The first document was loaded and it began to scan to the file on her computer. She peered out through the large picture window and into the corridor. Agent Myers was approaching and noticed Kate inside.

Myers leaned in. "Hey. What're you doing in here?"

"Just scanning some files for Agent Scarborough. He asked me to take a look at a few things and draft a report."

Georgia's brow creased. "What's he got you working on?"

"The sex trafficking case. He's got me cross-referencing the profiles of some missing victims."

"I see. I guess I didn't realize you were helping him out. In fact, I didn't realize you'd been assigned a field office."

"Well, I haven't officially and it's only been a few days, but I've been able to juggle it so far. He's not pushing me too hard." Kate wanted to diffuse a situation that appeared to have evolved into one.

"Okay, I'll let you get to it, then. Good to see you, Kate."

"You too, Agent Myers." While they occasionally went out socially, Kate never presumed to call her by any other name here and understood the chain of command.

The files were scanned. Kate grabbed the folders and walked back to the desk. As she opened each one and began cataloging the dates of birth, locations, identifying markers, etc., she began to get a sense of déjà vu and half-expected Marshall to come strutting down the hall as he used to do to check up on her. She hadn't done any real casework, and simulated exercises were not the same, since leaving the SDPD behind. Captain Hearn had offered her plenty of opportunity to stay, but in the end, he knew she couldn't possibly. So now here she was, doing the same thing. And it felt good.

» » »

Georgia set the dishtowel down at the sound of her doorbell and walked to the front door of her downtown apartment, only minutes from the field office. She was almost close enough to walk, or take the subway down one station.

"Hey. Come on in." She leaned in to kiss Nick as he entered.

"Sorry I'm late. It took longer than I expected."

"That's all right. I put the warmer on. Dinner will survive." She turned again to the kitchen. "Can I get you a drink?"

"Sure, that'd be great, thanks."

Georgia began to pour his favorite, Jack and Coke. Hers was Jim Beam and she didn't mind pouring them each a double. She held the two drinks in her hand and walked over to him as he stood facing the enormous window. In the distance was the Washington Monument. It was a spectacular view and his own apartment paled in comparison. He was at a higher pay grade than Georgia, but she'd been left a fairly good sum of money after her father passed away a few years ago. She invested the money wisely.

"Here you go, babe." She handed him the highball glass.

"Thanks."

"You want to sit down for a minute? The food will keep."

Nick took a seat on the edge of the stylish grey sofa sectional. He began to circle the rim of the glass with his finger.

"You seem preoccupied," Georgia said.

He inhaled deeply and tilted his head. "Sorry. It's just this case. I had Kate run a report for me earlier today. That's part of the reason I'm so late. She'd just finished with it and brought it to me."

"I actually ran into her earlier and she mentioned she was helping you out with some research." Georgia did her best to disguise her tone. She'd felt irritated that he had failed to mention the fact that Kate was working with him as if he was hiding it from her.

"Anyway, there's a suggestion that this could be crossing over into other communities. Still mostly from immigrants of eastern and southeastern Europe, but I think we're going to find it to be a much broader net."

"I am sorry to hear that. You sure that's all this is about?" Georgia continued.

Nick took to his feet and walked towards the glass doors that spanned nearly the entire distance of the room. He took in the view of the city lights.

Georgia knew how much he loved his job, but she began to suspect that it was tearing down some of his defenses and in a way that might make him careless.

He swallowed down the last of his drink. "Mind if I have another?"

FIVE

The sun fell behind the trees and the skies turned the color of fire. Kate admired the beauty from the chair on her front porch and, for a moment, shed the images that still lingered in her mind from the day's demanding task. Learning coping mechanisms helped her to stay focused on the case, rather than focus on the victims, and the Academy emphasized the importance of maintaining distance. Marshall, she once believed, had been the best at that. In the end, the discovery of who he really was only came after he was gone. It was a mistake that still chiseled away at her thoughts, but with the passage of time came perspective and so she tried to cut herself some slack.

Her thoughts turned to Will Caison. He was very kind, but she suspected he felt slighted by the fact that Kate had been given an opportunity to work on what was becoming a very significant case. There were times when Kate did feel privileged; given opportunities for which most would sacrifice their right arms. And really, what had she done to deserve them? Nothing except having been a victim herself. It was a double-edged sword.

Kate pulled the throw over her shoulders as the temperature lowered. She was still used to the warm southern California weather, but here, it seemed that early summer felt more like spring with its chilly night air. The lights inside the house began to glow through the windows as the outside darkened. Kate figured she should probably go inside, maybe fix a sandwich and settle in front of the television. She needed a break from the case, a break from her training, and a break from her own thoughts.

Just as she pushed up from her white painted rocker, a glimmer of light sparked in the distance. The front drive was long and it appeared to have come from the end of it, near the mailbox. She stared at the spot, but it didn't happen again. It was the second time she'd seen a sparkle of something and yet found nothing. "Now I'm starting to see things." She shook her head and walked back inside, locking the deadbolt immediately.

Maybe Nick had been right. Maybe she needed to talk to someone. Kate had hardly given herself a chance to recover from the life she left behind. Perhaps the flickers of light was her mind's way of telling her that something was there, still flickering in her mind and she needed to see to it.

Once back inside, Kate tucked her legs beneath her on the couch and watched TV. It didn't matter what was showing; she wasn't paying any attention to it. She'd have to get up early to get back into the field office tomorrow. Nick wanted to meet with her and Agent Jameson. It was the only day she could spend working entirely on his case. Sunday was her only day off from the Academy. Better to be working than sitting here in her empty home.

» » »

Madlena's father tried her cell phone again. Still no answer. It had been two days and he'd not seen or heard from his daughter. He didn't know many of her friends, but those he was able to contact hadn't seen her either. So far, his other daughter was unaware of her sister's disappearance. Instead, he did what any father would do and shielded her from it—for now.

"I need to call the police," he told his friend, who'd come over last night to help look for her.

"You can't, Alek. They'll send you and Marica home. Then what happens when Madlena returns?"

"She's never been gone this long. I don't know what to do. I have to find my daughter." Alek slammed his fists against the table in his small kitchen. "I knew what she was doing to get the money. I knew and did nothing about it. Nothing! We needed it for food and clothing. You know how hard it's been."

"You can't blame yourself."

"Who else is there to blame, then? Madlena is probably dead in some alley." His face turned red and his eyes pooled with tears. He was a large man who was unaccustomed to feeling such pain. He'd lost his wife, but that was after his youngest was born, almost fifteen years ago. Not since then had his heart hurt so much. "Moja djevojčica." *My baby girl.* "What can I do, my friend?"

"We'll find her. We'll ask everyone we know, but Alek, you can't go to the police."

Alek pulled open a drawer in the kitchen. "This is all I have." He showed his friend a recent picture of Madlena. "We must go and find her now. I cannot live like this. What am I to tell Marica?" He grabbed his keys and walked to the front door. "Are you coming or am I on my own?"

The two men began walking through the neighborhood in the north part of Richmond. Run down houses with boarded-up windows, power poles with lines hanging precariously low and cracked sidewalks with weeds and grass poking through.

This was where Madlena called home. Alek and his friend walked up to each home that appeared occupied and knocked on the doors. They were greeted with mostly unfriendly people who had no desire to so much as look at the photograph Madlena's father held in his hand. No one knew her, no one had seen her, at least, that was what they told him.

Hours had passed and Alek needed to go home. His other daughter would be home soon from school and with Madlena missing, he didn't want to leave her alone. "She's gone." His face was masked in anguish. "I have to tell the police. They'll find her."

"No. You can't, Alek."

"I won't just sit here and do nothing."

"Then let me go. I'll call and I'll be anonymous. It's the only way. You have to see that. They'll have her description and when she went missing. Will you let me do that?"

Alek looked at his friend, another expatriate who understood their options were limited. "Okay. Okay, thank you, my friend."

» » »

The task of filing the updates that would be sent to the multiple jurisdictions already involved in the investigation had been handed off to Kate. She'd spent the better part of the morning on the assignment.

Nick began to approach her and stopped short when he got a call. He raised his index finger, indicating he'd be just a moment. "Agent Scarborough here." A brief pause before he continued. "Yes, I'll be there as soon as I can. Thank you."

When Nick started towards her again, Kate noticed a change in his appearance. Whoever had been on the other end of that call had revealed some upsetting news. She looked at him with anticipation.

"That was Moreno. He got a call from Richmond PD. You want to drive down there with me? It's a long way, at least an hour and half, probably more. They got someone in custody they think could be a link to James Corbett."

"Of course. I haven't finished with the reports yet."

"They can wait, or better yet, see if you can get Vasquez to finish them. We need to get down there and talk to this person."

She'd compiled the information and asked Agent Vasquez for the favor.

"Reid, we're leaving. Get your things." Nick pulled on his suit jacket and reached for his keys, which rested on his desk.

Once they reached the garage, Nick began, "We're heading into the north side of Richmond. That's where the girl turned up at the police station." He pressed the remote, unlocking his Infiniti SUV.

Kate slid into the passenger side, onto the camel-colored supple leather seat. She knew Nick's career extended twelve years and his choice of vehicles was proof that longevity in the FBI must pay well. "And so you got the call because she gave a description that matched James Corbett?"

"Moreno did and he called me. Now, I have to warn you, this isn't exactly a good part of town we're heading into."

"I can handle it." Kate buckled her seatbelt.

"Just giving you a heads up." He turned the ignition and pulled out of the parking garage.

They'd made it in just under two hours. There were flights, but it would have taken just as long, and Nick wanted to get down there as quickly as possible.

As they neared the local precinct, Kate began to realize that he wasn't exaggerating with regards to this being a shady part of town. She hadn't traveled much apart from her small rented house in Woodbridge to the Academy to the FBI field office. So, coming into this part of Richmond was nothing like she would have expected. Run down houses, several abandoned. People standing on corners looking suspicious at the sight of them rolling along their street. No matter what one's political party affiliation, Kate was becoming convinced with each passing derelict home that the poor were not living a life of leisure on the welfare system and seemed to in fact be becoming even poorer. And she'd seen her share of down and out neighborhoods in San Diego. This was infinitely worse.

The station was just ahead about two more blocks. It would have been impossible for them to stand out any more than they already did. The sleek, silver luxury SUV flashed by like some sort of neon dollar sign glowing in the night. And the stares of the local inhabitants were pretty hard to ignore.

Nick pulled around to the back of the building, behind a gate where an officer stood watch. The man closed it again after they drove inside. "Come on." Nick reached into the back seat and retrieved his laptop bag.

Kate stepped outside into the warm and sticky air. She was used to humidity, but what usually accompanied it was a cool ocean breeze. There was no such breeze from any ocean or otherwise right now.

A rear entrance was just in front of them and the officer who let them inside the gate unlocked and opened the reinforced steel door. Was this place Richmond, Virginia or Belfast, Ireland?

"Detective Garrett? Special Agent Nick Scarborough and this is Agent-in-training, Kate Reid." Nick extended his hand.

"Pleasure." The detective returned the greetings and proceeded to his desk where four other officers were sitting. "Ms. Sala is in the back in our interrogation room." Garrett picked up a sketch from his desk. "This is what she gave us. Look familiar to you?"

Nick examined the picture and handed it to Kate. "No." He looked back to the detective. "Can we speak to Ms. Sala?"

Garrett nodded and led them to the small interrogation room near the back of the old building that had bars on all the windows.

The detective opened the door and inside was a young woman, not more than twenty, sitting at a table. When she looked over at the new arrivals, Kate briefly cast her eyes away. The woman had suffered abuse at the hands of her captor and it was a sight for which she was not prepared. "Has this woman seen a doctor?" Kate immediately asked.

"Yes, ma'am. She was taken to the local hospital before coming here. I can get you the report from the doctor, although we don't have the results of the rape kit tests."

"Thank you. We'll take what you've got," Nick replied. He stepped towards the too-thin woman who'd been given someone's spare clothes to put on by the look of her. "Hello, Ms. Sala. I'm Special Agent Nick Scarborough and this is Special Agent Trainee Kate Reid."

"You an FBI agent?" the woman asked Kate in what sounded to Kate like a Russian accent.

"I'm working towards it."

"That's cool." The woman returned her attention to Nick. "I already told them everything I could. I just want to go home now."

"Where's home, Ms. Sala?" Nick asked.

"Ukraine."

"You're a long way from home."

"They come and tell us we can make lots of money here. I had nothing back home. None of us do. And so I came here." She turned away for a moment. "But then they put us in this old shithole of a house. Told us we had to stay there until we were needed. And I thought, needed? Needed for what? Work? Except it wasn't no kind of work I was looking for." She wiped away the swell of tears in her eyes.

"Ms. Sala, what can you tell me about the man who held you captive?"

"Men. There were many men, but only one who mattered. They would take us, me and another one or two girls, and make us wear, eh..." It was clear she was trying to find the English word and began making gestures of flowing garments. "Pretty underwear, and we'd have to parade in front of these men. And if we were not chosen, we went back to the house."

"What happened when one of the girls was chosen?" Kate asked.

"I don't know. They never came back."

Kate looked to the detective and then to Nick. It seemed they all understood what it was this woman was intimating and it fit in with what they already believed this investigation was really about.

"How were you able to escape?" Nick asked.

"I told the detective that I waited until the man who was guarding us, I waited until he was, you know, with one of the other girls, because that's what he would do. And the drugs were starting to wear off and so I started feeling better and I knew if I didn't get out of there, I might never get out."

"You were drugged?" Kate asked.

"We were all being drugged. To keep us from running."

"We've already sent our guys to find the place," Garrett began. "She was able to give us the address, but when my men got there, it was empty."

"They moved 'em," Nick replied as he pushed up from the chair. "No doubt the moment they realized Ms. Sala was gone. Son of a bitch." He looked at the detective. "We're going to need to get her someplace safe and try to run this composite sketch through the database, see if we can find out who this man is." Nick turned back to the woman. "We're going to put you someplace safe, okay? We'll get you cleaned up and something to eat too. You're going to be fine, Ms. Sala."

Nick turned towards Kate, but before he could speak, the woman interrupted. "These men, they come to our neighborhoods and take the girls. They take them from the streets; anywhere they can. They had six girls when I escaped. Some couldn't have been older than fifteen."

"Christ." Garrett shook his head.

Kate approached the young, battered woman. "I'm so sorry for what's happened to you, ma'am. But please know that we will find whoever did this to you and we will find those other girls." She moved towards the exit, ignoring the telling look from Nick. She already knew she shouldn't have said what she did, but there was no way in hell whoever was kidnapping those women—girls was going to get away with it.

Kate waited outside for Nick and Detective Garrett to emerge.

"That was quite a claim you made, Trainee Reid," Garrett said, placing special emphasis on the word, *trainee*.

"I'm sorry, detective. I know I overstepped."

"Well, I only hope that you and Agent Scarborough can keep your promise." Garrett continued along the corridor toward the bullpen. "I'll keep you informed, Agent

Scarborough, of any progress. We've already got forensics out there analyzing the scene."

"You mind if we go and have a look?" Nick asked.

Garrett placed his hands on his hips. "Look, I know you feds got a job to do, but so do we. Now, I'd appreciate it if you let my team handle the crime scene for now. I'll be sure to hand over any information we find. No offense."

"None taken, detective," Nick replied. "It's only a matter of time before you see several of us feds hanging around anyway."

"When that time comes, Agent Scarborough, you'll have this department's full cooperation." Garrett sat down at his desk, having clearly ended the conversation.

"Thank you for your time, detective. I'm sure we'll be in touch. Good afternoon."

"Good afternoon, agents." Garrett didn't bother to look up, instead speaking at his computer monitor.

"Well, that could have gone better," Kate said, stepping inside Nick's SUV.

"You can't be too hard on the local guys. They're just doing their job and protecting their territories. We get that sometimes. Unfortunately, I don't think it'll be the last time we see Detective Garrett or Ms. Sala."

SIX

The passageway echoed with approaching footsteps that grabbed Kate's attention. Her own steps were soft and not like the lumbering thuds sounding from behind. She stopped and waited, noticing that it was Mike Hewitt jogging to catch up to her. He had been a cop for the past five years and was the type of man who seemed to relish in the defeat of others. The undesirable quality ensured he had few friends at the Academy. And Kate was hesitant to stop in the first place.

"Reid, hold up," he said.

She'd returned to campus from the visit to Richmond and the battered Ruxandra Sala and was on her way to get dinner from the cafeteria. "What's going on?" Those who knew her would easily spot the plastic smile she wore from a mile away. Fortunately, Hewitt wasn't one of them.

"Did you hear?" He placed his hands on his hips and appeared to pause with much anticipation in hopes she would take the bait.

She prepared for what was sure to be the conveyance of delightfully upsetting news. "I've been out all day. Hear what?"

"Munoz is out. She went home today."

"What? Why?" This was not the news she was expecting. There wasn't a chance in hell her roommate had failed any part of her training.

"I don't know exactly, but I guess it was her choice. She wanted to go home."

Kate looked into Hewitt's now sparkling eyes. He'd gotten what he'd wanted. Delivering the disappointing news and seeing the look of defeat on her face. This just didn't seem possible. Firstly, because Jocelyn hadn't called or texted her to relay the news herself, and secondly, because Kate had come to appreciate their friendship. She was one of the few female friends she had anymore—and now that was gone.

"Didn't she tell you?"

"No. I guess I've got the room all to myself now. Not much consolation, though."

Hewitt raised his hand to Kate's shoulder. "I'm sure she felt like she'd let you down and was afraid to tell you. It must have been hard for her to leave her family behind."

Perhaps he had felt the slightest bit of empathy. "I guess so," she replied.

"I gotta head back. I saw you and thought I'd let you know. See you later?"

"Sure. Thanks, Mike."

Kate continued down the hall, not noticing Hewitt swaggering in the opposite direction. With her appetite having vanished along with Jocelyn, she returned to the now-empty dorm room. Jocelyn's side had been cleaned out. She knew Kate would be out today and must have figured it was the best time for her to pack up and leave.

Dropping to her bed, she looked over the now vacant bunk next to hers. Kate reached for the chain around her neck and started twirling the ring that dangled on its end, an action that had become completely involuntary. It was the engagement ring Marshall had intended to give her. It offered comfort, familiarity, and Kate needed that right now.

Jocelyn's departure was a reminder that this was no easy path. In fact, it had been more difficult that she'd imagined. But with Nick's support, she pushed herself far beyond her comfort zone.

Whether it was this latest disappointing news or the fact that the memory of Ruxandra Sala's appearance simply couldn't be squelched, Kate began to consider what had happened to the young woman. Labeling her a woman seemed a stretch. She couldn't have been more than twenty years old, but she was beautiful. Even through her marked face and swollen eyes, anyone could see that. Thick black hair and caramel-colored skin, she could have easily passed for a model.

» » »

The young girl wore a blindfold, causing her to trip over the steps until finally reaching what she thought was the threshold — an opened doorway. The man behind her yelled at her in a language she understood little. "Molim, ja ne razumijem. Molim te, nemoj me povrijediti." *Please, I do not understand. Please, do not hurt me,* she said.

"Just get inside!" the man yelled.

"Sorry, sorry." The young Serbian woman had learned enough English to get by, considering she'd only been in the country less than a year. Most of the words learned were the result of watching television shows.

It had been three days and Madlena had been on the move almost the entire time. Never allowed to sleep more than a few hours at a time; awakened by the cries of the other girls who had the misfortune of traveling with her, and suffering the effects of drugs used to keep her sedated.

Hungry, filthy, and having been violated more times than she cared to remember, Madlena prayed they would push enough drugs in her arms to kill her because this was a fate much worse than death. She wondered if her father was looking for her and if her sister was okay. Thinking of them helped suppress the reality she now faced.

The girls were so tightly packed into the dilapidated homes in which they were forced to stay that the stench was unbearable. Urine, body odor, and sex. It was enough to make anyone vomit, but there was virtually nothing in Madlena's stomach left to wretch. Already too thin, she hadn't looked in a mirror in three days, but when she felt along her rib cage, she was sure they protruded more than what she remembered.

Now, as she stepped inside wherever it was they'd taken her this time, she'd regretted ever coming to this country. It turned out to be no better here, at least not for someone like her.

A hard shove to her back courtesy of the man that towered behind her and Madlena was on the ground. She pulled her knees to her chest and the high-heeled shoes she wore in a life that appeared would never see her return were making it hard to stay in that position, but she did her best not to move. There were consequences for such prohibited actions.

"Help me."

Madlena, still wearing the blindfold, turned in the direction of the sound that was more like a whimper coming from another girl next to her. "Shhh." She knew what happened to the ones who spoke out of turn.

A man, she had no idea who, or how many there were, yanked the blindfold from her eyes and the light made her squint. It didn't take long for her focus to clear and the comprehension to return that she was in yet another run-down house. Madlena's back rested against a wall and on that wall were spindles of a staircase. Next to her was the girl who whispered for help. Madlena had none to offer. None of them did.

In the room directly in front of her, she spotted three men. Two were seated and one paced as if trying to solve a problem. He must have felt her stare because he whipped his head around and glared at her. Madlena turned away, fearing retribution for her curiosity. And although she could no longer look at them, she listened — and waited.

The only indication of time was the sun shining through the dirty stained-glass panel inside the front door. It was noticeably lower than when they'd arrived. Three girls, including Madlena, still sat on the floor up against the wall of the staircase. Her legs were asleep and her secured arms ached, so the fact that her ass had turned numb didn't seem quite as bothersome.

That would all go away soon, though, because her mind was clearing. The sedatives were wearing off and when that happened, it meant they were going to be moved again, or taken away. Three days ago, when she'd been taken, there were five other girls there when she joined the group. Now, only herself and two others remained. The rest were gone; where, she didn't know, but they hadn't returned. With only three of them left, Madlena wondered who would be next.

She raised her bound hands to her right ear and carefully pulled out the cubic zirconia earring. Lowering her hands again, one of her captors glanced over towards her. She pretended to scratch an itch on her face. When he looked away again, she set the earring on the ground and rolled it behind her back.

If she was the one chosen today, someone, she prayed, would know that she had been here. That she had existed.

» » »

Kate offered her "expert testimony" in the mock trial that was part of her training. She'd felt fairly confident of her performance and because many agents were asked to testify in court, this was an important skill to understand. But it did bring back a time, not long ago, when she was sitting in the same courtroom as Lewis Branson during the Highway Hunter trial. She quietly observed from the back row as all three of her friends – Scarborough, Myers, and Agent Jameson – took the stand. There had been many times during the two-month trial when she'd wanted to confront Branson. Nick put a stop to any such reckless endeavors, though, and reminded her that it wasn't Branson she'd wanted to harm. It was Shalot, and he was already dead.

"Hey. You heading home?" Will had already begun packing up while Kate was still fumbling with the notes the instructor had handed out after the trial.

"Yes, definitely. I'm looking forward to sleeping in my own home tonight. Without Jocelyn, it just feels weird being in the dorm room now. I don't know why. I live by myself; I should be used to it. So what about you? What're you doing tonight?"

The end of another week had already arrived. It didn't seem possible that she had only eight weeks left here at the base. She'd been busy working odds and ends details for the investigation, but nothing had turned up on Corbett yet and so Nick just kept telling her to hang tight, something would break. It hadn't and the only upside was that she'd been able to devote more time to her studies. But the girls and the case never left her mind. In fact, the more she thought about it, the more she began to realize that she wasn't all that different from them. It was easy to identify with the idea of coming to America to start a new, and hopefully better, life. She'd pushed her own reset button for a second time already. Once when she left Spencer, and again when Marshall left her. Being here, at the Academy, was her new and hopefully better life. It was doubtful she'd get a third reboot.

"Nothing much, just study probably. I don't know. It gets pretty quiet around here on the weekends and I suppose I've got nothing but time. Don't have a place yet since I still don't know what field office I'll be assigned to. Are you planning on being here in the morning?"

"Do I have a choice?" They both laughed. "I'll be here." Kate felt the phone in her pocket buzz and cut the laughter short. "Hang on a second, I gotta take this." She answered the line, "Reid here. Yeah, of course. I can be there in half an hour. Okay. Bye."

"What was that all about?" Will seemed to notice the glint in her eye.

"I have to go to the field office. Agent Scarborough's got a lead on the case. I'll see you tomorrow?" Kate hardly waited for a reply before she was off, leaving Will behind.

"Sure." His halfhearted gesture of goodbye went ignored.

Kate scrambled for her keys and stepped inside the car. Her excitement at the news, however, made her careless. By the time she reached the guard gates to exit the base, she'd forgotten to retrieve her ID badge. The FBI had its own police force at Quantico and no one went in or out without identification.

The guard already appeared irritated by her lack of preparedness as the growing line of cars formed behind her. She fumbled in her bag a while longer and finally found her badge, showing it to the man who stood impatiently outside her window. A nod of his head and the gate lifted, and Kate was gone.

Heat ascended in waves off of the vast federal building known to those in the industry as the WFO, or Washington field office. As evening set in, the relentless temperatures remained above normal. Combined with the hour of peak traffic and summer tourists, Kate arrived hot, both mentally and physically.

"Sorry it took me so long." Her brow glistened and her FBI-issued polo shirt did little to hide the embarrassing dampness under her arms.

However, Nick seemed preoccupied and hardly took notice of her arrival. He glanced up at her. "That's fine. Come on in and have a seat." He continued to study his monitor. "Got a call earlier today from our friend, Detective Garrett, in Richmond. They found another drop house." He turned his attention to Kate. "Only it wasn't empty this time. There were two dead women inside. He says they're waiting on labs, but is pretty sure they overdosed."

She waited for the rest of the news before revealing any feelings on the issue because she was a little unsure what the issue was. Two dead women and a drop house. Where was this big break she'd been promised?

He seemed to sense she wasn't behaving as enthusiastically as he might have expected. "There was evidence that several people were occupying the home just a few days ago. Richmond police got a call from a concerned neighbor that he'd seen women coming and going for the better part of two weeks, but didn't bother calling because it seemed to stop. And that today, he'd noticed an odor. So they went and checked the place out. Two girls were dead. No identification."

"So we're heading back to Richmond?"

"Yes, you and I are going down there first thing in the morning."

"Got it. I'll have to get a pass on my classes tomorrow then." She didn't think that would be too difficult. Saturdays were considered light by comparison being only half-days.

"You'll have to make it up. If you think it's too much, then let me know."

"No. It's not too much. I can handle it." What she hadn't wanted to tell him was that the more involved she became, the more she learned about the women who fell prey to trafficking, the more she connected with them and wanted to see justice done.

"Okay. Garrett's sent over what they've got so far. Let's take a look at it." Nick punched a few keys and pulled up images of the drop house. "We need to check this with the other neighborhoods they've found these drop house in already. Find any similarities between them."

"Similarities like how? Size or style?"

"No. Like community. How are these places being chosen? Are the areas known to be suited to a particular religious preference? What about culture? Ruxandra Sala's Ukrainian. Are these locations in highly immigrant areas, like the ones Metro Police have found?"

Nick's cell lit up on his desk as he spoke. "Hang on." He glanced at the caller ID. "Hey, hon, you in town yet?"

Kate didn't need to guess the identity of the caller and felt vaguely awkward for listening in on the conversation.

"I'm not sure when we'll be done here. I just got a lead on the trafficking case and we're going through it now." Nick was quiet for a moment. "Kate." He glanced at her and winked. "Okay, sounds good, babe. I'll see you then, bye." Nick ended the call. "Sorry about that."

"Don't be. It's nice to have someone who wants to know what you're up to."

Nick stopped to look at Kate for a moment and pursed his lips. "You know what? I probably didn't need to make you drive down here. I can handle this tonight and I'll brief you in the morning on the drive down. Why don't you go on home?"

It seemed he was feeling guilty about his personal life; the fact that he had one. Why else the reason for the change of heart only moments after Kate's arrival? Had she appeared that desperate and alone that she couldn't handle him talking to Georgia? If she hadn't known him well enough, she might have taken offense. "No. I want to stay. Please."

"Okay." Nick rubbed his slightly rounded bristled chin, which was in need of a shave. "Then I'll tell you what. Why don't we pack this stuff up and we can head on over to my place? At least we can grab some Chinese and have a beer or two. Can't get away with that here." Nick cast a suspicious glance as if to imply Big Brother was watching. "Georgia will be there later anyway. This way, I won't still be here when she arrives."

"Yeah. Okay. That sounds good. I could use a beer."

They both lived in Woodbridge, but he had a condo overlooking Belmont Bay, a slightly more exclusive area. She pulled up behind him to the expansive building that reminded Kate of row houses. It ran along a curved road across from the bay. She'd been here before and felt grateful to have found a parking spot while Nick continued on to the underground parking structure for the tenants of the building.

Kate stepped out of her car and grabbed her things, locking it up behind her. The air had a familiar scent and although cooler than when she arrived at the WFO, a slight breeze carried the scent of the bay with it and put Kate at ease. She continued along the concrete path to the building's main entrance, where Nick would have to buzz her inside. The door clicked open after announcing her arrival and Kate walked towards the elevator to the fourth floor, where his unit was located.

Nick opened the door and she stepped inside his well-appointed home. He must've had a cleaner because no man she'd ever known would keep house so well. It was either that or the fact that it never got dirty because he was rarely home in the first place.

"Go ahead and put your things on the dining table. There's a Chinese restaurant nearby that delivers. Pick what you want off the menu and I'll call it in. Can I get you a beer?" Nick asked as he moved towards the kitchen.

"Thanks. That'd be great." Kate was drawn towards the sliding glass door in the living room and she peered outside to the deck, casting her gaze onward towards the bay. The night was clear and the moon shone brightly, reflecting off the water and the boats that were docked. "You know, you really should get yourself a boat. I mean, what's the point in living here if you can't enjoy the bay?"

Nick held two opened beers in his hand and strolled up next to her, glancing through the same glass door. "What? With all my spare time?"

Kate took hold of one of the beers. "You have a valid point."

They both looked out over the water in a long stretch of silence, as if each yearned to be out there, enjoying the evening on the bay. Instead, they had to find some connection between the drop house locations where it was suspected that a human trafficking operation was being conducted. It was a surreal way of life.

"Okay, let's get to work." Nick turned away from the calming view and booted up his laptop to retrieve the files.

Kate shuffled towards the table, not really wanting to depart from the scene, and sat down next to him. He spread out the photos of Ruxandra Sala, the first victim with which they'd come into contact. The bruises on her face and arms and chest made Kate wince as she had when she'd seen them in person. But the young woman had been brave enough to escape and, if she hadn't, they'd have virtually nothing to go by. Now, another drop house had been located. This time, two women didn't survive, although Kate had no idea how many others there had been, or if they were alive or not.

She began to run the locations of the two houses to search for any similarities. Both had been situated in poor neighborhoods and both had been abandoned. A buzz from the intercom fixed to the wall startled her.

"Must be the food." Nick pushed up from his chair and pressed the button, confirming the identity of the caller, and quickly buzzed him in.

A moment later, he opened the door and handed the man forty dollars. "Keep the change. Thanks."

The two continued on, eating, drinking beer, and working, for at least an hour, maybe longer—she'd lost track of time. Kate was beginning to feel like it was the old days, except that the old days were with Marshall, but it still felt good. It had taken her a long time to come to terms with the fact that she was here, training to become an FBI agent, a scenario that she'd played around with in her mind a long time ago, but never really believed it would happen. Part of her felt guilty for enjoying this moment—working on a case with the agent who helped save her life. Part of her knew she was only here because Marshall wasn't.

The front door handle jiggled and drew their attention.

"Oh hell, what time is it?" Nick pressed the button on his phone. The time showed eleven p.m. "Dammit. That's Georgia."

Georgia walked through the front door and appeared surprised to see the two of them amidst a stack of papers and dueling laptops. "Oh." She glanced to Nick. "I didn't know you had company."

"Georgia, I'm so sorry. I lost track of time. Kate and I got wrapped up in this case." He met her at the door and leaned in for a kiss. Her long, red hair partially covered her lips and Nick pushed it back behind her ear. He turned back to Kate. "Why don't we call it a night? We've got a long drive and I'm sure you'd like to get organized and get some rest."

"Of course." If there was ever a moment to feel like a third wheel, it was now. Kate quickly packed up her belongings in order to vacate without further disruption.

"It's fine if you two need to work." Georgia said, laying her purse on the sofa table.

"No. Really, I need to get home. You two enjoy some time together. I know you don't get much of it." Kate shoved her laptop into her bag and tossed it over her shoulder. "I'll see you at seven?" She passed by the two of them, noticing the puff of wind that raised Georgia's hair in her wake as Kate practically ran to the door.

"I'll see you then," Nick replied.

"Goodbye, Georgia. I'm sorry we didn't get a chance to hang out a little." Now she just felt awkward. It was the look in Georgia's eyes, like she was pissed that Kate had been there in the first place, an unusual expression that perhaps had some measure of truth behind it.

Nick closed the door after her. "I just completely lost track of time, babe. I am sorry. But now, I'm all yours. Can I get you a drink or a glass of wine? There's some Chinese left if you're hungry."

Georgia continued to walk inside, standing in the middle of the living room. "I really feel like an ass here, Nick."

"What? Why would you say that?" He walked into the kitchen to pour her a glass of wine.

"Why didn't you tell me she was coming over?"

"I didn't realize I had to keep you abreast of the details of my working arrangements." He moved towards her, holding out her glass of wine. "Are you pissed at me or something? We're working on a case, Georgia."

"It's just the more I think about it, it seems like you pulled a whole lot of strings to get her assigned to your office, and I'm just trying to figure out why."

SEVEN

Despite being on the receiving end of an undeserved silent treatment, Kate understood that something had transpired last night after she left Nick's place. The early morning drive to Richmond found her trapped in the car, feeling awkward, and although she'd attempted to engage in some lighthearted conversation, she soon realized it was entirely inappropriate, considering the destination they were approaching.

It was a failed attempt in any case and so Kate figured he'd talk when he was ready, but his reticence bothered her. They were about to confirm that the investigation had taken a deadly turn and they should have been discussing leads and coordination efforts between the jurisdictions. Instead, Kate spent the better part of two hours listening to talk radio, something she despised in the first place.

Upon arrival at the abandoned house where the two women were found dead, Kate began to notice something. She stood outside the home and looked along the road at the houses lined up and down the street. A few people came outside to check the happenings, having spotted police units parked in front of the home. As soon as she caught the stare of one onlooker, the old woman immediately turned away. A few young men stood outside another home about three houses down, and since the houses were close together, they were getting a pretty good view of the circus.

What she'd noticed was that of those interested neighbors huddled in conversation, she'd overheard a language that was definitely not English. Kate walked over to one of the local police officers who was taking pictures of footprints in the yard. "Hey, those guys over there, can you hear what they're saying?"

The officer listened. "I can hear 'em, but I don't have any idea as to what they're saying. Probably speaking Croatian or Serbian; they're pretty similar. Not sure, but this is a highly immigrant area concentrated with eastern Europeans."

"Makes sense. Thanks." Kate walked inside and found Nick typing something on his phone. "Hey. How's it going in here?"

"Good. It looks like these guys might have an identity on at least one of the victims. A young woman was reported missing last week and this one matches the description. They're working on getting the family to confirm her identity, but she'll have to be taken to the morgue first."

"Does she match our victim profile?"

"I don't know much yet. If she was here or her family was here legally, that doesn't mean our theory is off base. It just means we got lucky to have been able to ID someone."

"I was talking to the officer out there," Kate began, "and he mentioned this neighborhood has a lot of Croatians and Serbians. Similar to the demographics of the other neighborhoods, including the one Ms. Sala managed to escape from."

"Add it to the growing list then. Whoever is running this thing is starting to get careless. One escaped and now two are dead—assuming they're connected. In my mind, that's quickly becoming a certainty." Nick watched the officers photographing the scene. "I'd sure as hell like to know why we haven't found Corbett yet. I don't know if he's the head of the snake, but he's a part of it, and we need to consider employing other methods to find him before more girls wind up dead or being sold off to the highest bidder."

"I'm not sure which is worse," Kate replied.

The Richmond Police Department's forensics team was operating at full capacity, by all accounts. They were starting to bring the bodies down the staircase and take them to the waiting coroner's office mobile transport outside.

"We can talk to some of the neighbors, find out if they knew the victims, once we confirm their identities, or if they knew the men who brought them here," Kate said.

"That's why you're working with me," Nick started. "I don't know what the hell Georgia's problem is."

Kate suspected this had been the underlying reason for Nick's standoffish behavior. "She doesn't want us working together?"

"Hell, I don't know. I think it's just that she's been away so much lately and you and I have been working closely."

"Is she jealous? Of you and me?" A smile crept up on her face.

"Don't sound so surprised. I'm quite the catch, you know." Nick raised his hand to prevent her from issuing any sort of apology. "I don't think she's jealous, per se. I think it bothers her a little that I spend more time with you than I do with her. That's all."

Kate didn't know exactly how to respond to this. The last thing she'd wanted was to get in the way of those two. She considered Nick a mentor and a friend. It was hard to admit that the men who meant the most to her in her life had been mentors at one point in time. The idea seemed to prove Georgia's assumptions.

But the time had come for Kate to stand on her own two feet. And she couldn't let Georgia or anyone else get in the way of that goal. She was fighting for her own existence now and refused to crumble under the weight of her own guilt.

A small glimmer caught Kate's eye and she turned her head in the direction of the brief glow. An earring. A small, probably cubic zirconia, stud earring was wedged between one of the floorboards and the baseboard on the wall of the stairs. She leaned down to be sure.

"What is it?" Nick asked.

"Is that an earring?" She was careful not to pick it up. This wasn't her first rodeo.

Nick bent down on one knee to get a closer look. "It sure as hell is. How did you see that?"

"I don't know. The sun must've reflected off of it for just a second." It was surely a coincidence that Kate had seen, on more than one occasion, a glimmer catching her eye from her own home. It disappeared as quickly as it had appeared and she didn't know what it was, except perhaps her own imagination. It didn't feel like it was her imagination any more.

"Well, it could be something, it could be nothing, but that's a hell of a good eye you got there, Reid. Let's get those guys over there to bag it and tag it. Might belong to one of the victims."

"Or to one of the girls they took with them." Kate turned back towards the front entry. "I'm going to have a walk down the road. I'll be right back." She didn't think Nick heard her, but continued on anyway while he tracked a CSI down to collect the earring.

Kate stepped outside the home once again and walked across the dried, brown lawn and out onto the street. She began to head towards the men she'd heard talking earlier.

As she drew closer, their eyes followed her every step. Kate was in her NAT uniform, blue polo, light khaki pants, and black holster strapped to her waist. Her dark hair was pulled back in a ponytail. "Hello. I'm with the FBI and I'm working with the local police at that house just over there." She pointed to it.

One of the young men rolled his eyes at her gesture, then she realized it was fairly obvious where she'd come from. "Do you mind if I ask you two a couple of questions?"

"Nemamo pojma što govoriš." *We have no idea what you're saying,* one of them said.

A young girl stepped outside onto the porch of the home where the men lingered. "They don't speak English. Not much anyway."

"But you do?" Kate asked.

The girl of maybe twelve answered with a nod.

"Are they your brothers?" Kate asked.

The girl nodded; her thick hair falling into her face.

"Do you know what happened over there at that house?"

"Ono što je ona kaže, Nicola?" *What is she saying, Nicola?* the man asked, puffing on his cigarette, his eyes never leaving Kate.

The two exchanged several phrases that Kate had no way of following. She only waited patiently for the girl to translate.

"My brother says he knows that someone died there. A woman."

"Two, actually," Kate replied.

"He says he has seen the men coming and going from that house."

Kate felt a surge of anticipation rise. "Does he know these men? Does he know their names?"

The girl spoke to her brother in their native tongue once again, leaving Kate on the edge of her seat for an answer.

"He doesn't know them, but he has seen them at the bar where our cousin works."

"Do you think your brother could take me to see your cousin?" Kate asked and again waited for translation.

"He says he will take you."

"Good. Please tell him that I will be back in just a few minutes. I need to see my boss first. Please ask him to wait for me and I will return. I promise."

"Okay."

"Thank you, Nicola."

Kate jogged back to the house where Nick stood on the front porch talking with Detective Garrett.

"Where did you go?" he asked.

"I was just speaking with the neighbors down there. They've seen the men that were here. One of them said his cousin, who works at some bar, could identify the men. I guess they were in that bar a few times, I don't know, but we need to get down there. The only problem is that these guys don't speak much English. Only the little girl does."

"From what I gathered, this area has a concentration of Croatian immigrants. I bet we can find one of the local cops who can speak the language." Nick looked to Garrett. "You got anyone who speaks Croatian?"

"Not here. Not that I know of, but let me ask around. Give me a minute and I'll find out." The detective left the two of them alone.

"We need to get back there before the guy changes his mind. He didn't seem to be overly enthused in the first place," Kate said, glancing back at the home.

"Why did you go over there by yourself? I turned around for a minute and you were gone."

"I just got an idea, and I did say something. You just weren't listening. Aren't I supposed to be able to take the lead once in a while? What kind of agent would I be if I just sat back while you did everything for me?"

"It's not that. You need to be safe. There's no way I'd have let you walk over there without someone else with you. You don't know those guys, Kate. You gotta remember to be cautious."

"All right. Point taken." Kate checked her tone, realizing that she'd come off defensively. "Can we just get back there, please?"

The detective returned, shaking his head. "Sorry, no one here can help, but I'd like to come with you. The guy who works at the bar has to speak English."

The three of them headed towards the house where the two men now stood on the bottom step of the porch. Their basketball jerseys hung almost to their knees with shorts that could have been confused for pants.

Kate didn't know how long they'd been in this country, but they appeared to be American sports fans, or they were trying to blend in. She figured the kids couldn't have been much older than twenty, maybe twenty-one, and she assumed at least one was the brother of the girl called Nicola.

On approach, the men appeared leery, not expecting two other law officers flanking the woman they knew to be with the FBI.

"Policija?" The man turned to his sister.

She nodded.

"Nema lokalna policija, samo FBI," the man said.

The young girl with full lips and thick, dirty-blonde hair looked at Kate. "My brother says no police, only FBI."

"I see you've built a good rapport with those in the community," Nick said to the detective.

"Yeah, well, it's a work in progress. Look, you two go. Talk to the bartender and find out what you can about this house.

I'm going to be here for another couple of hours anyway. So, just give me a buzz when you know something." Garrett patted Nick on the back and nodded to Kate. He turned to the kid. "No policija."

The two men spoke words that meant nothing to Kate and Nick. But she would have believed it to be a discussion that verged on becoming an argument, noting the inflections and slightly raised tones. The one who appeared slightly younger went back inside the house and quickly returned with a cell phone in his hand and began walking towards them.

"Do you want me to come with you?" the girl asked Kate.

"I don't think that'd be a good idea, sweetheart. A bar is no place for a young girl. But thank you for your help."

Nick extended his hand to direct the man to his car, which was still parked in front of the crime scene. When they approached the house, the man turned towards it and spoke.

"Prostitutke."

"Prostitutes?" Nick asked.

The man nodded.

Kate hadn't asked the sister her brother's name and figured she should attempt to find out. "What is your name?" She pressed her hand to her chest. "Kate."

"Kate?" he replied. "Gregor. Gregor Bjurić."

Nick unlocked the car and opened the rear passenger door. He scanned the man's body. "Are you armed?"

He didn't understand and tilted his head.

"Gun?" Nick pointed to his own weapon.

"Oh. No. No gun," he replied.

Nick made a gesture to indicate he would need to pat the kid down. He seemed reluctant, but allowed Nick to check for a weapon. It didn't appear to be the first time he was patted down either, as indicated by his stance. "Okay."

Gregor stepped inside while Kate slipped into the front passenger seat.

"Well, I'm not sure how we're supposed to find this bar if the guy can't give us directions," Nick said, shutting his door and turning the key to the ignition.

Kate turned back to Gregor and then pointed straight. He nodded. After several of these same gestures, they reached the bar, which had only been a couple of blocks away.

Nick pulled into the parking lot and it appeared as though the place wasn't even open. "Now what?"

"Up." Gregor pointed to the staircase that led to a door at the top, just above the bar.

Nick got out and opened the rear passenger door.

Gregor followed and cast a cautious glance at Nick. He began to walk up the stairs alone and knocked on the door. They waited at the bottom, leaning against the car.

"Why do I get the feeling that this guy understands more English than he's letting on?" Nick asked.

The door opened and a man of similar build and age stepped just into view. The two began talking and, after a moment, the occupant looked down at Nick, then returned his attention to his cousin.

The two finally began to descend the stairs and Nick moved towards Kate. "All right. Let's see what this guy knows."

The man next to Gregor tossed his cigarette to the ground and thrust his hands inside the front pockets of his jeans. They continued to move towards the agents.

Nick immediately cast his eyes to the man, whose hands were now out of view. His stance firmed and he placed a hand on his revolver. "You speak English?"

"Yes," the man replied. He must have sensed Nick's alarm and slowly pulled his hands back out of his pockets and held them palms up to show the FBI man that he was unarmed.

"I'm Special Agent Nick Scarborough. This is Special Agent Trainee Kate Reid. Your cousin here said you might know something about what was happening at the house on his street."

The man eyed Kate up and down. "You're training to be an FBI agent?" he asked her.

"Yes, sir."

He nodded his head and returned his attention to Nick. "Greg says you found some dead bodies there or something?" The man didn't have an accent.

"Yes. Two female victims. If you don't mind, can I ask your name?"

"Julian Petrovich."

"You're from Croatia as well?" Kate asked.

"My parents are. I was born here. Greg's my cousin. His family moved here about two years ago. But Greg hasn't had much interest in learning English, so his sister translates a lot for him."

"We met her. Nicola?" Nick said.

"Yes. So Greg told you I talked to those guys who were living at that house."

"Did they live there?" Nick asked.

"Well, not exactly. I mean, it wasn't like they were paying rent or anything. That house has been abandoned for years and the city won't do nothing about it. Anyway, these guys came in asking where they could find companionship. Said they were hanging out at that house and wanted a taste of the local talent."

"It seems there are quite a few Croatians living here. Did they specifically ask for a Croatian companion?" Nick asked.

Greg started speaking to his cousin. Julian shook his head and continued, "There's a mix here. Croatians, Serbians, Hungarians, Romanians. They're all here, but don't hang around one another. In fact, they do the best they can to stay as far away from each other as possible."

"And yet, they all live in this community?" Kate asked.

"Yeah, go figure. Anyway, these guys were looking for pretty much any woman from Eastern Europe. I don't know. I guess that was their thing, but I told them where they could find the kind of women who wanted to be paid for their services."

"Do you think if I showed you a picture that you might recognize them?"

"Sure. I don't see why not. They both came in a couple of times. I remember them."

"So it was just two men?" Nick asked.

"Just two that came into the bar. Don't know if they had friends at the house or whatever."

Nick leaned into the car and pulled out the photo of James Corbett and the composite sketch they'd received from Ms. Sala's description. "These guys look familiar to you?"

Julian took hold of the pictures and examined them for a moment. "I recognize this guy for sure." He was holding up Corbett's picture. "This one could be the guy he was with. It's hard to say based on this drawing. He's bald, so it's possible this could be him."

They still had no identification on the man in the composite, but it appeared they were dealing with the same person.

"I don't suppose they ever gave you names?" Nick asked, concerned Corbett had been operating under an alias and hoping they could get some indication of who his partner was.

"No, I didn't ask either. Not my business." Julian went quiet for a moment. "Did they kill those girls in the house?"

"That's what we're trying to find out. You've been a big help. Would you mind if Detective Garrett with Richmond PD stopped by to ask you a few more questions?"

Julian looked at his cousin. "Um, yeah, I guess that'd be okay. I can give Greg a lift home."

"Thank you, Mr. Petrovich and thank you, Gregor," Kate replied.

They got back inside the car and pulled out of the parking lot. Kate looked back at the men through the side view mirror. "What's the deal with the local cops here?"

"No idea. Clearly, there are some issues. We need to stop at the station and inform Garrett of what we've got."

» » »

Madlena sat on the edge of the bed in the silky robe given to her by the man who now owned her, for a specified length of time, although she was not privy to that information and had no idea how long she would be here. It was better than the derelict houses she'd been held captive for the past several days. Here, a hot shower, clean clothes, and comfortable bed were being offered, but for a high price. Mild sedatives and heroin still coursed through her veins, and it was now much too difficult to decipher the day or time, only that she looked through a foggy lens. Perhaps it was better that way. Dulled senses and hazy memory kept her from fully realizing the horror she was living.

Her sale had come by way of an auction where she'd been examined by several men. She was forced to stand, half-naked in front of them, and they leered at her slender figure. Now she knew what had happened to the other girls, and since none had returned while she was there, Madlena likened this viewing to a death knell.

After the bidding ended, she was then placed onto a small plane that brought her to this place now. The man who paid for her seemed like just another John and she did what he asked. But now he kept her in a hidden room. No windows, but plenty of devices by which he used to bring her pain. Her body was worn, bruised, and swollen.

Madlena began to think of her family. Her sister would probably be in school right now, something her father would have insisted upon even as Madlena remained missing, if only to keep the child from worry.

The sound of a latch releasing caught her attention. He was coming.

EIGHT

A phone call from Detective Moreno with Metro Police during the drive back from Richmond brought unwelcomed news. After the day's long effort working with the local police and playing the go-between with Moreno and Garrett, the call was just fetid icing on top of a bad cake.

Moreno was following a lead on a tip regarding the location of James Corbett, but it failed to turn up anything and so the man for whom a BOLO had already been issued still evaded them.

"What about the composite sketch from Ruxandra Sala? Any idea who that guy is? We know he's partners with Corbett. The bartender confirmed as much," Nick said to the detective.

"Not yet. I ran it through our recognition software, but there was no match." His voice sounded through the car speakers. "I was hoping you guys could run it through your databases."

"We'll be back in the office soon. I'll have Agent Jameson get it into the national database and see what we come up with. If we can find out who this guy is, it might bring us closer to finding Corbett. We'll be in touch. Thank you, detective." Nick pressed the end call button on his steering wheel.

» » »

The time on his cell phone showed three p.m. The bar would be opening soon. Julian took the final bite of his sandwich and locked up his apartment. The commute wasn't bad, just a walk down the stairs and he was inside the bar. He flipped the light switch and a soft buzz filled the room. The sound came from fluorescent lights with green glass shades that hung over the pool tables.

The stools had been upturned onto the bar top and Julian returned them to the floor, but not before a quick wipe with his dishcloth. The bar was blessed with being the only one inside a mile radius of the tight-knit community and so, while it lacked a certain quality that would find it ranking low on Zagat's list, it was always packed with hardworking people, mostly of eastern European lineage. Julian's father had retired and now, after twenty years, it was his turn to run the place.

With his back turned, organizing the bottles of liquor placed strategically on the shelves, Julian noticed a sliver of light bouncing off the mirror behind the wall of booze. It was the front door and someone was opening it.

"We're not open yet. I'll need a few more minutes, please." He set a bottle of gin down and began to turn around. The light from the opened door cast shadows on the rest of bar and the identity of the visitor remained in disguise. As the person's steps drew near, Julian smiled as the shadows finally revealed his guest. "Oh. It's you. What are you doing here?"

"Trebali su držali jezik za zubima, Julian." *You should have kept your mouth shut, Julian.*

"Toma, wait!" He raised his hand to shield him from the gun that was now pointing at his head. "What did I do? What did I do?" His face masked in fear, the words stumbled from his lips as he looked through the spread fingers of his hand. The automatic defense mechanism would do little to stop the bullet from piercing his skull. A moment was all he had to understand why this was happening. And then it came to him. *Gregor.*

The gun fired point blank at Julian's head and he crumpled to the floor behind the bar. Blood and brain matter sprayed onto the bottles behind him. The massive bullet ripped through his head and carried on through to the mirrored wall, shattering the glass and bottles until they fell on top of the now lifeless Julian Petrovich.

Toma, a square-shaped man with ham hands and a face wrecked by tattoos, looked over the counter to ensure that his victim was not moving. "No policija, no FBI." He retrieved the dishcloth that rested on the counter and wiped the few spatters of blood that landed on him. Turning away, he headed to the entrance again. The door had remained open and he wondered for a moment if anyone had heard the gunfire. Then he figured, if anyone had, there would be no calls to the police. No one around here trusted them. Toma flipped off the lights and closed the door on his way out.

» » »

The CCTV monitors displayed the action on the streets of Hogan's Alley as the tactical training operation was about to begin. Agents responsible for coordinating the drills watched the screens and gave out orders to the actors. Kate was behind the scenes, watching the raid unfold.

Supervisory Special Agent Hawes stood next to her and began pointing to one of the screens. "This is where you seem to have the problem." The NATs involved in the drill were quickly assessing the situation and putting to use some of the techniques they'd learned. "When you get to this point," he continued, "your reactions are not adequate to the situation. You are too hesitant." Hawes turned to her. "Hesitation kills, Reid."

While she was hanging onto his every word, a disruption came by way of a call on her phone. *Damn it.* Agent Scarborough's name popped onto the screen. "Sir, it's Agent Scarborough. May I take this?"

The look on Hawes' face suggested Kate was pushing her luck, but he nodded anyway. "Thank you, sir." She stepped outside the surveillance room into the bright corridor. "Reid here."

"That kid from the bar the other day?" Nick wasted no time.

"Gregor?"

"No. His cousin, Petrovich."

"Yeah."

"Shot in the head. A couple of patrons found him behind the bar about an hour ago. Detective Garrett wants us to head back down ASAP."

"Oh my God." Kate glanced to the closed door behind her. "I'm right in the middle of training. Can I…"

"Let Hawes know what's going on. He'll let you leave. Meet me at the WFO in an hour." Nick ended the call.

Kate returned her phone to her pocket and stepped back inside the room. Agent Hawes looked at her as if he already knew what she was about to ask.

"Scarborough needs you?"

"One of the men we spoke to the other day has just been killed. Agent Scarborough wants us to get back to Richmond."

Hawes returned to view the monitors and waved an arm at Kate. "Go on, then."

» » »

Nick was talking on his cell and pulling on his coat when Kate arrived at the field office. She spotted him and followed him along the hall. His pace was quick and she had to jog to keep up with him.

Agent Jameson approached from one of the conference rooms. "You heard what happened?" he asked Kate.

"Yeah. Agent Scarborough asked me to come down. We're heading back to Richmond. You coming?"

"Right behind you."

Nick turned to the two of them. "That was Detective Garrett. His people are at the scene now."

"Do they have any idea who might have killed Petrovich?" Jameson asked.

"No one's talking." He glanced at Kate. "You ready to go?"

She nodded. "Have they checked for surveillance footage yet?"

"The bar's security cameras were disabled. He's got his team checking any other cameras in the area. Someone found out that we talked to the guy. I've already asked Garrett to check on Bjuric; make sure he and his family are okay."

"What about the little girl?" Kate asked.

"Don't know yet. We'll find out when we get there."

» » »

The hole-in-the-wall neighborhood bar was gaining attention from the people in the nearby shops and local markets. And the later it got, the larger the crowd became. Most were probably on their way home from work and either frequented the bar or lived nearby.

Just as Nick pulled on scene, a local news truck followed right behind them. The three got out of the SUV and approached Detective Garrett, who stood outside talking to a member of his team.

"I'll let you handle that." Nick pointed a thumbs-up in the direction of the news van.

"I don't want them to know the FBI is here. Why don't you guys go inside? I'll take care of this."

As soon as the three crossed over the police tape, one of the local officers immediately approached. "You can't be in here."

Nick figured the guy was protecting his territory and understood that, but he pulled out his badge to make his own assertions. "Special Agent Nick Scarborough, FBI. Detective Garrett asked us to come inside while he deals with the media. He's out there, if you want to ask him."

The officer stared at Nick's badge, then glanced at Kate and Dwight. "These two with you?"

He nodded.

"Okay. What do you need to know?"

"Has the victim already been taken by the coroner?" Nick took the lead and headed towards the bar area.

"About an hour ago. Clean shot to the head. It was a large caliber semi-automatic pistol. Ballistics has the bullet and casing now. Looks like it was a .50 caliber Dezzy."

"Jesus," Jameson replied.

Kate wasn't familiar with the nickname, but assumed because of the large caliber size, the gun was intended to make a statement.

Nick eyed the hole in the back of the bar. "So, we're talking wanna-be gangster?" Nick asked.

"Wanna-be or *is* a crime boss, would be my guess." Detective Garrett walked inside and approached the agents.

Nick turned around. "Like maybe in the upper echelon of a trafficking ring?"

"Maybe."

"What about Bjuric? Is his family safe?" Kate asked.

"We found the young girl and the mother, but not the brothers." Garrett replied. "I can only hope they went into hiding and aren't already dead. Something like this is going to spread around the community fast. If those boys aren't lying low yet, they will be soon."

"I'd like to have my team run background checks on Petrovich's family and Bjuric's too. Also, Petrovich identified James Corbett, but we still don't have a name for his cohort. We didn't get any hits from our database either. What about any other video from these cameras?" Nick glanced at one camera tucked away in the far corner above the bar. "If they were disabled, that means they were operating at one time or another. Anyone search Petrovich's home yet?"

"My guys are up there now."

Nick surveyed the bar. "Assuming this location, this community, is the hub of the operation, and I'm beginning to suspect that it is, why would Corbett and his partner have come here asking about the local talent? Wouldn't they have already known? There's no question in my mind that whoever killed Petrovich is linked with these guys—and that he's local." Nick turned to Garrett. "Why would they tell Petrovich anything or ask him any questions that might lead someone to believe they were looking for a particular type of girl?"

"Maybe they were recruiting?" Garrett replied.

The detective might have been onto something, Kate thought. But perhaps recruitment on a different level. "Julian Petrovich probably overheard a lot of interesting conversations," she began, "and was probably aware of any new people coming in or had at least been made aware of the happenings in the neighborhood. Maybe these guys were looking to recruit him? Have him help scope out the targets?"

» » »

"Što vam je rekao? Petrovich?" *What did Petrovich tell you?*

Gregor's hands were bound and his face bloodied. He recognized his surroundings because he'd been in this diner many times before, but never in this position; sitting on a metal folding chair inside the storage room where they kept the canned goods and condiments. "Ništa, kunem se." *Nothing, I swear.* His cousin Julian had told him nothing except what he said to the FBI. He didn't think Julian had anything to tell. None of this was supposed to be happening. He was going to be killed for opening his mouth. Why hadn't his brother stopped him? Why hadn't he told him? Now it would be up to Toma to decide if he was to live or die and only his brother could save him now.

"I don't think he knows anything. If he does, he won't be talking to the FBI or the police anytime soon. I'll keep him close to me, Toma. He doesn't need to end up like Julian."

"If it hadn't been for Gregor, Julian would still be alive. That kid didn't deserve to die for your fuckup." Toma looked at Gregor. "Now I'm just supposed to let you go? You think my boss is going to be okay with that?"

A tear fell from Gregor's eye. "No." His voice sounded scratchy from a dry throat.

"There were cameras in the bar. Were they recording?" The man who was speaking was scarcely older than Gregor himself.

"No," Toma began. "They weren't working, at least not when I walked in. I checked." He leaned against one of the steel shelving units. "Kovac wants another three for him by the end of the week. Can you do that?"

The young man, wearing an oversized basketball jersey of the Charlotte Bobcats, looked to Gregor, wiping his brother's blood from his knuckles. "What about him?"

"I don't know yet. I haven't decided."

"I told you, brother. No policija."

He understood now why Vito hadn't wanted him to go with those FBI agents. He was a part of it and now Gregor was too, whether he wanted to be or not. He closed his swollen eyes and, in his thick Croatian accent, he replied, "No more policija, brother."

» » »

The trainees lined up along the mats inside the gymnasium, wearing gloves and headgear. The instructor paired them off and the rounds were about to start. The purpose of boxing was to get the agents used to taking a punch and how to react when it happened. They'd also have to wrestle one another for forty-five seconds until one of them managed to get the other one down on the ground, hands pulled behind their backs.

There was no discrimination here. With only seven women remaining in their class of thirty-two, there would be no special treatment. They were expected to fight against another trainee and it didn't matter if that trainee was a woman.

Will and Kate were teamed up once again for this round of training. He hit his gloves together like a boxer and turned to Kate. "How'd it go the other day in Richmond?"

"I was only there for a few hours, but Scarborough and Jameson are coming back today. I'll know more later. They're checking for any surveillance video from public safety cameras, but I don't know if they came up with anything. Scarborough had me running on a piece of evidence I found in one of the drop houses, so I spent some time with Forensics, but nothing yet."

"Caison, Reid, you're up." The instructor blew his whistle.

"I'll take it easy on you," Will said, walking out onto the mat.

"Don't flatter yourself. I can hold my own, Caison."

Kate wanted him to take the first swing, but wasn't sure if he would. Someone needed to, though, because this was no game. This was training and they had to do it because it could save their lives someday. She could hear her breath echoing in her ears and the heat from it bounced off the chin guard and into her eyes. She blinked first and then stars filled her eyes.

He'd taken the first swing and struck her across her left cheek. It stung, but it was the shock of the blow that caught her off guard. She'd have to strike back. A right hook to his chin and Will stumbled back a few steps. Kate cracked a small smile.

He struck again. This time, it felt as though he was trying to take it easy on her, and it pissed her off. She nailed him in the gut and Will doubled over, but only for a moment. She could see him smile and shake his head. It was on now.

Two minutes and the whistle sounded and both stopped to catch their breath.

"Okay, Hicks and Goldman, you're up," the instructor said. "Good job, Reid. Caison, good defense."

They stepped off the mat and removed their headgear. Kate wiped away the band of sweat and the hair that stuck to it from her forehead. She still breathed heavily, but not from physical exhaustion. It was the image of Hendrickson's boot striking her head the moment Will's glove made contact that caused her pulse to rise and her breaths to deepen. She looked away from him, afraid he would see in her eyes what she felt in her head—fear.

"You all right?" Will asked.

"I'm fine. Are you?" She tried to brush it off. If something like that happened to her in the field, would she be able to get past it? Would it slow her reaction times, like what Hawes suggested was happening during her ops drills? If it did, it could cost her her life or that of another agent. This was a problem and one she was ill prepared to handle.

"You got a pretty mean right hook, I'll give you that." He rubbed his chin.

"Yeah, well, I've had some practice." Kate revealed a nervous grin.

Another round and they were up again. This time, no headgear allowed. The reasoning behind the technique was for the NATs to understand how to react rationally if he or she was hit. The shock of a bare-knuckled blow could throw people off. She could personally attest to that. Her concern now was that another vision would surface. She was frightened by the idea that she could no more control them than she could have controlled Hendrickson in the first place.

Recalling Nick's words that not all agents were faced with daily life-threatening situations, she closed her eyes for a moment to clear her thoughts. *Who the hell would want me for a partner?*

When the whistle blew this time, she understood what was required of her and knew that she wouldn't get a third chance. Failing this and struggling with ops training would find her on the way out.

Her eyes opened and she moved in to strike first. An effective blow, Caison stumbled back after she caught him with an uppercut to his ribs. He doubled over and quickly lost his footing. Caison face-planted onto the mat and struck his nose hard.

She reached for his arm to help get him to his feet. "I'm sorry, Will. Are you okay?" He didn't look it.

"Caison? You all right?" The instructor looked at him with only mild concern.

"Fine. I'm fine." He held his bleeding nose and stepped off the mat.

Kate noticed some of the other trainees showing some unease for his plight. She felt really bad, but also kind of proud. So it hadn't been her strength that brought him down, just his two left feet, but still. Her earlier concerns started to fade—a little.

"Again, I am so sorry, Will." Kate helped him put his gear back in his bag.

He pulled the tissue away from his nose to check and see if it had stopped bleeding. "Hey, no problem. You were just taking out your aggressions. I get it."

He was piling on the guilt, all right. "I—I wasn't..."

Will laughed. "I know. I'm just giving you shit. The least you can do is buy me dinner."

"Sure, but you want to go out in public looking like that?" Kate pushed open the gym door for Will and she followed behind.

"Maybe you're right about going out in public. How about we just grab some food from the cafeteria and hang out in your room again? We can go to my room, but you know what Lancaster's like. He'll give me shit about this for the rest of the night."

"Hang on." Kate reached for her phone as a call came in. "This is Reid."

"Kate, I'm still in Richmond," Nick began, "but forensics came back on that earring you found at the house. Jameson ran the DNA sample and got a match. An unidentified woman was found in Virginia Beach last week and the case was entered into CODIS. It's the same woman who was there at that house. We're heading to Virginia Beach shortly to talk with local police there. She was discovered behind a laundromat. Local cops think it was overdose again, but are fairly certain she was moved after her death."

"Do you want me to go with you?" Kate asked.

"No. I got it this time. But if this is the break that I think it will be, then I'll let you know and we'll go from there. Right now, I think you need to stay put. But, Kate, if you hadn't found that earring, we wouldn't be having this conversation."

"Thanks, Agent Scarborough."

"I'll call you as soon as I know something." He ended the call.

"Something happening with the investigation?" Will asked.

"I think so. We might be getting a break on this case after all. Another woman was found dead, but this time, we know she was one of the kidnapped victims. We just need to find out who she is."

They reached the dormitory. "So, we heading out for food, or just up to the room?" Kate asked, her thoughts still on the girl in Virginia Beach.

"Let's just grab something from the cafeteria. Actually, I'll hit the Marine Px and pick up some brews first. How about I catch up with you in say, half an hour? I'll just meet you at your room."

"Sure. Sounds good. See you then."

She'd wanted to be there with Scarborough. She wanted him to say, "Meet me in Virginia Beach." But they both knew that she could only do so much. The more she thought about this latest development, the more concerned she became about the rising toll of bodies.

As she walked to the building's entrance and showed her ID to the guard, she hiked the four flights of stairs to her room. Another woman had been found dead. Yet another woman in a string of deaths all related to a human trafficking ring. And they still had no idea where the leader was or who his partners were.

Kate reached her room and dropped her bag on her bed. She checked the small mirror on the desk and noticed her left cheek was a little red. Pressing lightly on the raised lump, she looked at the scar on her temple. She pulled her hair over to conceal it.

Will had arrived and now stood outside with his hands full. "Here. Let me get that for you." She grabbed the paper bag and peeked inside. "You managed to get this past the guard?"

"He took one look at my face and said I looked like I needed a beer, so he let me on up."

Kate smiled and stepped aside to let him in. "You want an ice pack for that? I think I have one in the mini fridge."

"No thanks. I'll survive." Will opened the pizza box and grabbed a slice. "Here. I just picked this up on the way."

"Thanks." Kate popped open a beer and took a big drink.

"How's it been without Munoz?" He sat down on the former roommate's bed.

"Okay, I guess. She sent me an email last week saying she was sorry for not telling me first. I don't blame her. It must have been hard leaving her kids and husband."

"Yeah. Well, they told us from the very beginning that not all of us would make it through."

"I know." Kate took another swig out of her can of beer. "I just didn't think it would be her. I mean, with her background. But then, I still may not yet survive this."

"You will. I know you will."

Kate could see that while he believed she would make it, perhaps it wouldn't be of her own doing. "You think Scarborough is going to make sure I pass, don't you?"

Will cast his eyes towards the window. "That's not what I'm saying."

"Well then, why don't you spit it out?" Kate felt a growing sense of irritation.

"Look, Kate, I'm not trying to start an argument here. I believe you are more than capable of passing this program. You've already proven your abilities… in more ways than one." He stopped for a moment. "I've read a little about you. I know some of what you've been through."

"I'm sure it wasn't too hard to find." It had only been in the past couple of months, since the end of the Branson trial, that the media attention finally died down.

"It's just that I think Scarborough feels responsible for making sure you pass. For making sure you get everything you want because he knows firsthand all the shit that you've been through. I mean, you've lost a hell of a lot, Kate. I was in

Iraq and I saw men die, but I didn't lose my childhood friend or the person I loved."

Kate had a hard time listening to anyone else talk about them. She could hardly talk about them herself. Her heart dropped into her stomach, but she pressed on. "So you think Scarborough is going to do whatever he has to do to see me through the Academy?"

"I think he'll help you if you need it and he'll make sure you know you've got a safety net. I just don't think you need it."

She set down her paper plate. "Excuse me for just a second." Rising from the bunk, she began walking towards the bathroom.

"I'm sorry, Kate. Are you mad at me?"

"No. I'm not. I just need a minute." She turned to him. "You might be right about Agent Scarborough, but I *can* do this without his or anyone else's help."

The bathroom was shared by the adjacent room and Kate went inside and locked both doors. She was upset by Will's honesty. If he was able to pick up what was happening with Scarborough, then others in her class probably could too.

"Kate? Your phone's ringing. It's Scarborough."

She pulled the washcloth from her face. "Can you grab it and tell him to give me a second. I don't want to miss his call," Kate said from behind the door. "Code is 3626."

Will entered her security code and unlocked the phone. "Agent Reid's phone. This is Agent Caison."

Nick was quiet for a moment. It seemed he wasn't expecting to hear Caison's voice. "Yeah, I need to talk to Reid."

"Hang on. She's in the restroom."

"Never mind. Just have her call me back ASAP." Nick hung up.

Kate stepped out of the restroom and reached for her phone, noticing the peculiar look on Will's face.

"He hung up."

NINE

Instructed to sit on the couch, the young woman who'd been too high to remember her own name followed the orders. Corbett reached for his camera. "Spread your legs." He began snapping pictures of her genitalia. His clients demanded to see the goods before making their deposits and the images could also be used for the websites to promote their offerings.

It was a lucrative industry, one that found Corbett on the receiving end of more money than he ever made in his previous life as a high school counselor or before that when he worked in the food service industry. Never an ambitious man, he was often preoccupied with the young girls for whom counseling services were offered or the part-time kids who worked in the fast food restaurants on his delivery route.

It had been all too easy for him to pass the background check and the tests required to work at the school. Of course, he hadn't had a criminal record, which helped. And their job requirements were a joke. But it gave him the idea to take his talents and put them to better use. From there, it didn't take him long to align himself with the man who was running the show.

What put all that in jeopardy was that he'd been required to submit fingerprints for the school district. That had been the reason his identity was so easy for the cops to obtain. That, and the fact that he'd failed to use a proxy server on one of his websites that led them to his door. Corbett hadn't wanted to leave his home, but there was little choice. Now he had to be constantly on the move, and it was becoming a hassle. The biggest danger was in transporting them. It would only take one person to witness him taking half-unconscious women and tossing them into the van. It was best when his partner could keep them. His place was secluded. But it wasn't always possible. The only good thing was that he could unload them within just a few days. Demand seemed to be at an all-time high.

His boss still had great concerns for the operation and what would happen if the feds managed to track Corbett down. No matter how many times he'd offered assurances, the only true assurance was for him to continue to deliver high-caliber assets, which he intended to do.

"Turn around," he said to the girl, taking more pictures.

Two more waited in the bedroom for him. Corbett wasted no time breaking in his latest acquisitions. Humiliation and denigration was the key to keeping them submissive. The drugs kept them from struggling.

» » »

The track was still slick from the morning drizzle as Kate made her way around it. She was preparing for the second of three physical fitness tests she would have to pass in order to graduate. The mile and a half run was just one part of it, but Kate wanted the practice. She checked the stopwatch and smiled as she crossed the finish line. Light sprinkles of water landed on her face as she tilted her head up towards the misty skies and tried to catch her breath.

Kate returned to the lockers. She was the only one inside the building, except for the maintenance man who opened it up for her. With all the time she had been away on the investigation, it would be on her to keep up with the rest of the class. As hard as it was to stay put while Scarborough and Jameson were working on the Jane Doe found in Virginia Beach, making up for lost time, lost practice, was the only way to make sure she didn't fail. Will might have been right about Nick, but she wouldn't accept that she couldn't do this on her own. They were all watching her now; the instructors, the agents in the WFO. Watching to see if she really has what it took to be a federal agent.

Whether it had been the run that cleared her head or the cool water that now flowed down her body as she stood in the shower, Kate couldn't be sure, but an idea sparked. Something she had missed before. Something they had all missed.

This couldn't wait; she had to talk to Nick. Kate jumped out of the shower and hardly dried off. Fumbling to get dressed, she reached for her phone to call him. "Come on, answer." The line continued to ring and finally went to voicemail. "Damn it." It was seven a.m.; Nick had to be at the field office. She knew he'd gotten in late last night, but also knew the man rarely slept longer than four hours, spending much of the rest of his time at the office.

The consequences of missing the eight a.m. class would have to be considered later. Kate needed to get to the field office now.

A few of her colleagues were on the track now as she left the building and headed towards her car, still parked at the dormitory. She waved, but did not stop to speak to them.

The car unlocked with a beep from the remote entry, and Kate tossed her bag onto the passenger seat, sliding inside. She tried Nick once again, but the line still went to voicemail.

"Where the hell are you? Pick up!" He'd hung up before she'd gotten a chance to speak to him last night and now he wasn't answering. Something wasn't right. She decided to try Agent Jameson. "God damn it! Where the hell is everyone?" Had there been some sort of staff meeting or some other bullshit that was keeping these guys from answering? Her patience had just about run out and, combined with the heavy rush hour traffic, Kate wanted to scream.

Finally arriving at the WFO, Kate rushed inside to find Nick. The obligatory security scans only irritated her further.

Agent Vasquez emerged from the break room, stirring a cup of coffee. Kate immediately stopped. "Have you seen Agent Scarborough?"

"I just got here, Kate. I haven't seen him yet. Is everything okay? You look upset."

"Sorry. I'm not upset; I just need to see him or Agent Jameson and traffic was hell and I'm missing my class…"

"Okay, okay. Calm down. Let's check his office first."

Vasquez was right; she needed to calm down. She just felt so damn stupid for not noticing it before. It was only over the weekend, when she'd had a chance to update the files that she'd seen it, but it didn't click with her then. It seemed that was just how her mind worked. It needed time to process information, work to find a solution. It was as if she'd begun to develop this ability, one that made it possible for her to pick up on the finest details and find a connection. Perhaps she'd always had it and never gave it a purpose, until now.

"Agent Scarborough?" Vasquez asked, now standing in his doorway with Kate anxiously waiting. "I think NAT Reid would like to speak with you." She stepped aside. "See? There you go."

"Kate. Aren't you supposed to be in class?"

She was surprised by his casual tone. Hadn't he checked his messages or seen that she'd called? Being irritated with him wasn't going to help. He didn't know why she was there or that she'd put her training in jeopardy because of it.

"I tried to call you a couple of times. Agent Jameson too."

"I saw the missed calls. Sorry about that. We've been busting our asses trying to light a fire under Virginia Beach PD to get us those labs and keeping up with Garrett too. Anyway, what it is? What's so urgent that you're here and not at the base?"

She stepped inside, but not before giving a nod to Vasquez, thanking her for her help. "The other night, after we returned from Richmond, I was updating the notes on the files and I came across images of the websites that've already been shut down."

"Okay. What about them?"

"I studied the pictures of those girls for a long time. I don't know why, particularly, except I guess I was just saddened by them."

"Kate, you and I have talked about this."

She raised her hand. "I know. I'm working on it. Anyway, I went for a run this morning at the base and when I was in the shower, it occurred to me that I'd seen tattoos on some of the women."

"And that's unusual?"

"It's unusual if they're virtually the same tattoo on several of them."

Nick slowly began to sit up straight in his chair. He folded his arms across his broad chest, waiting for her to continue. "I remember seeing tattoos, but not that they were of anything unique, or that they were the same."

"On at least three of the women that I can recall, each had a tattoo of a flower."

He pursed his lips. "Lots of women have flower tattoos."

"You're right. But what if he's marking them? Branding them. Maybe Corbett calls them by the names of their tattooed flowers. Rose or Lily or Daisy. I don't know. But, Nick, I think it's worth considering. What about the woman found in Virginia Beach, the one that came up as a DNA match from that earring we found? Does she have a flower tattoo?"

"Scarborough?" Agent Jameson appeared in the corridor. "You got a second?" he asked, eyeing Kate.

"Yeah, what's up? I was just talking with Kate and, um, she has found something that could be of interest."

Jameson moved inside to join them. "I just got a call from one of Detective Garrett's officers. He said Ballistics showed the bullet that was used to kill Petrovich was definitely from a .50 caliber Dezzy."

"We already assumed that, right?"

"We didn't assume that we'd find the gun, or the man who appears to be the owner of said weapon." Jameson puffed out his thick round chest and placed his hands on his hips, content with his role as messenger of these glad tidings.

"They found the gun? Did they arrest the man?" Kate asked, believing this news meant they'd be able to get the shooter to talk and that they'd find Corbett as a result.

"Apparently the gun was found next to the body of the man who, in all likelihood, fired the weapon at Petrovich. The guy turned up in an alley behind a strip mall not far from the drop house. He's been identified as Toma Soric. According to local PD, they'd been watching Soric for a while to get him on drug-related charges. And in fact, on initial discovery, they believed it had been a deal gone bad. But I don't think so and neither did the officer who contacted me. This is too much of a coincidence."

"I'd have to agree with you, assuming that not many people in the neighborhood carry a monster of a gun like that. The man kills Petrovich a day after we talked to him, then he winds up dead a few days later. What about Bjuric? Any idea of his whereabouts yet?" Nick asked.

"Not yet," Jameson replied. "No one in the area's willing to talk. Oh." He raised his index finger. "They did find a safe in Petrovich's apartment. Guess what was inside?"

Both Kate and Nick smiled, already knowing the answer.

"Surveillance tapes. I'm waiting on a call back from Garrett to see if they find Corbett on any of those tapes with his as of yet unknown partner. We know the cameras weren't working on the day Petrovich was killed, but that doesn't mean they weren't working prior. And if Richmond PD was surveilling Soric for dealing, they got to know who he was hanging out with. We can start talking to those people."

"When it rains, it pours." Nick leaned back in his chair and laced his fingers behind his head. "Kate thinks Corbett is branding his girls. Tattooing them." He directed his sights to Kate. "Can you go back through the files and pull up every image of the sites we've shut down and get with computer forensics to find any more that have popped up since. I want you to scour the pictures of the girls to find any and all tattoos. It might not just be flowers; who knows? Now, we just need to identify the Jane Doe and we might actually be getting somewhere."

» » »

The instructor raised his starter pistol and, although the sound of the shot always rattled her, Kate sprinted off the mark without hesitation. The afternoon skies were clear and the sun bounced off the red clay track as she pumped her arms and legs as fast as she could.

She passed by two of the other women in her class and was on her way to catch up to Sherman. He was fourth. Her mouth opened to pull as much air into her lungs as possible. Her legs were beginning to burn and her heart felt like it might beat right out of her chest. But she pushed on. A primal urge took over; to push past each one of them just to prove that she could.

Kate started to feel a new energy rise in her. Perhaps it had been due to her discovery about the case; she was feeling unstoppable. Her voice screamed inside her head as she raced towards the leader. Will was coming up on her right, but she didn't look at him. She could feel his eyes land on her and follow her as she passed him by. This was no longer a race to meet the goal of simply passing the test. She was only required to beat a time of 13 minutes, 30 seconds and she was well beyond that now. The goal wasn't to beat all her classmates either. The goal was to prove that she deserved to be here.

The ring she wore around her neck began to cling to her chest. The delicate silver chain stuck while the ring bounced beneath her clothes. Kate had become so accustomed to wearing it that she didn't notice it on most days. Today, however, it was a reminder. And it impelled her even further.

Just as she was nearing the final stretch, Hewitt remained the only person in front of her and he crossed only milliseconds before she did. She wished it hadn't been him that beat her, but she'd accomplished her goal. Kate slowed her momentum until finally coming to a stop. Her lungs burned with each gasp as she worked to bring her heart rate down. She doubled over and grabbed her knees.

"What the hell's gotten into you?"

She spotted Will's feet in front of her and she raised back up. With her hands on her hips, she tried to speak. "What are you talking about?"

"Oh, come on. You were clearly showing off," he said.

The only indicator that he might have been joking was the half-cocked grin on his face. Kate started to regain her breath and the redness in her cheeks was fading. "Maybe I just wanted to prove something."

"What on earth do you need to prove and who do you need to prove it to?"

"Nothing. Never mind." Kate began walking back to the instructor.

"Well done, Reid. You were only behind Hewitt by three-tenths of a second. That's your best time yet. Go on. You can go now," the instructor said.

Kate began walking back to the lockers and she heard Will jogging to catch up with her.

"Hey, wait up," he said, slowing his pace as he reached her. "You going home tonight?"

"Hell yes, I'm going home." Pulling double duty was starting to take its toll. She'd had to make up sessions from earlier in the week and had been spending most nights holed up in her dorm room reviewing the photos on the websites. So far, she'd tracked down fifteen with flower tattoos and her theory was starting to pan out.

"Well, why don't I pick you up around eight and we'll go out for dinner? We need to celebrate passing the second PT test. Wyman didn't make her time. She missed it by about half a second. But she'll get one last chance."

Kate shook her head knowing that not everyone would make it through. The physical demand alone was reason enough to give up. She considered Will's invitation and supposed she'd earned a break. "I would like to go out. Thank you. How about I just meet you at Corduroy's?" Giving him the idea that this was going to be some sort of date wasn't the impression she'd wanted to leave. "I'll see you at eight." Kate continued on towards the lockers.

» » »

It was the first time in nearly twelve weeks that Kate had put on something other than a t-shirt or polo shirt. When she arrived at the restaurant, she smoothed down the long, summer dress that had been in her closet for about two years. The reminder that Kate was, in fact, still a woman was nice. And it seemed Will noticed too.

"Wow. You clean up good, Reid." He looked up from the table as she approached.

"I thought it might be nice to look like a girl for once."

Will raised a bottle of beer to his lips, but stopped short. "Just so you know, you always look like a girl. Sit down. Take a load off."

The waitress approached their table. "Can I get you something to drink?" she asked Kate.

"Yes, I'll have a CC and Coke, please."

"Coming right up."

"Whiskey? I wouldn't have taken you for that kind of girl."

"Well, there's a lot you don't know about me, Caison."

"I guess so." He studied her face for a moment. "What's gotten into you today? You seem really, I don't know, different. Did something happen on that case you're working on?"

She lowered her menu to look him in the eyes. "Maybe I'm finally starting to realize that I don't need anyone's help. That I can do for myself."

Will raised his hands in surrender. "I never said you couldn't."

There was no argument to be had; Kate simply wanted to get her point across. She was grateful for the opportunity to help Nick with the investigation, but there was no way in hell she'd let it be the reason she made it through the Academy. The waitress returned with her drink. "Thank you."

Will raised his glass and waited for her to join him. "Cheers. And congrats to both of us for passing the test."

"Cheers." Kate looked to Will and smiled. Although he was aware of some of her past, mostly from what was splashed around in the media, he didn't know all of it. All the unpleasantness that led to her arrival to this very point in time. It was freeing and she began to understand that this was what it was like to start over. Fresh, with no baggage. Well, she had plenty of baggage, but it was much easier to leave behind when she wasn't being constantly reminded of its presence.

This was what they had wanted; the girls in the pictures Kate had studied for so long. At least, the ones who'd come to America believing it was the land of opportunity. Now they were nothing more than slaves. She was enjoying the food and the conversation, but her mind never left them and she would find whoever was taking the women, robbing them of the new life they'd so badly wanted.

Kate dabbed her lips with the napkin and reached for her purse when the waitress placed the bill on their table.

"Hey. Hold up. You aren't paying for this. I asked you to dinner, remember?"

"Will. Stop. I'm not going to let you pay for me, okay?" She retrieved a fifty-dollar bill and placed it on the table, but before she could let it go, Will laid his hand on top of hers.

"No. Please, this is my treat." His hand lingered in place.

Kate waited for another moment, then decided she wasn't going to fight this battle and really only wanted to pull her hand away. "Fine. Thank you. That's very nice of you."

"All right then. You ready to go?" he asked, leaving his own cash on the table to cover the much-too-expensive meal.

Kate put her money away. "I'm ready."

As they walked out of the restaurant, Will lay his hand against the small of her back. She flinched and tried hard to conceal it. She hadn't wanted to make Will feel bad. He was only doing what most men do, but the problem was, she hadn't been touched that way in a very long time and it was something that Marshall always used to do.

She brushed off the discomfort and walked outside into the warm night air. Warm by east coast standards, not by southern California standards. But it felt nice nonetheless. Kate reached into her purse and pulled out her car keys. "I really needed this tonight, Will. Thanks for the wonderful dinner and conversation." She unlocked her car.

"Do you want to go and get a drink somewhere? I mean, it's what, like ten o'clock?"

"We do have to go in tomorrow morning, you know."

"I know, but come on; we're having fun here, aren't we? Let's go grab a drink at some dive bar."

Kate noticed he'd moved in a little closer and, for a moment, she didn't mind. But then she remembered who she was. "Thanks for the offer, but I don't think so. I'm too old to be going into work hung over. Some of us aren't twenty-three anymore."

"I'm twenty-seven." He placed his hand against her car door.

"Will." Kate wasn't ready for this. Not now, not until a time that she couldn't even envision yet.

"What?" he whispered.

His lips were so close to hers, she could feel the heat of his breath on her mouth. The idea that he could be someone to offer comfort. She thought how good it would feel to be touched again. Her heart still ached so badly and for a moment, it was Marshall's breath she felt; his whisper in her ear.

Will's lips touched hers and she did not pull back. It could be him, just for a moment.

The tears pooled in her eyes when she remembered this man was not Marshall. She pulled away. "I'm sorry, Will. I can't." Kate stepped inside the car. As she turned the ignition, she saw the look on Will's face – disappointment, and she'd put it there.

"Kate, I'm sorry. Don't go."

"I have to." She pulled the door closed and drove away. In her rear view, she watched him standing there, alone. He finally walked away.

Kate turned up the radio as loud as she could to drown out her thoughts. Guilt over a betrayal that wasn't really there, guilt over treating a kind man that way. For a moment, all she wanted to do was keep driving. Just go back home. Not to her home here, but her home in San Diego. Only it wasn't hers anymore.

Kate's cell phone buzzed and the Bluetooth picked up the call. She immediately suspected it was Will wanting to offer an apology he did not owe, but instead, the caller ID on her dash showed Nick's name.

"Nick. What's going on?" She cleared her throat and hoped he hadn't picked up on her shaky tone.

"We got the labs back on the woman in Virginia Beach." He paused. "Kate, not only is it a match to the DNA found on that earring, they found foreign DNA too."

Kate was trying to absorb the information, pushing back the regret that had begun to consume her thoughts.

"I need you in the field office—now."

TEN

The streets were heaving with summer tourists, even at this late hour, but Kate made it to the WFO in pretty good time. She hadn't bothered going home to get changed and felt somewhat uncomfortable showing up in a dress and high heels.

On arrival, she noticed several agents still hard at work and soon spotted Agent Jameson. "Hey. You're here awfully late."

"Well, hey there." He turned around. "I guess I could say the same thing about you."

"Agent Scarborough asked me to come in. Said he's got the labs back. Have you seen them?"

"I have. I'm working on the files now. Looks like you were out having fun." Jameson eyed her slim figure, which her long dress so elegantly revealed.

Kate smiled. "I guess." She started to walk away. "I better go see what he needs. Catch up with you later." The corridor was carpeted and Kate suddenly found new appreciation for it. Otherwise, she would have been heard coming from a mile away in her high-heeled strappy shoes. "Knock, knock."

"Come on in," he replied, still staring at his computer screen. It was only when Kate moved in closer did he turn his eyes towards her. "Wow. Look at you. What, were you on a date or something?" He caught himself. "I'm sorry. None of my business."

"It's fine. No, it wasn't a date. Just friends having dinner."

"Gotcha. Thanks for coming down. I know it's late. I wanted to go over what we found and then talk about the websites and start to put the data together on the tattoos. See if there's anything there."

"Shoot." Raising her dress a little, Kate lowered herself onto the chair across from his desk. She was ready to get down to business.

"First, let me start with the foreign DNA found on Jane Doe's body. Have you heard the name Martin Druseburg?"

"Doesn't sound familiar." Kate leaned back in her chair. "Who is he?"

"A man who has enough money to pay for pretty much anything he wants. Apparently, he made his fortune selling off his small software company to one of the big boys."

"Okay. The guy's rich and he likes the company of eastern European women. Enough that he wanted to keep one as a pet?" Kate was startled by her own blunt tone, but chalked it up to the late hour and the whiskey that had settled on top of her meal.

"That's what I'm thinking."

"If that's the case..." Kate sat back up and leaned on the desk. "Wait, how did she die?"

"OD'd."

"So, we assume he gave her the drugs and she decided to take more than she should? Because I have to think that he wouldn't have wanted anything to happen to his investment."

"Exactly. I think she wanted out and thought this was her only way. But, Kate, we have a match. On this man who paid money for her and a match on the earring you found in that house."

"We don't have a name. Who was she? And why is this wealthy man in the system?"

"He had to give a sample a year ago to absolve him of charges from a woman who claimed he raped her. Turns out it had been someone else. Not that that alone would convince me of the man's innocence. I find it hard to believe the charges would have come from out of the blue. But anyway, once you're in the database, you stay in. And it gives us an idea of the type of person we're dealing with. Seems to fit right in with this current Jane Doe situation. As far as Jane's identity, I emailed Detective Garrett a picture of the body. Someone's bound to identify her."

"Okay. In the meantime, I think we've got something on this branding theory." Kate was about to elaborate, but Agent Myers walked in.

"Hey, Georgia. You just get in?" Nick's face lit up in an instant.

Kate recognized that look. She used to wear it all the time.

"A while ago. I freshened up a little and then decided to check up on you. It's been a long day."

"I'm sure it has," Nick replied. "But that's it, right? Case is over?"

Myers continued inside and sat down in the chair next to Kate. "You look nice. Let me guess, you were on a date when this one here called you in?"

"Something like that," Kate replied.

"It's good to see you're getting out and starting to make some friends, Kate. You deserve to enjoy yourself once in a while." Myers returned her attention to Nick. "Yes. The case is finished. Well, my part in it is. So what are you two working on that required taking her from what looked to be a fun night out?"

"I was just about to tell Kate that she and I are going to take a trip up to Virginia Beach. We got a female victim and found DNA on her that matched who we think was holding her."

"That's good news. When are you leaving?"

Nick turned to Kate. "I'm going to head up first thing in the morning and I'd like you to catch the first flight out after your class. Can you do that?"

"Yeah, absolutely. Won't be a problem." Kate pushed up from her chair. "Well, I'll leave you two alone. I'll go over the website images with Agent Jameson and see if we can put a report together for you. Good night." Kate moved towards the door, closing it behind her.

A large, open space occupied much of the fourth floor. Desks, computers, and wall monitors reminded Kate of a communications room or something along those lines. It served as the nerve center for the unit. Kate found Agent Jameson once again and was ready to get to work. "I'm back. You got some time to go over the photos from the websites?"

He turned from his monitor. "You bet. Sit down and show me what you've got."

Kate logged into the system and retrieved the files she'd been compiling. "I started to see these tattoos and didn't think much of it at first, but then I recalled that they were similar. So I talked to Agent Scarborough and mentioned that I think this guy could be branding the girls he takes." She clicked on the file that contained the images she'd pulled so far that all had the similar markings. "See here." Her pinky lined up with the girl's back. She was naked and standing with her back to the camera. "Just above her right thigh. You see that?"

Jameson zoomed in on the image. "It looks like a tattoo of a flower. Maybe a sunflower? I don't know; it's kind of hard to tell."

"I think it could be a daisy."

"Oh yeah, I can see that."

Kate proceeded to pull up multiple images and pointed out similar markings. All were flowers, but different in one way or another; species, or color.

"Holy shit." Jameson rolled his chair back. "You're right. This guy is branding them like cattle."

She nodded her agreement. "We need to know if this Jane Doe has a tattoo."

"If she does, then Druseburg knows James Corbett. Good work, NAT." Jameson cracked a wide smile and locked his pudgy fingers across his thick waist. "I'll take this to Scarborough. You should go home and get some rest. Tomorrow's going to be a long day."

Kate rose from the chair. "You're right. Better get some rest while I can. I'll see you tomorrow afternoon. Thanks, Dwight."

"Oh hey, congrats on passing PT."

A curious grin crossed her lips. "Thanks, but how did you know?"

"You realize this is the FBI, right?"

His deadpan expression brought her to laughter. "Right."

» » »

Kate flipped on the hall light and immediately kicked off her shoes. It'd been too long since she'd worn heels and her feet hurt like hell. If she knew what was good for her, she'd walk straight into her bedroom and go to bed. But she was too anxious now and had almost forgotten the disastrous end to her evening with Will. Almost.

With thirst nagging away at her, she walked to the kitchen and pulled a bottle of water from the fridge. Wine rattled again in the refrigerator door. "What the hell," she said, and poured herself a glass.

An uncomfortable and awkward feeling began to rise in her and the thoughts pushed aside her previous elation from Jameson's praises. She didn't mean to hurt Will's feelings, but then, he shouldn't have put her in that position in the first place.

"Forget it. I shouldn't feel bad," she said, walking to the couch. The late night talk shows were almost over, but it didn't matter; she just wanted the sound of people's voices. She curled up her legs and pulled the long dress over her knees. There was a chill inside this house. It didn't seem to matter that it was summer, the place never really heated up. Perhaps because it was surrounded by enormous trees that blocked out much of the sun's warmth.

Kate only sipped on the wine as she watched the television. Her initial desire for it having faded as the minutes ticked by and probably stemmed from a need to drown out her guilt over leaving Will that way. She soon recalled the look on Nick's face when Georgia walked into his office earlier tonight. It was nice to see and she did miss that, very much, in fact.

A lump began to rise in her throat and Kate tried hard to swallow it back down again. So many people had treated her with kid gloves since she lost Marshall. Like she would just break in two at the mere mention of his name. Some days it was like that, but she never let them know what it truly felt like for her—to lose him.

Still, she thought about the kiss and how it reminded her of him. Kate placed her fingers over her lips and closed her eyes, reliving the softness and the gentle touch. "Stop," she told herself. But it was too late; her eyes reddened and began to spill over.

Kate picked up her cell phone from the table and opened up Will's contact information. Her finger hovered over his number. *Don't.* She began typing a text to him. It would be easier than talking. *"Hey. You up?"* The casualness of the words felt contrived. She stared at the message. Finally, she pressed send.

Immediately, she regretted the action and put her phone down, standing up to go to her room. If he answered, she was just going to ignore it. Kate began walking away when the familiar buzz sounded. She stopped in the middle of the living room. A minute or longer must have passed because it sounded again. A reminder that she'd received the message.

"Go to bed. Just go to bed," she whispered, but loneliness was overpowering her logic and he reminded her of him. She turned to pick up her phone and read the reply. *"I'm awake. You okay?"*

"I could use a friend." She held the phone, waiting. Her pulse was rising and her hands trembled. Her thumb still hovered over the send button. Kate closed her eyes and touched the screen.

An immediate reply came back. *"I'll be there in 30."*

She had plenty of time to tell him not to come, that he should turn around and just go back home. But she didn't. Instead, she consumed all that was left of the wine in her glass, closed her eyes and simply waited, remembering the kiss, remembering how it felt to be so close – convincing herself that this was okay. Finally, the knock on her door came.

Kate felt weak, but she rose from the couch and carried herself to the door. With a click of the deadbolt, she momentarily postponed the inevitable and reconsidered the consequences.

"Kate? It's me, Will." His voice sounded through the door.

A deep breath filled her lungs and the door opened. "Hi." A fragile smile came only by force. "Come on in."

"Are you okay?" Will closed the door behind him.

"I'm fine. Come sit down. Can I get you something to drink?"

"I'll take a beer, thanks."

Kate returned with an opened bottle of beer. She sat down next to him, but didn't speak.

"You're not okay, are you? You want to tell me what's going on and why I'm here?"

No, she didn't because she didn't know why he was there, except that she missed Marshall, and seeing how happy Nick was with Georgia just made her feel even more alone.

"I just wanted a friend to talk to. Is that okay?"

"Of course it is. I am your friend, Kate."

"Thank you." A genuine smile appeared on her lips this time.

Will raised his hand and pushed the hair from her face. He ran his finger along the scar on her left temple.

Kate knew he'd seen it before. Her hair was always pulled back and, although it wasn't as noticeable now, it was still evident. "You want to know how I got that?"

Will shook his head. "Not in the least."

» » »

Her room was quiet, dark. Kate lay in her bed, staring out the window that let in a hint of moonlight around the edge of the curtains. This shouldn't have happened. All Kate wanted was to feel something other than grief and loneliness. She wanted to feel loved again. But this man next to her now didn't love her; at least, she didn't believe he did. And she didn't love him.

His arms around her offered momentary comfort, but now she regretted it, as though she'd just betrayed Marshall, and it did nothing to fill the emptiness.

Kate turned her head to Will. He was asleep. Her lips quivered as she looked at the man who was not Marshall. She had to get out of this bed. She had to get away from him.

Pulling the covers back, a chill pressed against her bare skin. Her feet quietly touched the ground and she stood. Guilt gnawed at her stomach and twisted hard. She had to make it to the bathroom before losing all control of her despair.

The small nightlight in the bathroom guided her way and Kate closed the door with quiet urgency. Her eyes reddened and she looked at her face in the mirror. Her diminutive features now appeared puffy and discolored, even in the scant light. "I'm so sorry." Kate reached for the ring on her necklace. She hadn't taken it off while she lay in bed with him and the realization of the fact was enough to bring her to tears.

Her hand trembled as she covered her mouth to conceal the sound of her grief. How could she have allowed herself to indulge in a moment of weakness? The need to be touched, to be loved was too powerful and now, as she peered down at her naked form, she regretted it. All of it. And she wanted nothing more than for Will to leave; get out of her bed and out of her house. But Will was a kind man, a good man, and that made her feel all the worse. She'd used him.

"Kate?" A voice sounded just beyond the door. "Are you okay?"

He must have awakened from the sound of her sobs and now he wanted to know if she was okay. Of course she wasn't. She cleared her throat and wiped her eyes with her fingertips. "I'm fine. I'll be out in a minute."

She filled her lungs with the cool air and worked to pull herself together. A small washcloth lay on the basin and Kate moistened it and pressed it against her stinging eyes to stem the flow of tears. Another deep breath and she pulled open the door. Will stood just outside, his waist wrapped in the bedsheet.

"Hey. I thought I heard something and just wanted to check to see if you were all right." He seemed to study her features with some concern. "You don't look all right." Will reached out for her shoulder.

Kate shuddered at his touch that only minutes ago had been welcomed.

He immediately lowered his hand. A thin, knowing smile appeared on his lips and he nodded his head. "I see. Um, I guess I should be going now." Will walked back towards the bed to gather his clothes that were heaped in a pile on the floor.

"I'm sorry, Will. I—I'm just not ready for this. I should've never..."

But before she could finish, he said, "Hey, you know what? It's fine." He lowered the sheet and pulled on his jeans. "I should've listened to you earlier. You told me you weren't ready, but I came over anyway. It was my mistake, not yours." The black t-shirt stretched over his head as he pulled it down to cover his toned chest. He moved to Kate, who had wrapped herself in the robe that hung on the bathroom door. "I'm sorry, Kate. I—um... well, let's just say that I guess I let my feelings for you get the better of me." Will leaned in and kissed her cheek. "Good night."

Kate remained in her room as Will walked away. She listened as the front door opened and then closed again. Her feet carried her to the living room and she pulled the curtain back just enough to watch him back out of the drive. When she reached the front door to turn the deadbolt, Kate pressed her back against it and slid down to the floor and, her knees pulled tight against her chest, she wept.

» » »

The instructor stepped inside the lab to waiting students and placed his briefcase on the desk. "Let's get you paired up and we'll get started on the assigned stations."

The forensics lab at the Academy was far superior to anything Kate had ever seen before. Maybe because it was used by the BAU headquarters as well as for training, but this was state-of-the-art.

Today, the trainees would be given hands-on experience with forensics. Although several of her classmates had some knowledge, this would introduce advanced techniques that included collecting fingerprints, running DNA samples, and understanding the uses for fluorescein, a chemical used in the detection of latent blood at a crime scene.

Each station had a different evidence collection technique and, for the first time in a long while, Kate began to feel at home.

"Reid, Caison, you two can start on the fluorescein station." The instructor pointed them in the right direction.

Since they first arrived this morning, neither had spoken to one another. This was exactly what Kate hadn't wanted. They'd slept together and she had made him feel terrible for it. For a moment, Kate considered a request to work with someone else, but then questions would be raised as to why.

The two had been paired up on several occasions and had not been a problem. If the instructor discovered the reason behind her request, it could possibly jeopardize all they both had been working towards. No, she made her bed and would have to lie in it.

The two made their way to the station. Kate had been familiar with the fluorescein technique, but only ever used Luminol. However, both chemicals would still fluoresce under LED or ultraviolet light to detect a bloodstain that had been cleaned. It didn't matter if bleach or other cleaning agents were used, the iron in the blood would still be picked up by these two compounds.

She began to spray the chemical onto the clothing sample. Kate noticed Will's standoffish demeanor and hardened face. She'd hurt herself and him in the process. With several more weeks left in her training, she began to realize it would be a very long and uncomfortable time. But what could she say to him that would offer any real solace? *Gee, I'm sorry I had sex with you because all I could think about was my dead fiancé.* That would be a morale boost for him. "Damn it."

"What's wrong? What happened?" Will moved in to see what the problem was.

"I put too much on the sleeve, I think. You see that?" She pointed to some very faint lines in the shirt.

"Yeah."

"That could be a fingerprint and too much of this solution will diminish the detail."

"Oh, maybe we should ask for another sample."

"No. Let's just keep going. Here." She handed the spray bottle to Will. "Why don't you try? My hands aren't steady enough, I guess."

Will held her gaze for a moment. "Yeah, all right."

They processed the samples utilizing the various collection techniques. This should have been fun for Kate. After all, she'd spent a year or better in this environment. But she'd ruined a friendship by making a bad decision and now who was left? Her roommate had quit and Will was the only other person who she'd grown comfortable around. He'd helped her too. With the tactical training, his experience had been invaluable. She'd lost that too.

Kate eyed the clock on the wall. It was almost over. Then she'd be on a flight to Virginia Beach to meet Nick and Dwight. She could only hope that on her return, Will might see his way to forgiving her for treating him so carelessly. Maybe she would have forgiven herself.

ELEVEN

The short flight from D.C. to Norfolk had been smooth until the turbulent descent hastened Kate's desire to land. An unenthusiastic flyer, she prepared by clutching the arms of her seat and stiffening her back as if bracing for impact.

Kate tossed her overnight bag onto her shoulder. She'd been given little instruction regarding the tasks ahead and prepared by packing a bag in the event she wouldn't make it home tonight.

Agent Jameson awaited her just outside the gate inside the main terminal and she soon spotted him. He was hard to miss, a result of his stature, and now his cheeks were raised in a smile so high that his eyes had turned to mere slits when he flashed his near-flawless teeth.

"Hey, how was your flight?" he asked.

"Bumpy."

"It's the heat. Come on; Scarborough's waiting for us." Dwight pushed the button for the elevator and held the doors so Kate could step on first. "I'm on the second-floor garage."

The flashing headlights were a beacon in the darkened parking structure when Dwight pressed the keyless remote entry on the rental car.

Kate slid inside the passenger seat. "How far is the coroner's office?"

"About half an hour. Maybe a little less." The engine turned over and they began to make their way out of the garage. "How was class today?"

"Awkward and uncomfortable" was what she'd wanted to say, but she thought better of it. "We were utilizing evidence collection techniques and I actually felt like I knew what the hell I was doing."

"Don't sell yourself short, Kate." With a quick glance and brief smile, Dwight pulled out onto the main road. "I know you and I haven't spoken much and I didn't really know Detective Avery all that well, but I just wanted to say that I think he'd be real proud of you."

"Thank you, Dwight. That means a lot to me." It was a nice sentiment and she did appreciate it, but right now, the struggle to come to terms with her actions was in direct conflict with the idea that Marshall would be proud of her. She doubted that very much.

Rather than continue to engage in conversation for which Kate was unprepared, she instead passed the time by pretending to do work on her phone. Brushing him off felt harsh and perhaps Dwight was able to pick up on that, but Kate had screwed up in a big way last night and the events replayed constantly, reminding her over and over that she wasn't worthy of forgiveness from Will or anyone.

"This is it." Dwight cut the engine after pulling into the parking lot of the coroner's office.

Inhaling the fresh salty tinge in the air as she stepped out of the car was a pleasant reminder and, for a moment, she felt like she was back at home. "Is he still with the coroner?"

"Yes, he just texted me." Dwight locked up the car and shoved the keys in his pants pocket. "Follow me."

Inside the lobby, a young woman sat behind a sleek black reception desk, complete with a raised glass top that spanned its entire length. Perhaps she was fresh out of college. The welcoming smile she wore had no hesitation behind it, as though she hadn't a clue that people couldn't always be trusted. Her conservative attire was likely the reflection of her place of employment. To dress provocatively here of all places would seem grossly inappropriate.

"I'm Special Agent Dwight Jameson and this is Agent Trainee Kate Reid." He confirmed his identity by displaying his credentials. "We're here to meet with Agent Scarborough and Dr. Reese."

"One moment, please," she replied and turned to her fairly advanced looking phone system for authorization. "Please, go ahead down the hall. Dr. Reese's office is the last door on the right. He's expecting you."

"Thank you." Dwight led the way down the hall, his polished, square-tipped shoes tapping against the stone tiled floor, a sound that announced their approach from several feet away.

Their arrival had been expected and the door buzzed open before Dwight could press the button mounted on the side.

"Good, you're here," Nick began, wasting no time. "Dr. Reese and I have been reviewing the autopsy report on our Jane Doe. As we've already been made aware, the labs came back with a DNA match for the man who we believe was the last person to see her alive. And," he looked directly at Kate, "we found this. Dr. Reese, would you please show the agents the tattoo."

Dr. Reese lifted the right shoulder of the body. Her black hair was pushed back to reveal what Kate had already suspected was present. "Agent Scarborough suggested there could be a connection between this victim and others you suspect are involved in a sex trafficking ring. And this tattoo is some sort of marker?"

Her skin was pale, making the fresh-looking tattoo all the more prominent. And while her complexion was falling victim to the ashen tone of death, a slightly reddish ring outlined the flower, indicating it hadn't been there long.

"That's what we believe and this seems to confirm that assumption. Any word yet on the woman's identity?" Kate asked.

"Not yet. If it hadn't been for the earring, and Virginia Beach PD inputting the sample in the database, we'd have no cause to suspect she was a victim of this operation," Nick said. "But we know she was at the house and we can now confirm she was connected to James Corbett, thanks to his unique branding. And as for Martin Druseburg, maybe he can shed some light considering it appears as though he was the last person to see her alive." Nick examined the girl again, as though her identity might somehow reveal itself.

"I spoke with Detective Garrett just after Jameson and I arrived this morning," he went on. "He made mention that an anonymous call came in last week offering a description of a woman the person believed to have gone missing. Apparently, the individual hadn't wanted to be identified. Unfortunately, an official report wasn't filed because no one came in to file it. All they have is a description, but Garrett thinks this could be the girl, based on the photo I emailed him."

"Does he have a name attached to the description?" Kate asked.

"Madlena Jankovic," Nick replied. "Garrett is looking for an address or the name of a relative, something, so that he can get a positive ID."

"I guess we need to pay a visit to Martin Druseburg. With his DNA on this dead girl's body, he might be willing to give up the man who sold her to him," Jameson said.

Nick gathered his files. "Thank you for your time, Doctor. Either me or a member of my team will be in touch with any further questions."

"Thank you, Agent Scarborough." Reese nodded to Dwight and Kate. "Pleasure to meet you and good luck. I don't want to see any more of these young girls turning up in my office."

Nick led the way outside the facility. "I've already touched base with the local authorities. Detective Franks has been assigned to this investigation and she's going to meet us at the home of Druseburg." He continued to walk toward the parking lot. "This is a very high-profile man and the local PD wants to be sure to keep this out of the media. We're simply going to question him. We have absolutely no hard evidence suggesting he bought and paid for this girl or that he might have been responsible for her death."

"We have her earring and the presumed connection to Corbett – the tattoo," Kate said.

"We do, but that's not enough to prove anything. She could just as easily have been a hooker he picked up and then she offed herself afterwards. No, we need to draw him out. I'm sure he'll want to bring in his lawyer, but let's just see what we can get out of him before that time. Detective Franks will then politely suggest that he go down to the station for further questioning." Nick opened the driver's side door.

The three of them stepped inside the rental car and headed toward the home of the wealthy Martin Druseberg.

» » »

The enormous structure slowly revealed itself as they made their way up the long, meandering single-lane road that ran parallel to the ocean. The house, or rather, mansion, was perched atop the cliffs and stood out among the distant neighboring residents due to its modern lines and concrete grey exterior; a stark contrast to the grand Tudor-style homes in the area.

"Well, we knew the guy had money," Dwight said, peering through the windshield, his eyes cast upwards to the top of the cliff.

"I guess money will buy you lots of things," Kate replied. "Including people."

Dwight turned away from the breathtaking view and lent Kate his attention. "I suppose so."

Nick remained silent, but spotted Detective Franks' patrol car in his rear view.

"I'd be surprised if Druseburg was there," Dwight said. "If this woman escaped from him, he's got to be shitting bricks right about now. No way is he going to just be sitting around waiting for us to show up."

"Maybe you're right," Kate replied.

They arrived at the bottom of the home's circular drive and the agents stepped outside.

"Nice place," Nick said.

"You could say that," Dwight replied.

Detective Franks emerged from her car and walked towards the agents. Kate took notice of the woman's appearance. Although she looked to be older, perhaps in her late forties, she was a stunning woman. Blonde, shoulder-length hair, neatly styled in a straight bob. Her reddish-toned skin made her appear as though she was blushing, but in an alluring manner.

Kate looked at Nick, who had clearly taken notice of the woman's beauty as well. If Agent Myers was here right now, she might have reason to be jealous.

"Detective Franks." Nick extended his hand. "We spoke on the phone. I'm Special Agent Nick Scarborough and this is Special Agent Dwight Jameson and Agent Trainee Kate Reid."

"Pleasure and thank you for giving us a heads up on this one, Agent Scarborough. Mr. Druseburg is very well respected in the community, so keeping this quiet until we know more is very much appreciated."

"Of course. Shall we?" Nick extended his arm in a gesture that suggested the detective take the lead.

They reached the top of the stone steps and now stood beneath the curved, covered porch that surrounded the front of the home and faced the ocean.

The front windows were obscured by shades, leaving the impression that no one was inside. Detective Franks rang the doorbell and they waited for a length of time that implied there would be no answer. But then the door opened.

"Hello. Can I help you?" A stocky, middle-aged woman with short grey hair stood in doorway, the cavernous foyer visible behind her.

"We're looking for Mr. Druseburg. Is he available? I'm Detective Sergeant Franks with Virginia Beach PD."

"I'm afraid he is away on business. May I ask what this is regarding?" She eyed the visitors with what appeared to be skepticism.

"We just have a few questions for him. Do you expect him back any time soon?"

"Tomorrow. He said he would be back tomorrow evening."

"Okay. Thank you," Franks replied. "We'll try to get in touch with him through his office. Thank you for your time."

The housekeeper closed the door without so much as a "good evening."

"We need to find out where Mr. Druseburg has traveled to," Franks said.

"We don't want to alarm any of the employees," Nick replied. "We've got some follow-up with Richmond PD. Why don't Reid and I handle that, and Jameson, I'd like you to coordinate with Detective Franks on surveilling the house here. We have to consider the possibility that Druseburg isn't out of town at all. And if he returns, then we need to be ready."

"Understood," Jameson said.

» » »

The hotel was just ahead; a moderately priced chain that was considered suitable accommodation by the Bureau because they were the ones paying for it.

"You've been pretty quiet. Is everything okay?" Nick asked.

"Just a little tired, I guess." The idea that she could confide in Nick wasn't a possibility right now. She felt ashamed and guilty, and the thought of disappointing him, well, that was probably her own hang-up, but she cared what he thought of her.

"Okay. We've got work to do. Let's get inside."

Nick approached the front desk and checked them both in.

"Here are your keys, sir." The man behind the counter handed Nick two key cards.

"And for you, ma'am."

"Thank you."

"Enjoy your stay."

"First thing we need to do," Nick began as they walked to the elevators, "is to get hold of someone in Druseburg's office, see if we can find out where he is without raising any red flags. I figured it would be better if I handled it rather than Franks." The doors parted on the third floor and the two stepped into the hall.

Kate suspected Nick was intending on skirting the rules a little by trying to get a location on Druseberg and hadn't wanted the detective to be made aware of his efforts. She'd noticed on more than one occasion Nick's propensity for operating in the gray area if he believed it would award him results. "Do you think we'll be able to track this guy down?"

"One way or another, yes. Why don't you get settled in, then come over, and we'll get started?"

The two had adjoining rooms and Nick would be sharing his with Dwight. Kate dropped her bag onto the bed and reached for her phone. She'd half-expected a call from Will, but there was none.

Minutes later, Kate knocked on Nick's door. He'd already tossed his tie onto the bed and the first two buttons on his white oxford were undone. "Come on in. There's some water in the fridge if you're thirsty."

"Thanks." She grabbed the water and walked towards the desk where Nick was sitting at his laptop. "Have you contacted his office yet?"

"A few minutes ago. His secretary said he was in L.A. and was due back tomorrow, just like the housekeeper implied."

"So where does that leave us?"

"Well, we need to touch base with Detective Garrett, see if they've gotten anywhere with neighbors in the area." Nick raised his index finger. "You know what? We could search tattoo shops or suppliers. Corbett's got to be doing his own work. It'd be too risky to have someone come to him or worse, take the girls someplace to get it done. No, I think he's branding them himself. We might be grasping at straws here, I don't know, but it wouldn't hurt to find out if anyone recognizes him."

"Or maybe his partner, assuming the sketch is accurate enough." Kate said.

"It's all we've got right now. I think we should work on developing a timeline too. When the other drop houses were discovered, when Ruxandra Sala escaped. Corbett isn't staying put anywhere for long, and if we can get some idea of any patterns in his movement, then we should be working that angle too." Nick stopped and seemed to examine Kate.

She believed that her stone exterior had been enough to deter him, but could now feel his probing stare. Perhaps Kate wasn't as good at poker face as she once thought. Or maybe this problem had weighed so heavily on her mind that her distant gaze was too easy to see through.

"So, are you ready to tell me what's going on yet?" He laced his fingers against the back of his head, pressing down on hair that had grown out since she'd first met him. His style had changed from those early days, it now appeared more laid-back, and maybe a touch grayer.

Kate sat down on the double bed across from the desk chair on which Nick was perched. Nervously rolling the water bottle between her hands, she cast her gaze downward. *Don't tell him. It won't do any good.* She couldn't even convince herself. "I screwed up."

"Screwed up? How? On one your exams?"

She raised her eyes to meet his. "No. It's not the Academy. Well, it is, I guess." In that moment, Kate began to reconsider her earlier thoughts. This wasn't Nick's problem. He'd done enough to help her and so what did she expect he could offer now? A lingering pause meant he would only ask again if she continued to keep quiet. "I—um, I slept with Will Caison last night." She almost expected Nick to explode, telling her what a stupid thing she'd done, but he didn't. Instead, he lowered his arms, inhaled a breath, and waited for her to continue. "I felt weak—and alone. I knew he was attracted to me, he'd made it clear, and I took advantage of that."

"Do you have feelings for him?"

Nick's sincerity put her at ease and she was able to continue. "No. I was lonely. I miss him so much." No matter how hard she tried, her eyes still began to sting and she hated crying in front of him, or anyone.

He leaned over, his elbows resting on his lap, and looked directly into her eyes. "I know you miss him. I know you loved him. But, Kate, he's gone and he would want you to live your life."

"I feel like I betrayed him. And I hurt Will. I know I did." She dabbed her finger under her eyes.

"Caison's a grown man and I'm sure he can handle it. In fact, I'd be more inclined to think that he should've known better. That maybe it was he who was taking advantage, not the other way around."

Nick was always the first one to absolve her of any responsibility. "That's what he said, but I'm the one to blame. Not anyone else, just me." She looked away for a moment. "I saw you and Georgia at your office last night and it was just really nice to see you both so happy. I miss that feeling, you know?"

"Of course you do, but don't idolize our relationship. She and I have our own problems. It's pretty hard having a relationship when you only see each other once or twice a week. Look, all I'm saying is that you have nothing to feel guilty about, Kate. Just try to pull yourself together because I know you want to find these girls and you can't let your personal life get in the way. I need you now, okay?"

Kate understood his intentions. He wasn't trying to brush it off as if none of it mattered. But there was no point in dwelling on it either. *What's done is done.*

"Jameson's calling," Nick said as he answered the cell. "Scarborough here. Son of a bitch. Okay, we'll be right there."

"What is it?"

"Druseburg. He just got home."

TWELVE

Smoke drifted in front of the man's face from a cigarette he'd just put to his lips. The crease on his forehead deepened as he listened to Gregor Bjuric's brother, Vito, explain the circumstances that brought the brothers to his diner.

Stan Kovac sat in his favorite chair in the small diner that specialized in ethnic foods, particularly Hungarian cuisine. His long-time friend was the proprietor and so it was common for Stan to take his noontime meals here. Now, listening to the nervous, stuttering man before him caused his appetite to vanish.

"Toma is dead. His body's already be found." Stan pressed the cigarette butt inside the black plastic ashtray. "You are the one who killed him. Is that what you're telling me, Vito?"

"Da."

"English, Vito."

"Yes."

"And you did this to save your brother." Stan looked to Gregor, who seemed to slink down at the mere glance.

"He was going to kill him, but Gregor did not know what he was doing when he talked to the police. I tried to convince him I could keep Gregor under control."

The table shook as Stan slammed his fist down. "You see? This is the problem. Gregor talked to the police. Talked to the FBI, and brought them to see Petrovich. So Toma did what he believed needed to be done and that was to make sure Gregor didn't open his fucking mouth again."

"Mr. Kovac, it was an accident. He pointed the gun at Gregor, and I just—I knocked it from his hands and then we struggled. I begged him to stop, but he didn't and when I grabbed the gun, it just went off." Vito glanced at his brother. "I'm sorry for Toma, I swear it, but I can take over his job. I can make it up to you."

"And what do we do about the fact that the police have already found Toma? Do you think they'll just forget all about him?"

"No, sir."

"No." Stan pushed up from the chair as it screeched along the vinyl floor. "You think you are ready for Toma's job? Then you do what Toma promised me. Find me three girls by the end of Monday." Stan picked up the cigarette butt and flicked it onto Gregor's face. "And if he talks to *anyone*, I'll be the one to take care of him. In the meantime, I've got to go and clean up your fucking mess." Stan made his way to the exit and then turned around a final time. "Three by Monday at midnight."

Vito waited until Stan left the diner. "You're lucky Stan was in a good mood. Now where the fuck are we going to find three girls for him?" Vito paced the now empty diner. "Toma supplies drugs to everyone around here. He used his cut from Kovac's operation for seed money to keep his business growing. It won't be long before his dealers hear what happened. They'll come after me."

"We can go to the police, Vito. This is too much danger," Gregor said.

Vito's eyes darkened as he began to shake his head. "You don't understand, do you? No one can help us now. Not the police, not anyone. If Kovac doesn't kill me himself, one of Toma's partners will. And then you'll be next."

» » »

Dwight's instructions were to stay put and to not engage Druseburg. He and the detective were parked at the base of the cliff where they could still see the property and anyone who drove up the long access road. A small hiking trail with a few parking spots was where they waited. They would have been easily overlooked, tucked behind one of trees planted around the perimeter of the lot, and it appeared they had been, as evidenced by the driver of the Lincoln Town Car that continued along the road. It was difficult to tell, but Dwight was sure the outline of a person in the back seat was Druseburg.

The hour was approaching dusk and the sun was just now setting over the horizon against an ocean backdrop that was magnificent. Nick's car soon appeared and pulled alongside Dwight and the detective.

Nick's window rolled down and he rested his elbow on the driver's side door, leaning out. "He still up there?"

"I'm fairly sure of it," Jameson began. "We saw his driver turn onto the private lane about thirty minutes ago. No movement since then. Are we going to go up there and have a chat with him or what?"

"Let's go. Hop in. We should take just the one car."

It took only a minute or two to make it up the drive. The view of the sunset was even more spectacular from the vantage point of the front of the home.

Nick stepped out and adjusted his shirt. "Must be nice." He turned his head towards the ocean view. "I think Detective Franks should be the representative. It'll be less intimidating," Nick said.

Kate understood his meaning; intimating that a local police officer would raise fewer red flags than a federal agent, but the way Franks responded to the comment appeared as though she felt slighted by the remark.

Franks rang the bell and a much quicker response occurred, but by the same woman as before.

"Oh, I see you're back. Mr. Druseburg arrived earlier and I told him you stopped by. Let me see if I can get him for you now." The woman pushed the door against the jamb, but didn't close it.

The breeze grew colder as the sun began to dip further beneath the horizon. The four of them waited for the man they knew to be Martin Druseburg, but there was silence between them all. No one was quite certain how this would play out. Druseburg was a man of high standing, a wealthy man who wouldn't want unwarranted attention and so it was likely he would cooperate. That was the hope anyway.

Footsteps sounded behind the partially closed door. The steps were heavy against a marbled floor and it echoed. The large and ornate door slowly pulled open and revealed a man who stood not more than five feet eleven inches, maybe slightly less. Pudgy around the middle; a beer drinker or someone who just enjoyed heavy meals. His eyes met with the detective's first. She was standing at the head of the pack.

"Mr. Druseburg?" she asked.

The man in the tailored shirt and pleated trousers glanced at the four law enforcement officials, although he didn't yet know their origins, only assuming they were the law by the guns holstered at their waists. He rubbed his forehead beneath a too-low hairline – plugs, most likely – and began to speak. "Yes, what is this about? My housekeeper mentioned you came by earlier today. How can I help you—Officer?"

"I'm Detective Sergeant Franks with the Virginia Beach Police Department and these are federal agents. We're here to talk to you about a woman who turned up dead not far from here."

"Oh." The man appeared taken aback. "Well, I'm certain I can't help you with something like that."

"Mr. Druseburg," Franks continued. "Your DNA was found on the victim's body. May we come in?"

All color drained from Druseburg's face. He pulled the door open and stepped aside. "Come in—please." He waited for the agents and Detective Franks to step inside the foyer. "It's a little late in the day, but can I offer you any coffee?"

"Thank you, but none for me," Franks replied.

The others dismissed the offer and followed Druseburg to his living room.

"Nancy, would you mind bringing in some water, please?" Druseburg asked.

The housekeeper made her way into the kitchen and Kate watched as she left. The house was stark, cold, and uninviting. Its marble floors gleamed beneath the stainless steel and glass chandelier that hung in the entrance. Kate turned back to see the others make their way into the main room. She followed behind, taking note of the lack of anything personal in the home. No photographs of friends or family, no books or magazines lying around or even on a shelf somewhere. In fact, it seemed as though the only warmth the home had to offer was the view of the sun over the ocean. It would disappear soon and so would its bright rays that still shone through the sliding glass walled panels inside.

"You'll forgive me if I seem stunned, because quite frankly, I am," Druseburg began as he hoisted up his pants and took a seat on the high-back leather armchair. "Can you tell me who this woman is—was?"

"We were hoping you could tell us." Nick pulled out a picture of the dead woman they believed was possibly Madlena Jankovic. "They found her behind a laundromat a few days ago."

Druseburg winced at the sight of the dark-haired girl, lying on the blacktop, sparsely dressed. "Well, I'm embarrassed to say that once in a while, I—um, how to put this so as not to offend anyone." He looked at Kate. "I occasionally request the company of a woman who, in turn, offers that company at a price."

"You hire hookers." Kate's brash retort seemed to take everyone by surprise. "For a man who appears to have a great deal of wealth, I find it hard to believe you would need to pay for any woman's company. At least, not in the traditional sense." She despised this man and looked at him through eyes that already passed judgment as to his guilt.

Nick cast a disapproving glance to Kate. "I think what my agent-in-training is trying to convey is that it seems unusual for a man of your standing to utilize the services of a drug addict-prostitute, which this woman was."

"Is that how she died? Drugs?" Druseburg asked.

"I'm afraid so," Detective Franks replied. "Mr. Druseburg, do you recall this young woman's name? We have yet to notify her family, as we've been unable to identify her, and if it hadn't been for evidence suggesting you were the last one to see her alive, then I'm not sure we would be here at all."

Druseburg eyed the agents. "Why is the FBI here? A woman dies from an overdose, someone whose services I utilized at one point or another; I can't exactly recall when just now. Can I ask why the FBI is involved?"

"There's been a series of unexplained deaths recently, mostly in the southeastern region. Women, not unlike this young woman here, and what perhaps could link them together is what we believe to be their countries of origin. It seems as though these women are mostly likely undocumented immigrants. And we have reason to believe they are a part of a trafficking ring specializing in the sex trade." Nick noticed Druseburg's eyes flicker at his explanation. "Now, I'm sure you'd like us to be as discreet as possible, so I'm going to ask you what the good detective here already did. Do you know who this woman was?"

Druseburg studied Nick for a moment and it appeared as though the two were battling it out for dominance. Druseburg seemed to concede and turned to the others in the room. "Well, I don't know if this was her real name or not, but she went by the name of Aster. I couldn't give you a last name. I never asked." Druseburg rose from the chair. "Now, I am sorry this young woman took her own life, but I'm afraid there's nothing more I can do to help you. If you don't mind, I've got a lot of work to catch up on."

Nick was the first to take to his feet. "I see we're done here, then. You've been very helpful, Mr. Druseburg. If you wouldn't mind, I believe Detective Franks would probably want you to take some time out of your busy schedule to come down and make a statement. Unfortunately, as it seems you might have been the last person to see—Aster, was it? Then we'll need to make sure we have all of the details from that final meeting."

"Of course," Druseburg began. "Detective Franks, I can be at your office by ten a.m. tomorrow morning. Will that suffice?"

"Yes. Thank you for your cooperation," Franks replied.

Druseburg showed them to the front door. "Good evening, gentlemen, and ladies." He closed the door and engaged the lock. Returning to the foyer, he stopped as his housekeeper approached.

"Is everything all right, Mr. Druseburg?" she asked.

"Yes, everything's fine, Nancy. Why don't you go ahead and call it a night. I won't be needing anything else."

"Thank you, sir. Good night."

"Good night, Nancy."

Martin Druseburg walked back into the living room and retrieved his cell phone from the side table. He ascended the large staircase to the first landing and turned to watch the headlights outside fade from view. Continuing up to his bedroom, he pulled open the door and switched on the light. His eyes shifted to the back of the room where a keypad lay hidden behind a piece of artwork on the wall. A combination of numbers were entered when he approached and the wall slid open. What was revealed inside was an opulent bed with thick coverings and pillows; a small bathroom was adjacent.

Druseburg's time with Madlena, or Aster, as he knew her, had been almost finished, but she'd decided she wanted a way out—a way out of everything, by all accounts. He inhaled the floral scent that still lingered in the room where she stayed, ready for him at any time.

He opened the contacts on his phone and pressed the name. "It's Druseburg. Apparently, they found her."

» » »

The room in which Nicola slept was little more than a closet, but her mother had just given her an old television handed down by a coworker and friend that made her accommodation slightly more palatable. At least she wouldn't have to sit in the living room with her brothers watching them play video games or some basketball game. Nicola didn't care for basketball, or any other sport, for that matter. She was a pretty typical twelve-year-old girl with the exception that she was an immigrant. Born in Croatia, her mother brought her and her brothers to America a couple of years ago.

It was a hard life where they lived before. Recession had gripped the country for the past several years. That was why, when Nicola's father died, her mother brought them here. He worked in the shipyards, building cargo ships, and had a fatal accident. Her mother had family already living in America and so they all packed up and moved to Richmond.

Nicola's mother was now working two jobs. A housekeeper at a hotel by day and a waitress at a local restaurant that her distant relatives owned by night. Of course, she was paid in cash. Her mother had no social security number. Nicola enrolled in middle school without any questions regarding her personal history, but she had no legal identification either. Nor did her brothers.

They could've worked, but Nicola thought they were just too lazy. Instead, they sat in front of the TV playing on the Xbox that seemed to magically appear in their living room one day.

Her brother, Gregor, was kind-hearted, but often fell into the shadow of Vito, the eldest of the children. Now, as Nicola sat perched on a small beanbag chair on her floor watching Cartoon Network, she began to hear the rumblings of the brothers' return home.

It was Vito's voice she heard. Harsh, like he was angry, and she wondered why. Nicola stood up and tiptoed to her bedroom door. She pulled it open just a crack and leaned an ear towards it.

"It's not like we have a choice, Gregor. You're in this now just as much as I am."

The two spoke in their native tongue mostly because Gregor's English was so poor. It was the only time Nicola was exposed to Croatian and she was glad to still understand it. It made her feel connected to her home, to her father. She continued to listen.

"This is your fault. You shouldn't have gotten involved with Toma. I told you he was bad news. Everybody knows that. How could you do those things, Vito? How could you be a part of finding innocent girls and taking them from their homes?" Gregor asked.

"I only did what Toma hired me to do. I never hurt any of them. I swear it. How do you think I got all that money? You think Mama brings home enough money to support all of us? I did what I had to do. It was what Dad would have wanted."

"No. No. Tata was a good man, a hard-working man. He would never do what you did. You took *our* people, *our* sisters and let them be sold to big, fat, rich American men."

Nicola gasped as she quickly pulled away from the door. Had she heard Gregor right? Were her brothers involved somehow in the deaths of those women down the street? No, it couldn't be. They wouldn't do that. She stepped back towards her twin bed and lowered herself down.

That lady, that FBI agent, Nicola thought. Gregor must not have known or else he would have never agreed to talk to her that day. Vito was a part of it and was dragging Gregor down with him. Nicola noticed that the voices stopped. Footsteps were nearing her door now.

"Nicola!" Vito pushed the door open wide. He studied her eyes.

She did her best to appear calm, as though she hadn't heard anything, but she sensed Vito knew better. "What is it? I'm watching TV, what do you want?"

Vito looked at the small television that rested on her chest of drawers and then back at Nicola again. "Nothing. I just didn't know you were home. I thought I heard something. Everything okay?"

"Fine. Can I go back to watching my cartoons? I already did my homework."

Vito cast a sideways glance to Gregor, who had caught up to him. "Yes, of course. So long as your schoolwork is finished. You wouldn't want to disappoint Mama." He closed the door.

"No. Don't want to disappoint Mama," she replied.

THIRTEEN

It was a relatively small police station by comparison, but this wasn't as large a city as San Diego. And as the agents waited in Detective Franks' office, other officers seemed to move with speed and purpose around them.

"We don't get a lot of this type of thing," Franks began. "I've dealt with my share of murders and violent crimes, but human trafficking isn't something I'm accustomed to handling. Especially considering the high-profile of our primary suspect." She dropped a file onto her desk. "This is what we've got so far."

Nick picked up the file that contained the coroner's report and the photos from the scene where the victim was found. "The sooner we get a statement from Druseburg, the better."

"I understand and we will make sure he's down here tomorrow. My guess is that he's already on the phone with his lawyer," Franks replied.

"We've got his DNA from the victim, but in no way does that prove he played a part in her death," Nick said.

"What about the tattoo?" Kate started. "Did you hear what he called her?"

Nick turned to Kate and revealed a knowing grin. "Aster. That's a flower, right? Agent Reid, wouldn't you say that the tattoo on the victim resembled a daisy-type of flower?"

"Yes."

"And am I correct in assuming an Aster is similar to that?"

Kate pulled out her phone and quickly Googled "Aster Flower." An image of a purple flower with petals similar to a daisy appeared. She held out her phone so they could see the image. "I'd say so."

"Phone records," Jameson began. "We need to know who he's been talking to, who arranged for the meeting with the victim. I'll give you three guesses as to who it was."

"What we need is a warrant to search his property," Kate said. "If we can search his car and check the traffic cameras in the vicinity of the laundromat, we might be able to find out if he was in the area that night and if there's any evidence to suggest she was inside that car."

"Then we need to get a judge to issue a warrant. On a guy like this, we'd better have a compelling reason to request one," Franks interrupted. "I think we need to hear his statement first, then we can talk to a judge."

Scarborough agreed. "There's not much more we can do tonight. Detective Franks, can you post a patrolman near Druseburg's place and let us know if he goes anywhere? If he does, we'll need to put a tail on him." Nick picked up the file. "You mind if I hang on to this? We'll be back in the morning and I'll return it then. I'd just like to have some of this data entered into our case file." Nick pushed up from his seat. "We'll head back to the hotel. Call me if you need anything or if Druseburg leaves."

The detective began to show the agents out. "Will do. Get some rest. I'm sure you've all had a long day."

"It's been a long week," Jameson replied. "Thank you. Pleasure to be working with you."

» » »

Because she'd been awake since five a.m., spent half the day in training and then hopped on a flight, Kate felt as though the hour was much later than it was. The hotel was just ahead and Kate envisioned her head hitting the pillow. She retrieved her cell phone to check for messages as Nick pulled into the parking lot. Two missed calls from Will.

He turned off the engine and, alert as ever, Nick asked, "Who wants a drink?"

This was not in her plan, but looking at Dwight, Kate noticed he appeared keen on the idea too. "Okay. Sure, one drink, then I've got to get some sleep."

Nick tossed his arm over the seat and turned toward her in the back. "I'm sorry, but aren't you the youngest in this little group of ours and *you're* tired?"

"It's the Academy," Dwight replied. "Don't worry, Kate. This one here might not remember what it was like, but I'm not that far removed and I remember it quite well. It's okay if you want to skip it."

"No, no. It's fine. One drink. It'll probably help me sleep anyway."

"That's what I say," Nick replied.

As they walked inside, the small bar tucked into the corner of the hotel lobby was empty. Then again, they were staying on the outskirts of town, far away from the excitement of the beach.

"Wow, the place is hopping." Nick raised his brow to emphasize his sarcasm and hiked up his pants. He strutted inside like he was some sort of peacock. Maybe because they'd finally gotten somewhere on the investigation, Nick seemed to be feeling pretty good right about now.

Kate sat down at the closest table and glanced at her phone again. Will hadn't left any messages, just missed calls.

"Anything urgent?" Nick asked.

Kate looked up, "Hmm? Oh, no, nothing urgent." She figured he could see through her, but he chose not to comment.

"What do you want to drink?" Nick pulled out his wallet.

"Just a house white, thanks."

Nick and Dwight returned with their beers and Nick held Kate's wine. "Here you go."

"Thanks" She sipped on the wine that was much too dry for her taste.

Dwight pulled out his barstool and sat down. "So, we wait until tomorrow, until we can get Druseburg's statement." He gulped from the heavy pint glass that left a small foam mustache on his face. He quickly wiped it away with his tongue.

"We can't wait forever. I need to get with Detective Garrett and find out if he's made any progress. Let's hope he has and someone was willing to talk." Nick replied.

"If I can get Druseburg's phone records, I have no doubt Corbett's name will turn up. If we find him, then we'll find his partner and we can put this to bed." Dwight replied, taking another large gulp. It appeared he had wanted to put the job behind him for a moment and turned to Kate. "So how goes the training? You've got what? Like seven or eight weeks left?"

"About that. It's going well." Kate glanced to Nick, assuming he wouldn't say otherwise, even if that was, at least, partially the case. "Just need to work on a few things, but I'm getting through it. I'll get through it."

"I'm sure you will. Scarborough wouldn't have recommended you if he didn't think you could handle it. I can tell you one thing, your skills were not being fully utilized where you were before. You're a pretty tough kid, Kate Reid."

"Kid? Really?" She laughed. "You're what, four maybe five years older than me?"

"Maybe—something like that," Dwight replied with a smile.

"I think that's the first I've heard you laugh in a long time, Kate," Nick said. "I almost forgot what it sounded like."

The three of them had been through a lot together. Kate felt like she owed a lot to the both of them. "Well, you'd think working with you two clowns, I'd be laughing every day."

The sound of their amusement echoed through the small bar and into the lobby, drawing the attention of the man attending the front desk.

Kate noticed his glare. "Oops. Guess we were a little loud."

"Ah, screw him." Nick swatted his hand. "He has no idea the kind of shit we deal with every day. We deserve a goddamn laugh once in a while."

"Okay, okay, calm down there, Sparky." Dwight patted Nick's shoulder. "I don't think the guy meant anything. We just caught his attention, that's all."

"Whatever. I need a real drink." Nick stood up. "Anyone else want anything?"

Kate still had half a glass. "I'm fine, thanks."

"I'll take another beer," Dwight replied.

Once Kate felt confident Nick was out of earshot, she looked at Dwight. "What's going on with him? He seems wound up tonight."

"Tonight? Try most nights lately." Dwight tossed a look over his shoulder to ensure Nick wasn't heading back. "I don't know. I think it's got something to do with Myers. I've known Scarborough a long time and he isn't much for being tied down. It's damn near impossible with this job anyway. But I think it bothers him that Myers expects him to be around more than he is."

"She's gone just as often. That doesn't make any sense," Kate replied.

"I don't know. He doesn't talk about it much, except when he's had a few. I'm not sure dating someone you work with is a good idea anyway."

Kate noticed the apologetic look immediately appear on Dwight's face.

"I'm sorry, Kate. I didn't mean…"

She raised a pre-emptive hand. "No, please, it's fine. I know you didn't mean anything…"

"I didn't. I swear. I saw the two of you together. I saw what you did for each other. You two were different. In most cases, I wouldn't recommend dipping the old pen in the company ink, but you and Marshall were different."

Kate grinned. "Thanks, Dwight."

Nick returned with a drink for himself and a beer for Dwight. "You sure you don't want anything else, Kate? That glass is looking a little low now."

"No, I'm good. I have any more and you all might have to carry me to bed, I'm so damn tired."

"All right, all right, ya wimp," Nick replied.

Kate turned up her palms and shrugged. "What can I say? It's hard to hang with you boys." She took the final few sips of her drink. "Well, that's it for me. I'm off to my room." She jumped off the barstool, dabbed the corners of her mouth, and set her cocktail napkin next to the empty wine glass. "I'll see you two bright and early." She reached inside her small purse for a ten.

"Put your money away, Reid. Good night," Dwight said.

"Night." Nick followed with a raise of his glass as if he was making a toast. He watched her walk away and turned back to Dwight, who had in turn been watching him.

"You all right, man?" Dwight asked. "You seem on edge. Is it this case, 'cause you know you can't let this shit get to you. I'm pretty sure you're the one who said that to me a long time ago."

"No. It's not the case. Well, maybe part of it. Hell, I don't know. I just got a lot on my mind." He tossed back the rest of his Jack and Coke.

"Uh-huh. Any of it have to do with that pretty dark-haired woman who just left?"

Nick appeared as though being unjustly accused of something.

"Come on, man. You feel responsible for her. I get it. I didn't stop Avery from going to Shalot's place. I feel responsible for what happened to him. And I gotta look into Kate's eyes and see it all the time too."

"You didn't know that was where he was going," Nick replied.

Dwight only shrugged. "You didn't know either. But for some reason, you feel as though her success at Quantico, as an agent, all rests on your shoulders. As if her failure would be your failure."

"Maybe it would be. You want another?" Nick twirled the ice cubes in his empty glass.

"No, man. I'm good. It's probably best if you get some rest yourself." Dwight pushed off the table and to his feet. "Maybe give Georgia a call. It'll do you some good to talk to her."

"Sure. You're right. I'll do that. Catch up with you in the morning?"

"Absolutely. Good night, Nick." Dwight turned away and headed towards the elevator.

Nick was alone and cast his eyes to the empty glass, seriously considering another drink. He'd been doing pretty well lately, keeping it in check, but something had set him off tonight and he wasn't really sure why it had. After considering Dwight's suggestion to get some rest, he set the glass down and pulled out his wallet. "What do I owe you?" he approached the bartender.

"Forty-three fifty."

Nick suddenly regretted picking up the tab. He dropped a fifty on the bar. "Thanks."

"Thank you, sir. Have a good night."

He had already begun walking away and raised his hand in reply. "Good night." Nick reached the elevator and pushed the button, staring at the light that illuminated each floor on its way to the bottom. He again thought of what Dwight had said as he stood there waiting. It wasn't what he'd ever intended—feeling responsible for Kate's success, but maybe that was what this was. He'd been with her that day, holding her because she couldn't stand on her own two feet when the doctor said Avery was dead.

The elevator finally arrived and its doors parted, inviting Nick inside. As they closed again and took him to his floor, he began thinking about what Kate said earlier. Admitting she'd slept with Caison. Maybe that was what really bothered him.

» » »

"Do you have any idea how careless that was?" Druseburg asked as he poured a drink from the wet bar in the billiards room.

The speakerphone blared to life again. "Martin, I can assure you they have nothing. She was just another prostitute who wound up dead in the streets. You have nothing to worry about."

"I trusted you, Jim." Druseburg tossed his head back and downed his drink. "You said these girls were untraceable."

"They are," Corbett replied. "No one has any idea who she was or where she was from. She'll remain a Jane Doe and this whole thing will blow over."

"Why in the hell was the FBI at my door, then? Huh? They don't get involved unless it's some kind of big fucking mess, which I gotta tell you, Jim, it's sure as hell starting to feel that way."

James Corbett – Jim, to his friends and clients – continued to clarify his meaning. "Martin, I know it's been a challenge lately and we've had some unfortunate incidents. But none of these women have been identified."

"Not that you know of." Druseburg turned over one of the highball glasses and set it down on the bar. A bottle of Johnny Walker Red sat nearly empty on the counter. He poured what remained into his glass and proceeded to swish it around over the single cube of ice.

"We'll cool things down for a while, okay? I've got my guys looking out for some fresh faces. These feds can't do jack shit and they know it." Corbett again offered assurances.

"It wasn't your DNA they found, now was it, Jim?" He turned towards the glass wall. "You know, you're right. Because if they do try and pin this on me, well, let's just say that I won't be the only one to take the blame."

» » »

The house had grown cold as the temperatures still dipped lower. Nicola pulled up the blanket that lay at the foot of her bed. The house was poorly insulated in any case and made it feel that much colder. Nicola hadn't been able to sleep and, even now, still peered out of the small bedroom window that overlooked her street.

The neighborhood was quiet; it was late. But when Nicola sat at the dinner table with her mother and brothers tonight, she looked at them and knew. They had been a part of it. She could see it in Gregor's eyes. The question now, as she sat perfectly still on her bed, would she tell anyone?

She began to think of the dead women that had been found in the house just down the street. She wondered how anyone could do such harm, especially her own brothers. It did not come as a surprise that Vito would have been involved. He always seemed to associate with the wrong people, but he was still her brother.

Nicola squeezed her eyes shut as she worked through a solution. Vito would know if she said anything. He knew the moment he walked into her bedroom earlier that she'd heard everything. But what if the lady could help her? The lady who was training to be in the FBI? She seemed nice. She seemed to care.

I wish I could just go home.

Nicola lay down and turned on her side, curling her legs to her chest. She looked at her bedroom door and considered for just a moment that she could leave. And go where, she didn't know, but away from here. It would break her mother's heart, but then so would knowing her sons were involved in such a despicable act.

>> >> >>

"Kate?" A knock sounded on the door inside that adjoined the rooms.

Sleep still gripped her, but as the sound continued, she began to rouse. It was still dark and confusion as to where she was and what time it was had set in. The ambiguity of living two lives was difficult to conquer. One life inside Quantico and one life outside of it.

It was that life that now called her to wake. The clock on the side table brightened and its white LED light began to clear. "Jesus. It's four a.m." She sat up in her bed and the knock continued. "I'm coming."

She pushed herself off the bed and slogged across the room wearing just a t-shirt. Unlatching the deadbolt, Kate opened the door. Nick had already opened his side and now he stood just inches from her. "What's wrong? What is it?" She peered inside to see Dwight moving in his bed, as though he'd been roused slightly by Nick's disruption.

"I got a call from Garrett." Nick nearly pushed his way into her room, disregarding the fact that she was half-naked. Then again, he was only in his boxer shorts, a fact that a groggy Kate easily overlooked.

It took a moment for her to digest his words. "What did he want? Please come in," she said, although he was already planted on the end of her bed.

"A girl was brought into his station about an hour ago," Nick started. "Vice was booking her on solicitation and she mentioned the fact that several of the girls she knew were no longer on the streets or in the clubs. She figured they had all ended up in jail."

Nick rubbed his face as if it helped him to speak with further clarity.

Kate soon joined him on the bed and waited for him to continue.

"The vice cop thought it was a little strange and of course made mention of it to one of the officers who'd been canvassing the area asking questions about our Jane Doe. Well, after a few more questions, the cops realized that this girl might know the victim. So they talked to Garrett – he was already home in bed – and Garrett told them to show the girl a picture of the victim."

"Holy shit." Kate was fully awake now. "She recognized her, didn't she?"

"You're damn right, she did. It's Madlena Jankovic."

"Oh my God," Kate replied.

"The girl knew where she lived and Garrett and another of his officers will be going to the house first thing in the morning to talk to the family. Find out when she went missing. That'll help us determine where Corbett was at the time. Again, we're looking for timelines to help establish a pattern of movement."

Kate could see the fervor building inside him. "What do you me to do?"

"We're going to get the statement from Druseburg in the morning and then I want you to copy the files we have from Franks and head back to WFO. Get everything into the system. Jameson and I will be heading back to Richmond shortly thereafter. We know Corbett took Madlena, thanks to the tattoo. Now that we know who she is and that she was kidnapped, which can easily be established because of the anonymous call Garrett received, Druseburg's going to have a hell of a time explaining how he'd come into contact with her presumably after she'd gone missing. It won't take much more than that for him to turn on Corbett, I'm sure of it. Then, we'll find him."

"I can't go back. I want to stay here," Kate said.

Nick placed his hand on her bare thigh. "I need for you to go back and work on the case file. That is just as important and Quantico is still your priority."

Kate looked at his hand and Nick quickly pulled it away. "I'll go back, but only after we get Druseburg's statement." Her conviction was forced because she really had no basis for which to demand anything. Nick was the Agent in Charge.

"Thank you." He rose from the bed. "Sorry I woke you. It probably could have waited till daylight, but sometimes, I get a little excited." He stepped back toward the door. "See you in a few hours. Hopefully, you can get back to sleep."

Kate dropped her shoulders and exhaled. There wasn't a chance in hell she'd be going back to sleep.

FOURTEEN

Security at the Quantico gate was tight and Kate wondered if something had happened while she was in Virginia Beach. Peering beyond the driver's side window, she noted about six cars in front of her. That figured. She was verging on being late and if things didn't start moving, there'd be no doubt of her tardiness.

Her flight had returned late last night and she should've just driven straight to campus, but she'd already missed the midnight curfew and ended up going home instead. Now, she cursed herself for taking such a late flight. But the day had been so hectic. Druseburg didn't come in to make his statement until late in the afternoon and, by the time Kate gathered the files and coordinated with Agents Scarborough and Jameson, she ended up missing the earlier flight.

Now, Monday morning had arrived and she only had twenty minutes before she needed to be in class. A brief weapons review and then they'd be off to the shooting range for drills. Her car inched along, but she was still far behind. "Damn it."

Kate retrieved her cell phone and texted Will. She hadn't spoken to him since leaving on Saturday and hadn't returned his calls. Would he reply in kind? Maybe. She'd pretty much left him out in the cold. *"I'm at the guard gate. It's backed up. Be there soon.*" She hoped he would acknowledge her and pass along the information to their instructor.

The line was moving along a little better now. Kate was three cars behind. She glanced at the time on her dashboard. Ten minutes and still—no reply from Will. What did she expect? Whatever friendship had been there was now in tatters.

Several more minutes ticked away and, finally, she arrived at the gate, identification in hand. The guard nodded and raised the post. It was all she could do not to speed down the road to the training facility.

A parking spot was just on the horizon and Kate pulled in, killed the engine, and jumped out, yanking her bag from the passenger seat.

Once inside the room, she gathered herself, smoothing her hair and clothes. Her assigned seat awaited her, and so did Will.

"There you are. I was wondering if you'd be here today. I mean, since you're working with Agent Scarborough," Will said.

"Didn't you get my text message?"

"No." Will leaned over to reach inside his laptop bag to retrieve his phone. "Oh. Here it is. Sorry. It's been in my bag. Well, glad you made it on time."

"Thanks." Kate pulled out her laptop.

"How's the investigation going?"

"It's going well. Agents Scarborough and Jameson are heading to Richmond today to meet with the local police. They got an ID on one of the victims."

"That's great."

"It's not over yet."

» » »

The day was warming to an uncomfortable temperature and Kate was now standing in the heat, pointing a gun at a paper target thirty feet away. Goggles, ear protection, and an aim that was far beyond anything Kate ever believed she could develop. She waited for the instructor's go-ahead.

The kickback was still the hardest part of shooting the .40 caliber gun. Kate wasn't weak, but the strength required to withstand the recoil and still hit the target was substantial.

Some of the firearms training included the removal of the ear protection in order for the trainee to become accustomed to the sound. The startling noise often reminded her of when she was shot. She occasionally joked about it with Nick, reminding him that he'd shot her once. It was generally only to get a rise out of him, and he almost always took the bait.

Still, Kate couldn't help but be a little sidetracked at the moment. She wanted to know what the hell was happening with the investigation. It was well past noon and, at last check, before stepping onto the range, she hadn't heard from Nick or Dwight.

The targets were retrieved and Kate examined her results. Time would tell, however, if she would achieve the same near-perfect results on a human being, should the need arise.

Time would also tell whether or not Kate would be successful in the Academy. This week would present her with another Hogan's Alley tactical training scenario and she was already dreading it. She would have to focus solely on it if she hoped to pass the test. It was a matter of desensitizing herself to it, to the fear that crept inside her as she hunted down the criminals. Even now, the idea began to throw her off her target. "Stop. Focus," she whispered.

"What's that?" Will stood at the next target over and must have noticed her lips move.

"Nothing." She shook her head. He hadn't yet mentioned a word about the other night, or her disregard for his phone calls. He was being a perfect friend and gentleman and Kate didn't understand why, unsure if she herself would have acted in such a manner.

Distractions. There were too many distractions and Kate lowered her weapon. The instructor took notice and headed her way.

"Everything all right, Reid? Your weapon jam?" He lowered his gaze to study the gun.

"No, sir. Just got a cramp in my hand. I'm fine now."

He pressed his lips tightly in a disapproving manner and continued on to check on the other trainees.

Kate resumed her target practice.

» » »

The words on the paper lost all meaning as Nicola held her pencil over the empty circles in search of the right answer. But there were other things on her mind unrelated to the spelling test she was now taking. Things that shouldn't be on the mind of a twelve-year-old girl. She had tried to listen in on the conversations Gregor and Vito had over the past two days, but they didn't divulge anything more than she already knew. In fact, it seemed the eldest, Vito, was keeping a watchful eye on his little sister, perhaps waiting for her to say something about what she might have overheard.

But Nicola was smart. One of the smartest girls in her class. And she knew better than to reveal that she had any inkling at all as to her brother's plans. That was not to say that she wasn't afraid. She was very afraid. The fear had prevented her from finding much, if any, rest over the course of the weekend. It was a very real possibility that Nicola would fail this test, but maybe the teacher would understand if she knew why.

The time showed she had only minutes to finish. Nicola pushed up from her desk and walked toward the teacher. "Ms. McIlroy, I need to use the restroom."

The young teacher with a face that still wore the enthusiasm of a newly minted educator looked to Nicola with a furrowed brow. "Can't it wait until after the test?"

Nicola pressed on her abdomen and cringed. "It's girl problems." She was lying and hadn't even gotten her period yet. She figured she was just one of those late bloomers.

"I see." A sudden compassionate look appeared on the teacher's face, as if commiserating on a level that all females understood. "Go ahead, but come right back."

Nicola revealed a grateful smile and exited the classroom. As she entered the quiet hall, she reached a conclusion and made her way along the empty corridor, her flip-flopped footsteps echoing against the walls and bouncing off the well-worn beige vinyl floor.

Upon reaching the front of the school, she looked up at the sign over the green metal door, "Administration," and walked inside. Several of the staff, most of which were middle-aged women, were busy typing on their outdated computers or on the phone or helping other students with various tasks. Nicola stood at the counter and waited quietly for someone's attention.

She hadn't sprouted up as many of her classmates had this year, so it was only her head that was visible over top of the counter. Finally, a kind-faced woman approached. "Can I help you?"

"Um, yes. I would like to see Principal Barnes?"

It wasn't often a student would actually ask to see the principal and so the woman appeared somewhat surprised by the request. "Oh, is everything all right? Are you feeling okay?"

"I'm fine. I need to talk to him. Please, it's very important."

"It's Nicola Bjuric, right?" Only she pronounced it with a hard j, like jerk, instead of a y.

Nicola was used to the butchering of her name and so agreed. "Yes."

"Are you sure no one else can help you?"

"Please, I need to see Mr. Barnes." Nicola turned on the most pathetic and sad look she could muster. That would surely get her where she needed to be. If only this woman in front of her knew that this really was a life or death situation, she wouldn't be so hesitant.

"Let me see if he has a moment. I'll be right back."

Nicola sat down in one of the blue molded plastic chairs that were intended for the students. There were a few nice padded armchairs, but everyone knew those were for the parents.

She must have done a pretty good job convincing the administrator of her desperation because it felt as though only a few minutes passed before the woman returned.

"Come on, sweetheart. He says he can spare a couple of minutes for you."

Nicola took to her feet and was ushered by the slightly plump woman to the principal's office.

The woman opened the door and pressed her hand against Nicola's back, nudging her inside. "Nicola Bjuric would like a quick word with you, Mr. Barnes."

"Of course, please come in, Nicola, and have a seat."

She waited until the woman had closed the door before she turned to Mr. Barnes. "I'm sorry to bother you, Mr. Barnes, but I need to talk to a lady I met the other day. She's going to be an FBI agent and her name is Kate Reid."

The principal narrowed his eyes just a little, seeming to try and figure out what an FBI agent had to do with either him or this young girl he knew to come from an undocumented family.

"You met an FBI agent?"

"She's training to be one, but her boss came over with her to talk to my brothers a couple of weeks ago about some people who died in a house on my street."

The principal appeared to show great interest. "Okay. And why do you need to speak with her again?"

"Because I know some people who might be a part of it."

"You know some of the people who were involved in a crime?"

"Mr. Barnes, I need to speak with Kate Reid, she's the only one who can help me. Can you find her?"

» » »

It seemed long lines were everywhere today as Kate now waited to approach the buffet counter in the campus cafeteria. Perhaps it was that her patience had worn thin throughout the course of the day and it was culminating in a growing frustration with people in general.

Or it was the fact that she hadn't yet heard from Agent Scarborough. Either way, her stomach was rumbling and irritation was setting in. As she waited, Kate surveyed the room for an open table, preferably one at the back where she could be away from the chatter. It wasn't just her fellow-trainees that were there. Quantico offered training and other similar resources to a multitude of law enforcement agencies. Right now, Kate saw a whole lot of people wearing DEA shirts.

On further inspection, she noticed Will sitting with a few of their classmates. He'd behaved in a very respectful and professional manner, of which Kate was most appreciative. A twinge of guilt still surged inside her at the recollection of her actions.

Kate approached the counter and began to dish out her meal. The food wasn't bad here and she was hungry, so she piled it on pretty high.

Stepping away from the buffet, she spotted a small table in the back corner. Perfect. The sun dangled low in the sky and its light caught her eyes as she sat down, placing her phone next to the tray of food. She continued to glance at it with high hopes, but it remained silent while she ate her dinner.

A reflection appeared in the window as she stared out among the grounds of the campus. A moment's hesitation gripped her and then Kate finally turned to see Will standing next to her table. A smile acknowledging his presence appeared, but nothing more until she could swallow the food in her mouth.

"Can I sit down?"

She nodded, grabbing a napkin to dab her lips. Finally, she answered, "Sure."

"Why didn't you come join us? I thought you saw me wave you over?" Will asked.

"I didn't. I'm sorry."

"Eh, don't worry about it." Will folded his arms across the table. "So, any news from Agent Scarborough yet?"

"No." Kate glanced longingly at her darkened phone.

"He'll be in touch soon enough. These things take time, I'm sure."

Will turned away and the two were silent for a moment, both staring out the window. He turned back to her. "Do you think we can just forget about the other night?" he asked. "Because I see now that it wasn't the right thing to do and I really like having you for a friend. I don't want to screw that up, if I haven't already."

"You haven't, Will. And I would like for us to still be friends. I need your friendship probably a lot more than you need mine."

"I doubt that, but thanks. You know, for what it's worth, I think you're an incredibly strong woman and you will make a great agent."

Kate's heart lightened at his words. She smiled in reply.

He slapped the table. "All right, enough of that."

Will was a lot like her. He was pretty good at downplaying his feelings too. She could stop now. Let it go and move forward as his friend. It wouldn't change what she'd done, but it meant she still had someone to lean on—for now.

"Enough of the mushy sentiments," he continued. "We're supposed to be NATs, right?"

Kate began to laugh and felt eased by his offer of resolution. Although everyone in her class were called NATs, the image of an actual gnat always appeared in her mind when the instructors used the term. It was the little things like this that made her feel normal, and the laughter was sorely needed.

The tension finally broke, and optimal timing as usual, her phone sprang to life on the table. Kate looked at it and then to Will.

"Guess you'd better get that."

She picked up the call. "This is Reid." As she listened to the caller, her brow furrowed. A moment later, a brief grin formed on her lips. "Yeah, I can be there in a few hours. Thank you, Agent Scarborough."

Kate ended the call and inhaled a deep breath. She looked at Will again. He appeared eager to be informed of the exchange. "I've got to go to Richmond tonight."

"Really? What's going on?"

"Apparently, a young girl I met a couple weeks ago wants to see me. I guess she's got some information, but she only wants to talk to me."

» » »

With little traffic on the darkened highway, Kate was making good time and expected to be at the station in Richmond within minutes. Earlier, Scarborough had emailed her the audio transcript of the woman claiming to know the victim in Virginia Beach, Madlena.

With the Bluetooth connected, the audio file began to play over the speakers. The woman's accent was thick, Romanian perhaps? Kate was no expert in eastern European dialect, but the inflections were just slightly different from what she recalled when she listened to Gregor and Nicola Bjuric. But one tone was most discernable: fear.

She went on to describe to the detective how it felt like her friends were being picked off, one by one. Some of them worked in the local strip clubs and on the streets like she did, but a couple worked in the shops, bakeries, florists, and the like, mostly in the back and mostly out of sight. This woman feared deportation, but she feared being the next to go missing even more.

"They were just gone," she said. "I was starting to think that immigration had caught up with them, but then I still saw their families, brothers, sisters, moms. There are posters everywhere that the families are putting up on walls and streetlights. Anywhere they can find a place for them. I don't know what's happening. They're just gone."

As Kate's eyes fixed on the sparsely illuminated highway, she was reminded of the kinship she felt towards these women. They were here to start a new life. To be given a new beginning, only to find themselves being taken against their will into an inexplicable life of sexual servitude. And if the discovery of Madlena's body was any indication, the women were being drugged in order to keep them contained and unable to put up a fight.

The thought of finding the men who held so little value for women, selling them off to those who valued them even less—these thieves of hope—was growing stronger.

She stopped the recording and finished the journey in silence.

It was approaching nine o'clock before Kate reached the Richmond police station. Nick stood outside, clutching a paper cup with steam rising upwards. Her headlights shone in his eyes and he squinted as she pulled into the parking spot directly in front of him. She killed the lights and opened her car door.

Nick pushed off the wall and approached. "Looks like you made quite the impression on this little girl."

"She's still here?"

"Yes." He headed toward the entrance. "Her mother is here too, but he doesn't speak much English." Nick tossed the cup into the garbage can in front of the door. "Coffee tastes like shit."

Kate followed him inside. "What should I ask her?" Interrogation was a process that Kate was only just learning in her training. And this was different. Nicola was a witness. And a child.

"She wants to talk to you, so just let her talk. Don't ask any questions. Not yet. You're here to listen."

"Got it."

If the local police were trying to avoid intimidating the girl, they didn't seem to be doing a very good job. They had her and her mother inside one of the interview rooms. If she'd had her choice, Kate would have preferred to put the child in a conference room. But she supposed they would need to record her statement and this was the best place for that.

"Ladies first," Nick said as he held the door to the interview room.

An instant smile appeared on the girl's face and she leaned over to her mother and said something in Croatian. Kate assumed it was something to the effect that she was the one they were waiting for.

"Hi, Nicola. It's very nice to see you again." Kate pulled a chair from beneath the table and sat down.

"Hello, Agent Reid," the girl replied.

"I'm not an agent yet. You can call me Kate." She laced her fingers together, resting them on the table. "I understand you wanted to talk to me about something?"

Nicola looked at her mother. The exchange was easily recognizable. It was that of a mother giving approval.

Nicola began to pick at her fingernails. "I overheard something on Saturday. I was in my room when my brothers came home."

"Gregor and Vito?" Kate asked.

She nodded. The mother placed her hand over the top of Nicola's and shook her head. Nicola stopped picking at her nails.

Kate sensed her apprehension. They all did. And she looked at Nick with a silent inquiry. He nodded his approval to proceed.

"It's okay, Nicola. You can talk to me. You aren't in any trouble."

"I don't want my family to be sent back home. Are you going to send us home?"

"No, honey." Kate reached out for Nicola's hand. "No one is going to send you or any member of your family away." She cast a brief glance to Nick, wondering if she should have implied such a statement.

"I think my brother, Vito." A breath of air filled her lungs. "I think he might be involved with those girls who died in that house."

Kate looked to Nick again. He wasn't going to offer any more help. She was on her own. "What makes you think that, Nicola?"

"They were talking about finding more of them."

"More girls?" Kate asked.

She nodded. "I think so. Vito said if they didn't have more by tonight, then they would be in trouble."

"What kind of trouble?"

"I'm not sure, but I think they might be killed."

"Nicola," Kate began. "This is very important. You said they had to find more by tonight. Do you know where they were going to find these girls?"

"No. But Vito said it had to be tonight."

FIFTEEN

A logical start to the search for the Bjuric brothers as well as the potential victims they were attempting to acquire was at one of the many gentlemen's clubs in the city, a place that promoted fantasy, desire, and perhaps, if one was willing to pay the price, favors to fulfill such fantasies. This was Detective Garrett's city and he was well versed in the reputations of these places. Some catered to a more sophisticated client – i.e. ones with money – while others catered to those of less discriminating tastes.

It was those establishments that Garrett believed would most likely hire a staff member of questionable background or no background at all. This was where he and Agent Scarborough would start.

Meanwhile, the order came down for Kate to stay with Nicola and her mother at the police station. She wasn't happy about the order, but Nicola was afraid and she only trusted Kate. Her only consolation was the reminder that she was not yet a full-fledged federal agent and so her powers and abilities were limited. She couldn't hold that against her mentor.

Garrett and Scarborough approached the bar where a man with slicked back hair and a square jaw tended to the thirsty customers, or at least changed out their twenty-dollar bills for ones. Garrett leaned in, resting his forearm on the bar's edge.

He held a picture of the two brothers and one of James Corbett. "Good evening. I was wondering if you could help me out." Garrett retrieved his badge from his wallet and laid it on the bar. The man seemed unimpressed.

"Can you tell me if you've seen any of these men in here before? Specifically, have they been in here tonight?" He placed the photos over his badge.

The bartender picked up each picture and appeared to study them for a length of time that would be considered suitable. He shook his head.

"You sure?" Garrett continued. "I understand they were in here looking for something very particular."

"What's that?" the square-jawed man replied.

"A few young, pretty eastern Europeans. Croatian, Slovenian, maybe Romanians. That general area."

The man only shrugged his shoulders. Although difficult to tell for sure in the scant light, and he used too few words to decipher any sort of accent, but it seemed possible that his olive skin and brown hair suggested he was of similar origin.

It appeared Garrett was hoping to draw out some sort of kinship or loyalty from the man, but it wasn't working. At this, Nick decided to offer some assistance. He set his badge next to the pictures and this seemed to get the man's attention.

"Are you sure you haven't seen any of these men? If not tonight, maybe they were here on another night?" Nick said.

The bartender picked up the picture of Vito and began to reconsider his earlier hasty conclusion. "This one. He was here a few hours ago."

"Did he talk to any of the girls? The dancers?" Garrett asked.

"A couple of the girls who had just finished their shifts left with him. I don't know anything more than that."

"Willingly?" Nick asked.

"They weren't kicking and screaming, if that's what you're asking."

"Thank you. You've been very helpful." Nick snatched his badge and the pictures off the bar top. "We'll be in touch if we need anything else."

"I look forward to it." The man revealed a contemptuous grin.

Garrett pushed open the door, exiting the club to the sounds of cars rushing by, street peddlers, and music from a nearby nightclub. "The brothers must have split up. He said he only recognized Vito."

The two approached Garrett's car. Before Nick stepped inside, he retrieved his cell. "This is SSA Scarborough with the Washington Field Office. Can you put me through to ASAC Lansing? Thank you." He waited for Garrett to unlock the car door and slid into the passenger seat. "Yes, ASAC Lansing, this is SSA Scarborough. I need a favor. A big one."

» » »

Kate pulled onto the drive of Nicola's home. The girl had already fallen asleep in the backseat of the car. Her mother stepped out of the front passenger seat and opened the back door to wake Nicola.

"Let me help you get her inside." Kate stepped out and walked around to the other side while Nicola's mother was attempting to rouse the tired girl.

The house was dark except for a single source of light that shone through the front room window.

Kate glanced to the window. "Did you leave the light on?" she asked the woman.

"No."

According to Scarborough and Garrett, the brothers were together somewhere, but hadn't yet been located. Kate's concern rose, as did her pulse with uncertainty. With one eye on the illuminated window, she continued to assist in getting Nicola awake and out of the car. She looked to Nicola. "Tell your mom that you two need to stay right here, okay?"

Nicola seemed fully awake as if she sensed Kate's apprehension and nodded her agreement.

Kate placed her hand on her weapon and stepped carefully to the front porch. Her other hand reached for the door handle to check if the door was locked. It was. The curtains were closed, but as she approached the window, a small parting exposed a fraction of the room inside, but she could see no one.

Returning towards the two still huddled next to Kate's car, she tried to appear calm, but her palms were sweating and she recalled how similar this felt to the operations training she'd experienced. And how she'd failed. "Do you have a key?"

Nicola turned to her mother and asked the same question. A moment later, a key emerged from the woman's purse and she handed it to Kate.

Kate stepped with caution towards the front door. This time, she inserted the key and it clicked open. "FBI. Identify yourself."

She pressed the door open a little more, bringing into view the living room of the small home. "FBI. Identify yourself."

Still, no one answered. Kate drew her weapon and stepped over the threshold, elbowing the door further for a better view. Behind the armchair in the living room stood a kid, trembling with a gun in his hands. It was Gregor Bjuric.

"Gregor. It's Kate Reid. You remember me? I need you to put your weapon down. I'm not here for you. I've got your sister and mother outside."

"Why are you here then?" His fractured English seemed even more so underneath his fear.

"Gregor, put the gun down and we can talk, okay? You don't want to frighten your little sister, do you?"

"Nicola? She knows, and my mother?"

Kate nodded. "Where is Vito?"

"I don't know." His eyes were starting to pool with tears and his brow began to form tiny droplets of moisture.

"Gregor, it's okay. Calm down. Please—put the gun down. I promise you, I am not here to hurt you or take you from your family. I just want to talk to you." This was what she was training for, but her confidence wavered. "You were very helpful before and I need your help now, but I can't talk to you with that gun in your hand. Do you understand?"

He raised the gun higher and it now pointed toward Kate's head. He was shaking so violently that she feared he would accidentally fire. "I didn't want to take them. I swear, but he would have killed us."

Her life was in his hands, but she couldn't let him see her panic. Kate gripped her own weapon harder, and released the safety. "Put the gun down." This time, her words came across with steely conviction.

The click of the safety release seemed to get his attention. "Okay, okay." Gregor finally began to lower his gun. "But you have to keep my family safe. Promise me."

"I'll keep them safe, Gregor. Let's just sit down and talk for a minute." Kate took a step forward.

The frightened kid placed the gun on the seat of the chair in front of him.

A momentary inclination to collapse overcame her, but Kate steadied herself. The gun was still within his reach and this would not be over until it was in her hands. Kate walked to the chair, her eyes never leaving his. She lowered herself down, still aiming the weapon at his chest. Once his gun was firmly in her hands, her heart started again. "I'm going to bring your mother and sister inside now, okay? Just sit down and relax so we can talk."

Kate stepped backwards towards the door, afraid to take her eyes off of Gregor. She waved the two of them inside and, finally, she reengaged the safety and holstered her weapon.

The mother ran to her son and pulled him close as he sat on the chair. Nicola could only watch as her brother sobbed like a baby in their mother's arms.

Gregor sat back up and looked to his sister.

"I had to, Gregor. I know Vito made you do these things. But she can help." Nicola pointed to Kate, who'd secured the front door before returning.

Kate's top concern now was Vito's return. He would not be as submissive as his brother. She was feeling out of her depth and while she hadn't wanted Gregor to sense her growing concerns, she needed to reach out to Nick and get someone down here. One of the two brothers they'd been on the hunt for was sitting right in front of her. He could tell them where the victims were and if Corbett had them. "Gregor," Kate sat down in the recliner across from the sofa, still displaying calm, "where is Vito taking the girls?"

Shame instantly masked his face as he looked to his mother, but then he returned his attention to Kate. "Kovac. He was the one who told us to get the girls because Vito did something very, very bad. But he did it to save me."

"I need to call my boss, okay? He will be able to help you." Kate pulled her cell from her pocket.

"No. Please, no more police," Gregor replied.

"I have to. If I'm going to protect you and your family, we need his help."

Kate raised the phone to her ear, her eyes still fixed on the three members of the Bjuric family. Where the fourth was remained unknown, but Kate didn't want to be the only one there if or when he arrived. "Agent Scarborough. I'm at the Bjuric's home. Can you please come or send someone ASAP?"

"What the hell's going on?" Nick replied.

"Gregor knows where the girls are. He's here with me now." A final pause and Kate ended the call. "He's on his way."

Based on the inflections in the words Gregor spoke to his sister, Kate assumed he'd been angry about her bringing the FBI to their home. Their native language sounded harsh anyway, but Kate thought there was more to it. Finally, the mother spoke up and there was an immediate end to the discussion.

"I know you must be angry with Nicola," Kate began. "But she may have just prevented you from going to prison. Whatever this is that you and your brother are involved in..."

Gregor began to speak to Kate, but not in English. Kate looked at Nicola for translation.

"He says our brother, Vito, only agreed to take the girls because Gregor would have been killed. Instead, Toma was the one who died and Vito had to answer for it." Nicola looked to Gregor as he continued. "He says Stan Kovac is the man behind all of it. He's the one who has the girls."

Kate considered the idea that this Kovac person was Corbett's partner that they'd been working to identify.

Several more minutes ticked away while Kate attempted to gain a further understanding of how these two young men had become involved in something so heinous. Dragging their sister and mother into it only further endangered them all.

A knock on the door, and Kate heard Nick's voice call out, "Agent Reid, are you inside? Are you safe?"

Kate rose from the chair and moved to the door. Upon opening it, she spotted Nick and the detective. "I'm okay. We're all okay." She stood aside, allowing them entry.

"Detective Garrett is going to take you and your mother to a safe place for now," Scarborough said to Nicola. "Please, go with him and we'll make sure nothing happens to your brother."

The two of them quickly moved towards the detective.

Nicola looked back to Kate. "Thank you." A tender smile flashed on the frightened girl's face before returning to her mother's arms.

The three walked outside and only Gregor, Nick, and Kate remained in the house.

"What happened?" Nick lowered his voice as he huddled in front of Kate.

"I was just taking them home like you asked and, when we got here, Gregor was in the house. He was armed." Kate pointed to Gregor's gun on the side table next to her chair. "He's scared and I think he'll help us. He says a man by the name of Stan Kovac told him and his brother to find the girls. Vito must still be with the victims or Kovac."

"Okay." Nick pressed his hand against Kate's shoulder. "You did good here, Kate." He turned towards the kid. "Where did Kovac arrange the drop off of the victims?"

Gregor seemed to understand the question perfectly. Perhaps now he realized his brother was in danger and he could drop the act. Nick had been right all along. The kid knew enough and could understand enough English to get him further than he originally let on.

"A small diner a few miles away."

"When was he supposed to meet him?" Nick pressed on, moving in closer as he spoke.

"About an hour ago, maybe more. I came home. I didn't stay with him."

Nick sat down next to Gregor. "Can you call your brother and find out where he is?"

"Da." Gregor pulled out his cell and dialed Vito.

He began speaking to his brother in their language and this made them both extremely nervous because neither knew what he was saying. He could have been warning is brother.

Gregor ended the call. "He says he's on his way here and the girls are with Kovac."

"Did you tell him we were here?" Kate asked.

Gregor closed his eyes and shook his head. "He does not know you are here."

"We need to get eyes on Kovac," Nick began. "If he hasn't already met with Corbett, he will." Nick stood up and walked towards the kitchen, phone in hand. "He just made the call. Do you have a location yet?" The man on the other end of the line began to speak.

"Thank you. No, I'll call it in." Nick returned to the living room.

"What was that all about?"

"I asked our local field office to help us out with surveillance. A small plane has been circling the city, particularly the area where the girl mentioned her friends, like Madlena, had disappeared. They had the Stingray mounted in the aircraft and have been waiting for the ESNs registered to either brother to show up. They just did."

Kate was familiar with the technology and the ESN was a cell phone's electronic serial number. Once Gregor called his brother, Vito's ESN would have been discovered and, along with that, his location. She hoped they would find the girls before it was too late.

» » »

A small cabin cruiser bobbed up and down in the slip while James Corbett worked to secure it to the dock. A light sliced through the darkness just ahead and Corbett raised his eyes after a double check of the rope. The man had arrived and, with him, the precious cargo for which Corbett would be paid a great sum of money. He raised to his full height of not more than five feet, ten inches and placed his hands on his hips.

The van drew nearer and finally rolled to a stop along the edge of the boardwalk at the commercial docks. The headlights already dimmed so as not to call forth any attention. Corbett waited, staring at the van that had dark tinted windows in the front, but no windows in the cargo area.

The driver's side door swung open and Stan Kovac jumped down. He scanned the immediate area and spotted his partner in the distance. Corbett raised a hand in acknowledgement and Kovac proceeded to the back of the van and yanked hard on the double doors. On opening, he looked inside at the cargo. Three woman, bound by their hands and feet, drugged to the point of near unconsciousness. Kovac's nose wrinkled and his lips curled at the stench that wafted out. The odor of urine was overpowering. It happened sometimes if the girls were drugged too heavily, but least they were all still alive and he would be paid.

Another man stepped out of the passenger side and joined Kovac at the rear. Vito Bjuric tossed his cigarette to the ground. The conversation he'd had with his brother advised that he'd be better off not going back home. After this shipment drop, he would be leaving Richmond for a while.

"Corbett's over there," Kovac said. "Help me get the cargo out."

Vito jumped into the back of the van and lifted one of the girls from beneath her arms, dragging her to the edge.

"Can she walk?" Kovac asked, but instead opted to slap the girl's face to confirm a response.

The dark-haired girl wore little more than a tank top and shorts, but seemed unmoved by the strike to her cheek. If and when she returned to full consciousness, she might recall the last thing she'd said to the man in front of her now. "We're closing; you'll have to come back tomorrow." She worked in a smoke shop and Vito had inquired about making a purchase.

"No. You'll have to carry her," Kovac replied.

Vito swallowed hard, not because he couldn't carry this girl. She couldn't have weighed more than ninety-five pounds, but it appeared as though he was having a sudden attack of conscience. The girl looked half-dead and this was more than he thought he had signed on for. But there was no backing out now. Kovac would see him dead before letting him walk away. "Okay, give her to me."

Vito's legs were unsteady at first from the extra weight, but he soon regained his balance. He looked down at the girl's face. Saliva had pooled at the corners of her mouth and her eyes were half-closed, fluttering away at him. It looked like a perverse sort of flirtation. He knew this girl. He'd been to the smoke shop plenty of times. This was why Kovac allowed him to take Toma's place. Vito knew plenty of his expatriates and she was the sister of a friend who'd come over from Ukraine.

The two had been smuggling pot across the state border for the past six months, working for Toma on his side gig. It was the only reason Vito was still alive.

His legs were growing heavy as he continued to carry the near-lifeless body, but he made it to the boat.

"I'll take her from here," Corbett said.

Vito handed him the girl and stood there for a moment.

"Well." Corbett's eyes narrowed. "What are you waiting for? Go and get the others. We don't have all night."

» » »

"There's no one here," Agent Jameson said as he spoke to Nick on the phone. "The place is empty." He continued to scour the diner, searching the storage area, the walk-in refrigerator. It was completely empty. This was where the call had come from, but they were already too late.

"Damn it. They can't be that far ahead of us. Are there any signs of where he might've gone?"

"Not yet, but I'm still looking."

"Just come back to the station. We're bringing Gregor Bjuric in now. I have a sinking feeling he warned his brother."

Jameson slid his phone back into his pocket as he continued to search for anything that might indicate where the women had been taken, if they had been there at all.

A camera was mounted in the corner of the storage room and an idea came upon him. He continued to the back of the building, where a small office was tucked away. If the cameras worked, any surveillance equipment would likely be kept in there. The door was locked, but he pushed his elbow through the glass insert and turned the handle. Jameson pushed open the door and stepped over the shards on the ground. His hand felt along the wall for the light switch. A fluorescent fixture hung in the middle of the small office and immediately lit up the room. The office appeared as he would have expected. A small metal desk, a computer that was a little outdated, a ten-key calculator with an empty tape roll, and a few filing cabinets along the walls.

Jameson pressed his lips together and rubbed his cheeks, sure that he'd struck out, and was about to turn around and leave until he spotted a metal panel in the wall. It looked like an ordinary electrical panel with a metal door, except that it was larger than normal. He glanced over his shoulder, always feeling as though someone was behind him. It was a hazard of the job, he guessed, but he continued towards the panel and noticed a small padlock that kept the door secured.

He quickly turned back to the desk in search of a key and, as he pulled the drawers out, he rummaged through the papers and pencils and miscellaneous receipts inside. Reaching into the back of the drawer, he felt around with his fingertips. A key.

A smile spread across his face as he held out hope that it had been the key to the panel and not one just for a filing cabinet. On examination, it appeared larger than a file cabinet key and so he moved back to the panel.

Much to his relief, the padlock dropped down and Jameson slid it off of the door. This was what he'd been looking for. It was the recorder for the CCTV system. And it was running. Jameson pulled the SD card from the slot and closed the door. He needed to get back to the station now to find out what the hell was on this memory card.

» » »

Vito unloaded the last of the girls and waited by the van for further instruction. Corbett and Kovac were deep in conversation near the boat. Vito lit up another cigarette and leaned against the back bumper.

The two continued for a while longer and Vito thought that someone could come along at any moment. Late night shipments were nothing unusual here and he began to grow concerned by the length of time, considering there were drugged women on that boat. Kidnapping, trafficking, and God knows what other charges law enforcement would come up with if they were discovered.

He puffed on the cigarette and the breeze coming off the bay blew it into his eyes, briefly obscuring his vision. He dropped the half-burned stick to the ground and noticed that Kovac was finally returning. What concerned Vito now was the fact that he looked pissed off, like the deal had gone south.

He pushed off the back bumper and stood firm on both feet. He studied Kovac's face. His pulse elevated and his mouth dropped slightly as Kovac approached. Vito cast his eyes toward Corbett, who grinned and turned away, stepping onto the boat.

He knew then what was about to happen. Vito pushed off in a sprint, running in the direction from which they came. Kovac was going to kill him. His lungs began to burn as he pushed his legs faster. A quick glance behind him and Kovac was gaining ground, his gun already drawn.

"Fuck!" Vito yelled and continued to pump his arms, running as fast as he could. If Kovac killed him, he knew his family would be next. They wouldn't leave any loose ends. Vito had done all of this to protect his brother. All because he talked to that girl FBI agent.

Light fixtures hung against the building that housed some of the boats, mostly those in service. Vito needed the cover of darkness if he hoped to escape Kovac's bullet. He was pulling ahead, but needed more distance. Kovac wasn't likely to pull the trigger if he thought he'd miss. People might hear the gunfire and call the cops.

Vito could hear the distant sound of a boat jetting off into the river towards the sea. Corbett was gone. Kovac was tasked with killing Vito and this would not end until he was dead. But there had to be a way out. Sweat began to drip into his eyes, stinging them and clouding his vision. He had put some distance between himself and Kovac; now he needed to find a place to veer off. He was nearing the main road to the entrance of the port. There would be traffic. This might be his only chance. If he could reach the street, Kovac likely wouldn't fire on him.

It was past midnight now and none of the shops would be open for him to dart inside. He cast a glance over his shoulder. Kovac was losing steam. He was an older man, as far as the young Vito was concerned – Kovac was at least in his late thirties.

A small wave of relief began to surface, but he still pushed on. Because even if he survived this, his family would not be safe. He would need to warn them. That meant he would need to tell the FBI everything. At this point, however, Vito began to realize he'd either end up dead or in prison. Maybe prison was the better option from his current vantage point.

What looked to be an alleyway was just ahead. It could have been a niche between the buildings, but it was too hard to tell until he could get a closer look. On arrival, confirmation appeared in the form of a narrow alley. Vito turned sharply, almost losing his balance. He couldn't see what lay ahead at the end, but that mattered little at the moment.

The alley was just wide enough to get a garbage truck through, which would explain the several dumpsters along the sides of the buildings. The smell was strong, rancid, and Vito considered the idea that maybe tomorrow was pick-up day. The odor filled his nose and he didn't want to breathe, but his lungs screamed for air.

The other end of the alley was approaching. Vito began to slow, realizing he had lost Kovac. Light from the street lamps shone against the sidewalk just head. He slowed to a stop at the end and bent over, his hands resting on his hips as he tried to regain his breath. A shadow crossed in front of him and then two feet appeared.

He knew he was about to die and rose to look at Kovac's face. That was the last thing Vito Bjuric ever saw.

SIXTEEN

Jameson pushed open the police station doors, searching for any signs of Agent Scarborough or Kate. He jogged to the front desk. "I need to see Detective Garrett and Agent Scarborough. Please, it's urgent."

The woman behind the desk didn't inquire further; Jameson's eyes said all she needed to know and she immediately picked up the phone. "Detective Garrett, there's someone…."

"Agent Jameson," he interrupted.

"There's an Agent Jameson who needs to see you right away." She set the phone down. "He'll be right up."

Jameson nodded and turned to the direction of the hall where he'd expected Garrett or Scarborough to emerge. He stared down that hall as if that alone would cause their appearance.

Finally, he spotted them. Jameson approached, holding the SD card in his hands. "We need to see what's on here. Now."

The two men quickly turned on their heels and began heading back the way they came.

"What is this?" Scarborough asked.

"It's surveillance footage from the diner. It was in a locked wall panel and I was able to retrieve it." Jameson looked at Nick. "What about the brother?"

"Nothing yet."

"Well, depending on what we find on this, we may not need him anyway," Jameson replied.

The three entered Garrett's office, where Kate had stayed with Gregor. Nicola and her mother were in the small kitchen, which had a couch along the back wall. At last check, the girl had curled up and was sleeping in her mother's lap.

"What'd you find?" Kate leapt to her feet.

"Some video from the diner," Nick said. "We need to get it loaded up and see what the hell's on this."

Gregor's attention piqued at this news. He watched as the agents huddled around the computer monitor on the detective's desk.

Grainy black and white video appeared on the screen.

"This is the storage room," Jameson began. "I didn't see any other cameras, but that doesn't mean there weren't any. I didn't hang around for too long. But we may find something on these other files."

The metal shelves were half-full of food items; large containers of mayonnaise, mustard, and other condiments as well as some canned goods and a few boxes of napkins and silverware. Otherwise, there wasn't much else inside the room. A small door from the room led out to the back of the building. A delivery entrance, most likely.

"How far back does this video go?" Garrett asked.

Nick studied the image and quickly pointed to the timestamp in the bottom corner. "Looks like this is from tonight." He looked at Jameson. "Can you find an earlier file? Say from around nine o'clock this evening, and we'll start there?"

Jameson closed that file and searched for another. They were labeled with the date and military time. He pulled up the file with today's date that showed 2100. "Here it is."

The same image appeared. A quiet storage room, devoid of any movement or sound. A few minutes passed and they waited. Something was going to happen; they just needed to wait. Kate cast her eyes between the agents and Gregor. She moved back toward the kid. "Still no word from Vito?"

He shook his head.

"Did you tell him we were waiting?" Kate asked in a hushed tone

"I didn't want him to be caught." Gregor raised his eyes to meet Kate's. "He saved my life. Kovac would have killed me."

"We could have helped your brother. Now he's out there alone with no one to help him."

"There, look." Nick pointed to the screen. "They're coming in now."

Kate returned to the monitor, discouraged by Gregor's admission, but she was hesitant to mention it to the others. "What is it?"

Jameson looked over to Gregor. "You know what Kovac looks like, right, kid?"

He nodded.

"Good. Come over here." Jameson waited. "Is that him?"

Gregor studied the image. "That is him."

Another man appeared in the video. "And that is my brother, Vito."

"But you don't know where they were taking the women?" Garrett asked.

"No. I don't know anything more than I've already told you."

Kate was beginning to doubt his words.

They continued watching the video when a few young women appeared, being nearly dragged inside the storage room. It appeared as though they'd already been drugged.

It was disturbing and Kate struggled to watch, but looking away would only draw the concerns of the men around her. She didn't want to appear frail, because she couldn't afford to be. Never again had she wanted to see pity in the eyes of the men around her. And they did pity her, even if they would never admit it.

These girls were hardly able to stand on their own two feet. Their hands were tied behind their backs. Kate watched as Vito appeared almost hesitant to continue, like maybe he'd been having second thoughts.

"Wait, hang on. Can you go back a minute?" Kate asked.

"Yeah." Jameson began to roll back the video. "What is it? What'd you see?"

"There." She pointed to the screen. The back door of the storage room was propped open as they were taking the women out back, presumably to a waiting vehicle. And Kate thought that she spotted a small trace of that vehicle. "What does that look like to you guys?"

"It looks like the front bumper of a car," Garrett said.

"I don't think it's a car," Nick began. "A van maybe? Take a look at the wheel well. Much larger than a car."

"And it's got a mud flap," Kate continued. "I'm thinking it's a van."

"We need more. Keep going. Let's see if we get a better view of the vehicle," Nick said.

Jameson pressed play again.

They waited until all the women were loaded up. The men now stood outside the storage room, the door still propped open.

"Let's go," Kovac said.

"Turn it up. What's he saying?" Nick asked.

Jameson rolled it back just slightly and pressed play again.

"Let's go. We're meeting him at the docks in thirty minutes," Kovac said and then closed the door of the storage room.

"The docks," Kate started. "What docks?"

Detective Garrett spun around to his desk and picked up the phone. "I need to contact the marinas. Both of them, but I'll start with the commercial docks first. If they were there, we'll have video and a shipping manifesto."

Kate headed back towards Gregor. "Can you try your brother one more time, please? This could mean helping those girls. We need to find him." She'd hoped he understood now what was at stake. That this was the only way to help his brother out of the mess he'd created for all of them, and perhaps, if the local FBI office was still running surveillance, they'd get a location.

Gregor called his brother once again. This time, the line answered.

"Gregor. I'm so glad to hear from you. Where are you?" the man on the other line asked.

"Where's my brother? Where's Vito?"

"Oh, he's waiting for you. Don't worry. He is occupied with one of the girls. I'm sure you can understand. Now, tell me, Gregor, where are you? We could use your help. It could mean a lot of money for your family."

Gregor immediately hung up and looked at Kate.

She could already see in his face what he was about to say. "Vito's dead, isn't he?"

"He would never let anyone else answer his phone. He always kept it on him. Yes, I think he must be dead." Gregor's lips quivered, but he tried to keep it together.

"Who answered the call?" Kate asked.

"Kovac. He asked where I was at and that they could use my help."

» » »

The boat pulled into the slip and was docked by two men standing nearby. Corbett recognized one of them as the Arranger's security guard. The other, he'd never seen before tonight. The women would be transported from here via another van with others who'd already been taken by Corbett's counterparts. The organization spread far and wide and Corbett was just a small piece of the puzzle.

Stepping onto the deck of the vessel, he waved a hand to the men below. "Hey, you two wanna give me a hand?"

The men climbed aboard and began transporting the women to another van that would take them to their second and final destination. One of them, Corbett had on reserve as an apology for the trouble brought to Druseburg's doorstep. He'd hang on to her for a while until the feds realized they had nothing on his client and backed down.

These were large men who had no trouble with the limp cargo. They unloaded the women with ease and placed them into the waiting van.

Corbett didn't know where they were going or who would take charge of them. It was how the business functioned. Different factions, operating in different areas. Corbett had a contact, the Arranger, and was given instructions from there. But so long as the money kept coming, he didn't question it. And it had been his call to silence Vito Bjuric. He couldn't risk him getting soft again as he had with his brother. Far too much was at stake and Corbett had a boss too.

"I'm keeping this one," he said to the men. "I already checked with the big man. You can call him yourself if you don't believe me."

The man looked at Corbett. "Fine. If you say so."

"It's an apology to one of our best clients."

"Whatever, man. I don't give a fuck," the muscular, bald man replied.

Corbett raised his hands as if a gun was pointed at him. "Okay, I hear you. Just wanted to let you know it was copacetic."

The man began to walk away. "You'll get a call with another order soon."

Corbett agreed and jumped onto the dock to untie the ropes. He needed to get back to find out if Kovac had taken care of the kid. It would be a mess to sort out if he hadn't. But if the kid was gone, no one would really notice. His brother sure as hell wouldn't go to the cops, if he valued the lives of his family and his own.

» » »

"You should get back to the base," Nick said. "I'm sure you could use a few hours of sleep. There's not much more you can do here tonight."

"What about Nicola?" Kate asked.

"Assuming Vito's dead, and I'd say that was a safe assumption at this point, Garrett will get them home and post a patrolman at their house. Right now, Gregor Bjuric is the only person who can identify Stan Kovac, so we need to keep them safe."

"What's going to happen next?" Kate stepped away from the others to have a private word with Nick.

"I doubt we'll find Vito's body. Not soon enough anyway. Best bet is to get those phone records from Druseburg. Find out if he's contacted Kovac or Corbett. We've still got a shitload of evidence on him."

"Circumstantial," Kate said.

Nick grinned. "Glad to see they're teaching you something over there in Quantico."

"You forget, I worked in evidence handling and spent a lot of time helping Marshall with some of his cases."

"I didn't forget. And you're right. We don't have anything concrete on Druseburg—yet, not enough to charge him with murder or trafficking. In the meantime, we'll still try to track down Kovac and Corbett, but Druseburg's phone records will be our best bet." He picked up her laptop bag from beneath her chair. "You've got class in the morning. I'll be in touch with you later." He glanced at his watch. "Later today, by the looks of it. I didn't realize it was so late. Will you be okay to drive back to base?"

"Yeah, of course. I'm fine. In fact, I'm not tired at all, actually."

"Adrenaline. It's some pretty powerful stuff. You'll start to feel the drag soon enough. I just hope you get home before it hits." He opened the door of Garrett's office.

"I'll see you guys soon. I've gotta head back to base," Kate said.

Gregor pushed up quickly from the table.

"Don't worry. Agent Scarborough will make sure you and your family are safe." She'd wanted to be angry with him. After all, he knew about and participated in this latest drop. They could've already saved those women if he'd come forward earlier. But looking into his eyes, she could see he was protecting his brother. Although, in the end, it was his little sister who made it possible for them to have gotten this far.

"I'd like to say goodnight to Nicola."

"Come on, then." Nick walked with her down the hall toward the break room. He pushed the door open slightly. "Looks like she's still asleep."

"I'll be right back." Kate walked inside and headed towards Nicola's mother. She knelt down in front of the middle-aged woman, who was stroking her daughter's thick and beautiful dirty blonde hair.

"Your daughter is very brave," Kate whispered.

The woman smiled, although her eyes expressed a fear that only a mother could feel. "Like her father."

"Agent Scarborough and Detective Garrett will see that you are safe in your home."

"What about Vito?"

Kate turned her gaze towards the girl because she feared that her eyes would betray her and reveal the truth she couldn't bring herself to admit. "We haven't heard from him yet. But Agent Scarborough will keep you and your children safe."

"She looks up to you," the woman said, glancing to Nicola. "She wants to be like you, I think."

Kate pushed aside the feeling that was bearing down on her. The feeling that she'd believed her own child would have looked up to her someday. "Your daughter can be anything she wants to be. That's what's so great about this country."

"Maybe your daughter could." The woman stopped to look at Nicola again before returning her attention to Kate. "I don't think mine can." The smile on the woman's face faded.

Kate rose to her feet once again. "They'll be taking you all very soon and you'll be able to get some rest. Good night, Mrs. Bjuric." Kate turned and walked back to the door, the woman's words reverberating in her ears. She looked back a final time, but the woman did not look up at her.

"You ready to go?" Nick asked.

"I'm ready."

"Hey, everything all right? What happened in there?"

"It's fine. I just feel bad for that poor woman. She came here to give her kids a better life. Doesn't seem to have really panned out for them."

Nick opened the door to exit the station and continued walking Kate to her car. "What you did tonight, disarming Gregor and getting him to confide in you. Kate, that was no easy task. I mean, shit, that was Tactical Training 101 right there. And you passed with flying colors."

"Maybe you're right."

Nick opened the driver's side door for her. "Do me a favor. Just text me when you get home? I'll sleep a lot better tonight if I know that you made it home safely."

Kate slid inside the car. "You mean you're actually going to get some sleep? Ha! I'd pay to see that."

He pushed the door closed. "Yeah, yeah. Even us superhero special agents need our rest. You get it? SSA?" Nick leaned into the window, a wide smile on his face. "Be safe. I'll talk to you later." Two slaps of his hand on the car door, and he stood up.

Kate rolled her eyes at the terrible joke he'd made and waved a final goodbye before backing out and heading for the road. She watched Nick wave back in the rear view mirror.

Music would help keep her alert and so Kate switched on the car radio. She really wasn't all that tired, but she hoped the music would drown out the thoughts in her head. Had Nicola's mother been right? Would Nicola be afforded the same opportunities as any other American kid?

SEVENTEEN

With frequent stolen glances at the phone discretely tucked between her thigh and the seat, Kate struggled to maintain focus on the instruction. She was operating on less than three hours' sleep and needed to know what was happening. She was impotent to do anything from here and only wanted to go back to Richmond and find those girls.

"How would you handle that situation, Reid?" The instructor focused his attention on Kate, and now, so did everyone else.

Her eyes raised to meet his, embarrassed that she had no idea what he'd asked. "I'm sorry, could you repeat the question?" Kate's cheeks flushed in an instant.

"Are we keeping you from something, Reid? Do you feel this training is unnecessary in some way?"

"No, sir. I apologize."

He looked at her for a moment longer. "Hewitt, how would you handle that situation?" The instructor moved on to ask the one person whom Kate had come to dislike and, of course, he provided an answer with no delay.

"Are you okay?" Will leaned over, trying to keep his voice low enough to not draw any more unwanted attention her way.

"It's been a long night, that's all." If he was wanting a more comprehensive answer, it would have to wait because she was unwilling to suffer the wrath of an irritated instructor should she draw his attention once again.

This investigation was already causing Kate to slip in not only attendance, which she would have to make up, but if her distractions continued, it was likely her scores would suffer too. She was jeopardizing all she had been working toward.

"Tomorrow, you'll be interviewing witnesses. Please prepare by reviewing the case files and have your questions ready. This is an important skill that you will need to master." The instructor aimed his sights on Kate. "We will analyze your technique and you will be evaluated, so please do not take this assignment lightly." His hold on her finally released. "You are dismissed."

She'd been called out, and rightly so. Kate packed her things and prepared to leave when the instructor approached.

"Do you have a minute, Reid?"

At the front of the room was a small desk and the instructor took a seat on the edge, folding his arms, a sure sign she was about to suffer some sort of reprimand.

"I understand SSA Scarborough has you working on a fairly significant investigation, Reid, but that does not absolve you of your training. We had an agreement that assisting him was to complement what you are learning here, and to offer guidance on some aspects that you are struggling with. What I'm seeing now borders on a disregard for our rules here at the Academy. I cannot let the behavior continue. Some of your colleagues are also working outside of the training here and yet, I don't see the same distractions coming from them."

"I apologize, Agent Hawes. There's no excuse, you're right. Being here is what's important to me." While that was true, she couldn't help but think about Nicola.

"We've discussed where we can improve on some of the areas you're lacking in, Reid, but I need your cooperation. Do we need to refocus your energies? Maybe request that you take a less critical role in this investigation?" Hawes continued.

"No, sir. Again, I won't let it deter my focus from class again. I can assure you that this training is my priority."

"Okay. I don't give third chances, Reid." He pushed off the edge of the desk. "You are no more or less important than the other trainees."

"Thank you, Agent Hawes. You'll have my undivided attention from here on out."

"Fair enough. Goodbye, Reid."

The dormitory seemed a far walk as she drifted through the glass-enclosed breezeway, replaying the instructor's words, knowing she was putting everything at risk. And for what? Did she think Scarborough and Jameson couldn't handle the case on their own? Nick was under the impression that this investigation would shine a spotlight on her talents, whatever those were, and that everything else would just fall into place as a result. It hadn't. And they needed her like she needed a hole in her head. Kate stopped and looked out at the grounds, her reflection in the glass staring back at her. She examined her lucent features. *Who are you? Who do you want to be?*

Marshall had made her out to be better than she was, stronger than she was, and it was time to stop seeing herself as he had. Her past did not make her special, it made her a survivor. She needed to come to terms with the fact that no one here would cut her the slack that he did. It was time for her to stand on her own two feet. She would need to convince Nick of the same.

Returning to her room, the long-awaited call finally came. "Reid here."

"Vito's body was found early this morning floating near the docks." Nick spoke with urgency. "Garrett's team is searching Kovac's home now and we've got people posted at the diner in case he shows up. With two dead bodies linked to him, though, I'm not going to hold my breath that he'll show up at either place."

Kate immediately thought of Nicola. Her brother was dead and while she suspected as much, the reality would devastate her and her mother.

"Jameson's pulled phone records on Druseburg. Can you get to the WFO? I'll have the files waiting for you there. Get with Agent Vasquez and she'll walk you through it. His attorneys will have him under lock and key by now, so we need dates and times of any conversations with Corbett after Madlena had gone missing. We're looking specifically for numbers registered to Corbett, or Stan Kovac, assuming they're traceable. I just need some ammunition. Franks is on board, but she wants more before hauling him in because if we can't make charges stick, you'd better believe he'll be gone before we can."

"Nick," She hesitated to ask, but the question burned. "Why are you doing this?"

"Sorry?"

"You don't need me. You've got a team of highly qualified agents."

"We talked about this at the beginning, Kate. I asked you to be involved so that you can prove you deserve to be here. That you shouldn't be judged solely on the results of your operational training." He paused for a moment. "Was I wrong?"

"No. I'm sorry. I know you're trying to give me every chance to succeed." She'd wanted to tell him that that was the problem, but this wasn't about her, not right now. It was all too easy to slide down that slippery slope of questioning her worth, but she would need to put an end to it now and focus on the task at hand.

"I don't understand where this is coming from," Nick continued. "Last night, you were pumped; you were ready to tackle anything. What's changed?"

"Nothing." Kate closed her eyes. "I'll get down to the WFO and get with Vasquez." She ended the call, keeping from him the reason for her second-guessing. Self-doubt aside, she had a job to do.

» » »

The main hub inside the field office was where agents conducted much of their work, including background inquiries, database searches inside the many programs available to all law enforcement as well as several other daily operations that brought few accolades. It was the grunt work. These were the agents behind the scenes, performing necessary and critical operations that often brought praise to the field agents. This was where Kate wanted to be; in the background, far from the center of attention where she'd spent the better part of the last three years.

She opened the files they'd received from the telecom provider. The phone numbers would be cross-referenced to find matches to either Kovac or Corbett. Right now, Kate stared at a screen that showed her hundreds of numbers. "Thank you for helping, Agent Vasquez. I'm not that familiar with how this works."

"No problem." Vasquez punched a few keys and brought up another screen. "Give me a minute here, and we'll be able to get these matched." She continued to punch in commands of which Kate hadn't yet learned.

"So, how's your training going?" she asked, continuing to work on the information.

"It's not easy."

"No. It's not easy," she replied. "But Agent Scarborough is convinced you can handle it." She looked to Kate. "He's the best agent I've ever worked with and I've worked with some of the best. If he has confidence in you, then you should too." A short pause. "Here," Vasquez pointed to the monitor. "See the highlighted numbers? Those numbers come from VOIP applications. They show up as data usage on the telecom records, but we can see the assigned numbers."

"Voice-over internet protocol? Internet phone numbers," Kate replied.

"That's right. And the data usage gives us an approximate location to Richmond and Alexandria. Druseburg was using his cell phone to call these VOIP numbers."

"So, no cell phone numbers are coming up as registered to James Corbett or Stan Kovac?" Kate supposed it was a long shot that those men would use a registered number, but at least they would know for sure."

"Not that I can tell, but we can get more details on these records and apply for other information," Vasquez replied.

"What kind of details?" Kate asked.

"Emails, text messages, pretty much anything and everything relating to electronic information sent from his cell phone. For this information here," she pointed to the screen again, "we only needed a court order showing reasonable cause. But for historical information and access to emails and such, that requires a subpoena to the cellular provider. But it's easier to get than you might think."

"I'll need to show this to Agents Scarborough and Jameson. Can you email it to me?" Kate relayed her address.

"Of course." Vasquez's fingers glided across the keyboard. "Heading your way now."

"Thank you, Agent Vasquez. You've been a tremendous help." Kate rose from her chair.

"Good luck."

Vasquez had sent the report. It wasn't what Kate had hoped to find, but it did prove that Druseburg was in contact with someone in Richmond the day after Madlena Jankovic disappeared; a day after Corbett was seen in Petrovich's bar. What many people don't understand about most smartphones was that they almost constantly transmitted GPS locations and telecom companies held onto that information.

She hustled towards Nick's office to make the call, coming upon Agent Myers' office along the way. "You're here?" She stopped in front of her doorway, offering a welcoming smile.

"I am," Myers replied. "You look like you're in a hurry. What's going on?"

"Phone records. I was going to give Agent Scarborough a call and let him know what I found. Does he know you're back in town?"

"Sadly no. Not yet. I just got back and need to finish with a few more reports."

"Well, it's good to see you. Hope we can grab some dinner soon. It'd be nice to catch up."

"Sure thing," Georgia replied. "You'd better get in touch with Agent Scarborough."

With her cell phone in hand, Kate pressed on the contact button to call Nick as soon as she stepped foot inside his office. After the third ring, she expected his voicemail, but he finally picked up.

"It's Kate, I got those records and Vasquez was able to get a general location on calls made by Druseburg to VOIP numbers, they appear to center around Richmond, and the dates coincide with Madlena's disappearance."

"Email it to me and copy Jameson."

» » »

Detective Garrett returned to his office with papers in hand. "Here." He had printed the report and placed it in front of Nick. "What do we have?" Garrett sat down and began to examine the records.

"According to Reid," Nick began, "and now that I have a chance to look at this in a little more detail, it looks like Druseburg was in contact with someone in Richmond a few days before Virginia Beach PD found Madlena's body. I think we have enough to subpoena the contents of these records and get an exact location on the VOIP calls."

"We still got eyes on Druseburg?" Jameson asked. "I'm ready to bring the son of a bitch in."

"Franks has been keeping him under surveillance." Nick understood where his partner was coming from and was beginning to feel the same. The sheer amount of red tape bullshit was hard to overcome. And while they were getting closer to obtaining what they needed. The time it would take to get something solid was time they didn't have.

Detective Garrett opened up his files. "I spoke with security at the marina earlier this morning. Here's what they've sent me."

"What are we looking at exactly?" Nick asked.

"I asked them to run the names of the lessors of their slips, see if we can match any of them to Corbett. No luck there, but they also have records of who purchased fuel at their docks. Last night, a purchase was made at the pump after hours. We're tracking down the buyer, although it appears that it was a purchase made on a prepaid card. We're looking to see if that card was registered online."

"So we still don't have any assurances that Corbett was there last night and Kovac's nowhere to be found?" Nick could feel the heat rise under his collar and he was starting to side with Jameson. "Fuck it. You know what? I'm bringing Druseburg in now. His DNA was found on Madlena's body. I'll haul his ass in for solicitation if nothing else. I don't give a shit how high profile this guy is or how good his lawyers are. We know she was one of Corbett's victims, thanks to his arrogance in electing to brand the women. I'm not waiting for a subpoena." Nick slammed down the lid of his laptop. "I'm done screwing around. I won't wait for more girls to be taken and sold as goddamn slaves." He stood up and looked to Jameson. "We'll find Corbett too. One way or another, this shit ends now. "

EIGHTEEN

Martin Druseburg walked into his spacious and pristine closet to retrieve his luggage, which was tucked beside a built-in chest of drawers made from rich cherry. He told his office he was going to Tokyo to meet with a software engineer, however, none of that was actually true. The truth about Druseburg was about to come out; he was about to be hauled into FBI custody. The attorney, who was very well paid to help hide his extracurricular activities, had many contacts, one of whom informed him of the FBI's intent to bring charges. Of course, he immediately suggested a deal could keep him out of prison, or at the very least, ensure a lesser charge, but that would do little to salvage the wealthy man's reputation.

He hadn't wanted her dead. The girl took the drugs of her own accord. Druseburg had no choice but to get rid of the body when he discovered her with foam around her mouth and eyes rolled into the back of her head. Then that son of bitch, Corbett, decided he needed to brand his girls, like cattle. If that damn tattoo hadn't been on her body, no one would have known she was linked to Corbett. *Stupid fuck.* The girl was supposed to be untraceable; a byproduct of a dysfunctional immigration system.

Druseburg fumed as he tossed his shirts into the bag. He'd already made the call to his pilot and the jet was waiting for him at the airport. A small box rested on a shelf inside his closet. He lifted the lid and opened the cylinder inside. The bump of coke would be enough to keep his nerves in check until he boarded the plane.

He zipped up the bag and headed downstairs where his driver waited outside in the car. Getting out of the country before the shit storm hit was his only chance. Extradition, if he got caught, would take years, and he had enough money hidden in offshore accounts and it would take even longer to shut them down. Those feds thought they were smart. But he was smarter.

Standing at the front door, he looked behind him, shaking his head because leaving this house was tough. Sons of bitches were driving him out and it pissed him off more. He pulled open the door and pushed his sunglasses onto his face. "Get in the car. We need to get the hell out of here now."

The man he was speaking to raised his head. It wasn't his driver. "Mr. Druseburg? This is courtesy of Mr. Mercer." The man fired the weapon and Druseburg dropped to the ground.

» » »

Kate was beginning to feel that she was on the downhill slide at the Academy with only seven weeks left, and that she'd found her focus once again. This was partly due to what had transpired over the course of the investigation, and partly thanks to Nicola and the strength she and her mother had shown through all of it. Kate was starting to believe that her life could be transformed and that she could do this on her own.

She'd faced down a scared kid pointing a gun at her; disarmed him with skill and intelligence. Kate deserved to be here and she had nothing to prove to anyone, except herself.

"You ready to do this?" Will asked, securing his vest.

"I'm ready." Kate pulled down the shield on her helmet, ready for the hostage rescue. A Hogan's Alley training operation was about to begin.

Four members were on her team and they now stood outside the fictitious bank. Inside was a band of robbers, holding five people hostage. Armed with automatic rifles and handguns, the bank robbers were ready to take the innocent lives if it meant saving their own.

This was a cakewalk for Caison, or so Kate believed. He'd faced far worse conditions searching for Taliban in Iraq. Only they were usually armed with bombs and didn't mind dying, and if they took their hostages with them, then all the better.

The instructor gave the signal. The mission was on.

Caison took the lead. "Diaz, Fillmore, flank the rear entrance. Reid, head to the side of the building, but stay in view."

The team did as instructed. Will made the call to the leader inside. He would attempt to negotiate before authorizing any action.

Kate remained at her post, waiting for the go-ahead. She felt more confident than before. Perhaps it had been because it was not a one-on-one situation; that she was operating inside a team. She would not question where her strength was coming from, just that she was grateful to have it.

One of the hostages was emerging through the front entrance. It appeared the negotiations were working. Her hands were raised and the man behind her with the gun kept it pointed directly at her back in the event someone attempted to charge ahead.

"Over here. You're okay. Come on. I got you." Kate moved towards the hostage once the gun-wielding man was back inside, and led her to the waiting ambulance.

She looked to Caison, who waved for her to get back into position. He continued the dialog, but no further hostages were being released.

The radio on her jacket came to life. "Diaz, Fillmore, take the back entrance," Will said.

Kate waited at the side, weapon raised and ready to leap ahead at his command.

Once the others were inside, gunfire erupted and she witnessed one of the thieves going down.

"Now!" Will bolted to the front entrance with Kate on his heels.

They pushed through the doors.

"Get down!"

The hostages dropped to the ground while the bandits continued in a gun battle with Diaz and Fillmore.

Kate came face to face with one of the men wearing a skullcap and a bandana wrapped around his mouth so only his nose and eyes were exposed. Her heart pounded and her body buzzed with adrenaline. "Drop your weapon." Her voice carried more weight than she had expected, but the thief still held on to his rifle. "Drop your weapon now!" This time, her demand was firm. Her resolve, complete. Not that different from the night she faced down Gregor Bjuric. "I've got this gun pointed right at your goddamn head. Drop the fucking weapon."

For a split second, she believed the man was going to fire, but she watched the gun and it didn't flinch. Not a single shift in his stance, not a movement of his fingers. If she pulled the trigger before exhausting all other options, it could mean a failure.

The man lowered the gun to the ground and when he stood, raised his arms in surrender.

"Kick it over," she said.

Caison and the other teammates managed to either take down or get the remaining operatives to surrender. They were now working to free the hostages and Kate was facing the final threat.

The man kicked the gun towards her. With her weapon still pointing at the criminal, Kate walked towards him, spun him around, and pushed him to the ground. Once her gun was holstered, she straddled the man and cuffed his hands behind his back.

Inside the control room, Nick watched the events unfold along with the three instructors.

"Well, son of a bitch. Did you see that?" A sly smile slowly formed across Nick's face.

Agent Hawes conveyed a reluctant grin. "Guess she had it in her all along. Just needed to pry it from beneath the weight of her own doubts."

"I wasn't wrong about her."

"No. You weren't wrong," Hawes replied.

Nick patted Hawes on his back and left the dimly lit control room. He'd wanted to be the first to congratulate his protégé. He arrived out on the streets just as Kate was returning her gear. "Hey."

She turned around and noticed the look on his face. "So, I guess I did all right?"

"You know you did."

A rare coy expression masked her face because she knew he'd seen it. They both knew she passed the test.

"I couldn't be more proud of you, Kate." Nick squeezed her shoulders.

"Well, after that night with Gregor Bjuric, I figured it was a 'them or me' kind of thing. I'm never going to let it be *them* again."

"I know you won't. You know, it's getting close to dinner. You want to grab a bite? I'd like to run a few things by you on the Corbett case."

"Sure. Let me just say good night to the team. Meet you in ten minutes?" As she turned around, Will approached.

"Sound good." Nick looked to Will. "Hell of a job today, Caison. Well done."

"Thank you, sir." Will waited for Nick to fall out of earshot. "You're off to have dinner with the boss?"

"He wants to get me up to speed on the case."

Will shoved his hands in his pocket. "That's great. You did great today, Kate. You really did."

"Thank you. You're a good team leader."

"I got my field office assignment. It looks like I'm going to be working out of Louisville," Will said.

"Oh my God, that's great. That's where you wanted to go, right? They're involved in a joint terrorism task force, aren't they?"

"They are. It was my second choice, so yeah, I'm pretty psyched about it."

"Well, that is really fantastic, Will. I couldn't be happier for you." The smile she was wearing began to diminish as she studied his face. "What's wrong?"

"Nothing. I'm thrilled to be going to Louisville. It's an honor. I guess I'm just going to miss hanging out with you."

Although he'd insisted on starting over after what happened between the two of them, she now questioned his conviction. The look on his face was telling a different story. "We still got several more weeks together. I'm sure you'll tire of me before the end." Kate glanced over her shoulder, feeling uncomfortable and looking for a way out. "I better get going. Boss is waiting." She started to walk away. "See you tomorrow?"

"See ya."

» » »

The days were growing longer and by the time they'd reached the restaurant, the sun still shone high enough over the horizon to suggest early evening, but it was approaching eight p.m.

"I asked Georgia to join us," Nick said. "I hope you don't mind."

"No. Not at all. It'll be nice to spend some time with her. But I thought this was a working dinner?"

"It is. Georgia won't mind. She's used to shop talk." Nick held the door open for Kate and the two stood at the host station.

"I see her over there," Kate said.

A young college-aged woman approached the podium. "Party of two?"

"Actually, three, and it looks like the first is already here," Nick replied. "Can we go back?"

"Certainly. Go right ahead. Enjoy your meal."

They approached the beautiful redheaded woman whose features appeared much softer than in the harsh light of the office.

Georgia rose to greet them. "Kate. It's good to see you." The women embraced for a brief moment.

Kate took a seat across from Georgia and waited for the two as they exchanged in a polite kiss.

"So, Nick tells me you kicked ass today in Hogan's Alley."

Kate chuckled. "Well, I don't know if 'kicked-ass' is the right term, but I did all right."

"Don't be modest." Nick waved his hand. "You kicked ass." He scanned the restaurant. "Where's the waiter? I could use a drink."

The waiter appeared as if he knew he was being summoned and took the drink order.

As much as Kate had wanted to celebrate her accomplishment, it was the middle of the week and she still had to be on the track first thing in the morning. "Just an iced tea for me, thanks."

"What? You're not joining us in a drink to toast to your success?" Nick asked.

"How about we hold off on any celebrations until I actually graduate?"

"She's right." Georgia looked at Kate. "Not about waiting to see if you graduate, of course. I have no doubt about that, but I remember what it was like at the Academy, and going in with little sleep or a hangover is not recommended."

"You mentioned getting me up to speed?" Kate shifted the focus away from her.

"I got a call from Detective Franks in Virginia Beach late last night. We won't be bringing Druseburg in." Nick took in a breath that appeared intended to calm him. "He was found dead on the doorstep of his home. The housekeeper stays on the property and she got up in the middle of the night to go to the kitchen and noticed the front door was open. His body was laying across the threshold."

Any enthusiasm she'd felt about her success today had all but faded into oblivion. This was a huge blow to the investigation. "What happened?"

"A shot to the chest. I didn't want to tell you before you had your drill today."

At this moment in time, she was glad he'd waited to drop the bomb. There was no doubt it would have thrown her for a loop. Nick appeared completely deflated too. "And the housekeeper didn't hear any gunfire?"

"This was a professional job. Shooter probably used a silencer."

"How the hell—I thought Franks had surveillance on him? I don't get how this happened." It took a moment for Kate to realize that her voice had raised an octave and that people were beginning to turn their attention toward her.

"The only person he'd spoken to in the past two days, according to the phone records, was his lawyer. He knew we were coming after him."

Kate was completely destroyed by this news. This meant Nicola was still in danger. Kovac and Corbett were still out there, running around, collecting more victims. "Goddamn it." She turned away.

"Kate, I know this is a setback, but we've got a lead on a location for Corbett, thanks to the phone records you gave me. I had no trouble getting the subpoena after what happened and I forwarded the information from the cell carrier to Detective Moreno. I'm waiting to hear back from him, but it looks like they found an address linked to him. And, the subpoena was extended to include emails and whatever was on Druseburg's computer." Nick paused for a moment. "This isn't over yet."

"I'm sorry," Georgia began. "I know how hard the both of you have been working on this."

The waiter placed the drinks onto the table and took the dinner order. "I'll be right back with your food."

"Thank you," Nick said. "Anyway, Jameson's been combing through the emails and came across an exchange between Corbett and Druseburg that mentioned a person by the name of Mercer. Didn't mention a first name, but the email suggested this individual was the one who would authorize the gift that Druseburg was to receive in exchange for the loss of his last house guest."

"This Mercer could be the man in charge?" Georgia asked.

"I'm thinking he's at least higher up on the food chain than Corbett. Kate, I'd like you to come with me tomorrow afternoon to go and check the house we think belonged to Corbett. It's doubtful he still occupies it, but we might find some indication of where he is."

"Okay." The offer was genuine, but it felt like a consolation prize. Druseburg was the key to bringing down Corbett and now he was dead.

"Good. It won't take us long. The place is just outside of Alexandria."

"That close?"

"Yep. Just down the goddamn road." Nick picked up his Jack and Coke and tossed it back.

» » »

The keys jingled in the lock before it finally clicked open. Georgia walked inside and Nick followed behind, rubbing the back of his neck.

"That was a nice dinner, all things considered," Georgia said, already at the fridge and pouring a glass of wine. "You want a drink?"

"Sure, thanks." He tossed his keys into a bowl that lay on the side table. "It was good for all of us to spend time together. We haven't done that since Kate started at the Academy."

"She's almost through it now." Georgia returned with drinks in hand.

"Thanks. She has come a long way." Nick pulled open the sliding glass door that led to the deck overlooking the bay.

The breeze was cool and the waters lapped gently against the shore. Georgia stepped outside. "My God, it is gorgeous out here. I forget sometimes, being in the middle of the city."

"I forget for the simple fact that I'm hardly ever here." Nick raised his glass. "Cheers."

Georgia leaned against the railing and let the breeze lift her hair. "I wish it wasn't such a challenge, us spending time together."

"I know it's hard." He put his arm around her. "But we're here now and we should make the most of it. Chances are, by week's end, you'll be consulting on another case."

"Or you'll be back in Richmond, or Virginia Beach or God knows where with Kate and Dwight."

"Maybe, but for tonight, it's just you and me. No more shop talk." Nick touched her red-stained lips with his and kissed her the way she wanted. Soft, but firm enough that she knew she was being kissed. He pulled away and looked her in the eyes.

"What's wrong?" she asked.

"Nothing." He held her gaze. "I just forget sometimes how beautiful you are. I won't make that mistake again."

» » »

Nick sat at the edge of the bed, looking over his shoulder at Georgia. He didn't want to wake her and stepped quietly to the floor and pushed off the bed. He walked into the hall with bare feet and wearing only boxer shorts.

The corridor was almost black and his eyes hadn't yet adjusted to the sparse light that shimmered through the glass door. But he knew his way well enough and made it to the kitchen with little thought. In fact, he wasn't sure if he was quite awake. The reflection from the water on the bay inside the apartment formed a hazy illusion.

Thirst was his primary concern and Nick retrieved a glass from the cabinet above the toaster. Placing it beneath the faucet, he filled the cup. It took but a few moments for the water to soothe his cotton mouth—a side effect of too much drink.

He shuffled to the balcony door and stared at the moon that hung low in the sky. As the minutes ticked by, Nick became more alert, sober, and an idea took root in his mind. He fired up his laptop and looked up his contacts at Interpol. A quick glance at the time and he realized the man would already be awake. It was morning in London.

Nick didn't have much interaction with the Washington command center for Interpol, but he'd met Inspector Montrose a couple of years back when he was working a case where the suspect had fled to England. His contact might be of some use if he could run the name Mercer and see if anything caught by way of a watch list. It was a long shot, but he didn't have anything to lose.

In an email, he briefly described the investigation and asked him to check on the name. He included Corbett and Kovac. Might as well cover all the bases, since he was asking.

Nick reached for his phone, which he'd taken with him from the bedroom. He never went to bed, he never went anywhere without his phone. Hazards of the job. A call could come at any moment, and his response could be critical.

The screen didn't indicate any missed calls, or any texts, he found as he checked it in the off chance he hadn't heard it ring while he was sleeping. Still, he felt something was missing. This case was splintering into several directions and he needed to gain a foothold on it. Of course, he thought he had one with Druseburg, but that had vanished.

Now his two suspects were keeping an even lower profile as a result. That didn't help matters. He looked at his phone again. Finally, he unlocked the screen and typed a text message.

"You up?"

It was cruel to drag someone else into his insomniac misery, but he wanted to bounce ideas off of her. He waited for a while and began to lose hope. Moments later, he finally gave up and stood in a long stretch. Then he'd return to the warm bed with the woman he loved waiting inside it.

A message lit up his phone. *"I'm up. Everything ok?"*

She answered. Kate answered and he knew she would. Nick sat back down at the table and started typing a reply. *"Just had an idea and wanted to bounce it off you."*

Almost in an instant, her reply followed. *"Shoot."*

For the next twenty minutes, Nick and Kate exchanged messages and hashed out a plan for tomorrow. It was what he needed in order to find sleep again; just get it off his chest, and she was there to listen.

The hall light glowed, catching Nick's attention. He cast his gaze down the corridor and watched as Georgia emerged. "Hey. I'm sorry, babe. Did I wake you?"

She moved in closer with a sleepy shuffle. "I looked over and you weren't in bed. I just came to see if everything was okay. What are you doing up?" She looked down at the phone in his hands. "Who are you texting?"

NINETEEN

At first glance, it was difficult to know for sure if that was Nick's car traveling along the two-lane blacktop towards the Jefferson dormitory. An illusion had formed that made the roadway turn to water. The heat was the cause and when it combined with the humidity, it could sap the energy from anyone.

Kate waited for the SUV to emerge from the depths of the pooling road and, when she was confident of his identity, she reached down to retrieve the laptop bag that lay against her calf.

The late afternoon arrival was necessary in order for Kate to finish the day's training, but Nick had planned ahead and sent Jameson to the last known residence of James Corbett; information that Detective Moreno with Metro police conveyed earlier. After a few late night texts, she knew he'd reached out to his contact with Interpol London and was anxious to find out if it had led anywhere. The case was beginning to drag and that was never a good thing. Certainly not good for the dead women and not good for Nicola's family. Kovac likely wouldn't stop until he rid himself of the final loose end—Gregor Bjuric. But with Richmond PD keeping eyes on his home and the diner, the man had yet to show his face.

The silver SUV rolled up to the curb and Kate stepped inside. "Thanks for picking me up."

"No problem. It won't take us long, Jameson's waiting there now." Nick grabbed the gearshift and put it in drive. "I heard back from Montrose." He turned to Kate, wearing a knowing grin.

"Must be good news."

"Well, I'll start off by saying that Jameson found a few more names in the correspondence between Corbett and Druseburg. I gave the names to Montrose for him to put together in various patterns and he got a hit on a Richard Mercer."

"Who is he?" Kate asked.

"He's suspected of human trafficking. Malaysia, Thailand, and Southeastern Europe primarily." Nick stopped at the guard gate and handed his ID to the attendant. Finally, the gate opened and he drove through.

"Suspected. So that means they don't have anything concrete," Kate replied.

"No. And after a fairly lengthy conversation I had with him earlier, it looks as though we might have the biggest lead tied to him. The man's been extremely cautious and the only reason Montrose even found the name was because one victim had managed to escape and gave his name to the authorities some time ago."

"And that wasn't enough to bring him in?"

"Well, they didn't have a location on him for one thing, and two days later, the girl who gave the name turned up dead."

"So I bet Montrose is pretty interested to see what we've got."

"You could say that."

The conversation seemed to reach a conclusion and while they held out hope of finding something in Corbett's home, the case had already taken so many wrong turns, each had become weary of a good outcome.

"Listen, I want to apologize for disturbing you last night. It's just, I don't know, I woke up and my mind started going full speed ahead."

"You don't need to apologize. Are you kidding? Anytime you want to talk, I'm here." Kate peered through the passenger window. "God knows you've been there for me plenty of times."

"Thanks. Sometimes, if I can just get the ideas out of my head, I can sleep again."

"I understand," she said.

A final right turn down the street of a middle-class suburb of Alexandria and they had arrived.

"This is it." Nick shifted into park and shut off the ignition. "Looks like Jameson's still here."

The modest house with the grey exterior and white trim wasn't exactly what Kate expected to find. For a man who earned his living through the enslavement of others, she expected a more boastful accommodation. Instead, this home looked perfectly ordinary in a perfectly ordinary neighborhood.

Agent Jameson stepped outside as they approached the front porch. His hands on his hips, Jameson began shaking his head.

"Well, that can't be good," Nick said as he climbed the steps. "What'd you find in there?"

"Absolutely nothing. This house has been empty for a while, at least three weeks, maybe a month. Landlord said he hadn't seen Corbett since he dropped off his last rent payment in that same amount of time. Cash, of course."

"Yeah, I'm sure the landlord was meticulous in who he decided he would rent to. Cash is king." Nick peered over his shoulder. "Come on; let's get inside before we draw a crowd."

Kate trailed behind, stepping through the doorway to see that the home hardly looked lived in at all. Sparsely decorated, furnishings that were outdated and well worn. "This place must have been already furnished."

"What makes you say that?" Nick asked.

"Because this is a man who doesn't stay in one place for long. Pays cash for rent, probably uses prepaid cards for utilities." She continued to examine the living room where the three now stood. "These are not his things. He needs to be able to pick up and leave at a moment's notice."

Jameson turned to Kate. "You're right. It was already furnished, according to the landlord. We've got no computers, no papers, not much of anything. But we can run prints and determine if any match-up to Druseburg or Kovac."

"Or Richard Mercer," Nick said.

"Who's Richard Mercer?" Jameson hadn't been privy to the information Nick obtained from his contact at Interpol, but was quick to be filled in on the interesting news.

"All right, then. Let's collect some prints and we'll go from there. If we can tie Mercer to either of our guys, we might just be able to enlist the help of Interpol."

» » »

"Without Vito or Toma, I have to recruit someone else to find the girls for me." Stan Kovac raised his hand and scratched his shaved head, which was already revealing a five o'clock shadow.

"Maybe we just need to take care of this shit ourselves," Corbett replied. "I'm telling you, nobody's reliable anymore." He walked to the dining room table and pulled out a chair. "The Arranger's going to be calling in a few days, looking for more assets. If we don't have anything, well, let's just say the man in charge has no concept of forgiveness. You'll be gone, I'll be gone, and they'll find another couple of schleps to replace us. So I suggest we get our shit together and fulfill the order."

Kovac pressed his cigarette into the ashtray and exhaled the final puff of smoke. "This whole thing's turning out to be a giant pain in my ass." He sat down at the table. "I got the cops chasing my tail. Can't go back to the diner, can't go home. Where the fuck am I supposed to go, Jim?"

"We need to scope out a few places tonight. Figure out if they're worth revisiting tomorrow to get what we need. I gotta couple of guys I can call. They'll give me some idea who's invisible. Then, you can just go back to your hotel. Let's get this done before these guys decide they doesn't need us anymore."

Corbett pushed back and got up from the table. "Get your shit together. We're leaving now."

The streets and gentlemen's clubs were usually the best place to scope out an asset. Having little to no family was usually preferred and that could be ascertained with just a few questions. Determining the legal status was the next step. It was generally pretty easy to tell if an asset had legal identification. It usually started with a question like, "Are you sure you're not underage? I don't believe you; let me see your driver's license." And while a driving license wasn't that difficult to get a hold of, it was the address they were looking at. If there wasn't a driver's license, the next step was almost unnecessary.

And finally, the accent. Most of the communities were divided up by ethnicity. Seemed people preferred to hang out with those who shared a common background. The bartenders at these fine establishments could often be counted on to inform them as to whether or not a certain area was heavy with immigrants from a particular place.

Armed with all that information, determining who would make a suitable asset wasn't that hard. The hard part was in getting that asset alone long enough to take her.

» » »

Nick drove Kate back to base and the belief that they would find something of value inside Corbett's former residence had evaporated along with the clouds as the sun burned through them.

"Hey, thanks for coming down with me this afternoon. I'm sure you could've used the time to study." Nick didn't look at Kate as he spoke. Instead, he kept his eyes on the road and a tense grip on the steering wheel.

"You wanted me to prove myself and that's what I'm doing." This was Kate's attempt at easing the tension. She'd known Nick long enough to see when he was approaching the end of his rope on a case. He had almost reached the frayed end today.

"I was wrong to say that before, Kate. You don't need my help. You were able to work through the problem on your own."

"Only because of what happened with Gregor. And that was because you wanted me on the case."

"You put your life in danger, and I'm not okay with that."

"Maybe so, but it taught me what I needed to learn in order to get past the problem. I'm not saying that it'll be smooth sailing from here on out in my training. I'm just saying that I was faced with something real and it forced me to find a solution, not shrink away."

Thinking about that night brought Nicola to mind. With Kovac still on the loose, she was afraid for her. "I'm worried about that little girl, Nick."

"I know, but Kovac would be foolish to show his face right now. Everyone is looking for him and Corbett. We'll get to him before he has a chance to get to the Bjurics."

"Martin Druseburg's dead; who's to say someone won't get to them?"

Nick turned toward her for a moment, but didn't speak. She was right and she knew he'd seen that too.

"ID please," the guard asked Nick as he pulled up to the entrance of the base. The man examined Nick's credentials and quickly returned them, signaling his authorization to raise the gates.

The tree-lined, single-lane road wound its way up to the base and it only became apparent that it was a military facility on the final approach, remaining obscured from view along most of the path.

"I'll give you a call if I hear anything." Nick checked the time on his dashboard. "The cafeteria will still be open. You should get yourself some food. You must be starving."

The sound of a vibrating phone arose from the center console of the SUV. Nick shifted a few papers out of his way and dug out the device. He raised an index finger to Kate, suggesting that she wait a moment. "Agent Scarborough. Yes." Nick went quiet, but his expression seemed to indicate that something had happened, something good. "Thank you, Inspector. I'll be sure to keep you posted. Goodnight."

Nick tilted his head and a thin, tight smile played on his lips. "That was Inspector Montrose. He said Richard Mercer booked a flight to Richmond—for tomorrow. We'll trail him. Find out where he's going and who he's meeting." He hit the steering wheel with his palms in triumph. "Jesus. Finally." Nick returned his attention to Kate.

"I'd like to come with you," Kate asked, knowing it would put more pressure on her schedule.

"I'll find out when he's due to arrive and get back with you. You might have to cut your day short. Will that be a problem?"

"No." It might be, but she wanted to go. Mercer would lead them to James Corbett. She wasn't about to miss that.

"Okay then. I'll shoot over the details when I get them."

"I'll see you then." Kate closed the passenger door and nodded her goodbye.

» » »

The moment Kate walked into the field office, signs everywhere pointed to the fact that this was going to be a major operation. Several agents could be heard coordinating efforts with local authorities, surveillance equipment was stationed at the ready for the field teams, and she was the only one who hadn't yet been given a job to do.

She began to approach Scarborough and Jameson. "Is there anything I can do?"

"Kate, glad you're here. We'll be saddling up in the next thirty minutes or so. Mercer's flight arrives at six p.m., so I'd like you to help Agent Jameson prepare to head out. You ready to do this?" Nick replied.

"I'm ready."

"Come on over with me," Jameson said. "Let's get you up to speed." He led the way over to Agent Vasquez, who would be monitoring communications. "Agent Vasquez, have we coordinated with the TRU on surveillance support yet? We need to be up and running within the hour."

"Yes." She began to punch commands onto her keyboard. "They'll have the secure support online shortly."

Agent Jameson appeared to notice the slightly confused expression Kate was wearing. There were so many facets of the Bureau she had yet to understand and it was clear TRU was one of them. "Have you had an introduction to this yet, Kate?"

"No. I'm afraid not. Is it that obvious?"

"Don't worry. I wouldn't expect that you've been exposed to this in your training yet. The TRU is the Technical Response Unit. They're a part of the OTD, the Operational Technology Division."

As he began to explain, Kate recalled just how difficult it could be to keep all of these different departments inside the Bureau straight. It was an intricate web of sections, divisions, and units touching on every aspect of criminal activity inside the United States, and they all supported one another in their specialized capacities.

"They provide surveillance, support, and secure communications," he continued. "We need their help to keep our field operatives safe and ensure that no one outside the command center knows the position or directives being given to run an effective operation."

"So what will happen once the teams are in place," Vasquez began, "is that we'll utilize the electronic surveillance support to keep tabs on not only our guys, but on the suspects as well."

"Kate, you'll be riding with Agent Scarborough and me. We'll be tailing Mercer in hopes that he will lead us to James Corbett and possibly Stan Kovac. Once we get our sights on those three, we'll take them down. However, it'll be our field operatives running the show from the ground. Scarborough and I will monitor, but only engage if necessary."

Neither one had any intentions of allowing Kate to find herself in harm's way. She was to observe from a training perspective while the big boys handled the fight. This wasn't something with which she was completely on board. Understanding that she was not a full-fledged agent, Kate had already become involved to the extent that the outcome mattered a great deal to her. She would see Corbett and Kovac go down for what they'd done to those girls and make sure Nicola stayed safe.

» » »

A slight tip of the plane's right wing and the descent had begun. Mercer, full black hair and refined features, locked his tray table back into position. The window offered a spectacular view of the city that reflected the lowering sun's golden rays. But Mercer wasn't there to see the sights the city had to offer. He was landing in Richmond to do business and, with his profile, that was already a risky proposition.

He'd been appalled by the near total breakdown of not only the chain of command, but the organization itself, thanks to the debacle of his wealthiest client and the attempts at cleaning up the mess that Corbett had made. Others were beginning to talk and Mercer had no choice but to fix the situation or put an end to it. Much more was at stake than

Corbett could possibly realize. This was an organization with ties to a great many important people, none of whom could afford having the FBI snooping around their businesses.

The wheels skidded against the runway, bouncing and jarring him and the flight attendant. Mercer now waited for his corporate jet to come to a full stop. His intent was to return by midnight, if not sooner, and head back home to London. Being in this country too long brought with it many risks and Mercer didn't like to gamble.

The automated gangway extended to the small plane and the attendant opened the door for Mercer. "Enjoy your stay, sir."

He grunted, hoisting his leather bag over his shoulder and stepping onto the enclosure.

Mercer emerged onto the concourse and proceeded to the south exit, where a car waited for him.

"I have visual," the agent broadcast to the team through a small wireless headset as he spotted the target from inside the terminal. He began to trail Mercer from a safe distance.

Another team member was sitting on a bench just outside the south entrance, scrolling through his cell phone, seemingly oblivious to the world around him. However, he too waited to acquire visual on the mark.

Kate was in the car with Agents Jameson and Scarborough. They were waiting for the go-ahead to tail Mercer to his next location. She'd been close to danger more times than she could count, but this was different. Even as she tracked Hendrickson down, he was ultimately the one who found her, not the other way around. Now Kate was operating as the hunter. It was a strange sensation; exhilarating and terrifying. But she had Scarborough to fall back on. It wouldn't always be that way. Not once she was a full agent. She would be the one leading the team, or taking her part to ensure the team accomplished its goals.

"He's heading your way. Black Cadillac Escalade. Sole passenger," one of the operatives announced over the secure frequency.

Nick started the engine. "Here we go. Black Escalade."

All eyes were pointed in the direction in which the vehicle was expected to arrive. Kate's heart pumped faster. She stared out the right side of the windshield, around Jameson's shoulder.

"There he is," Jameson said.

Kate spotted him too. A sleek black SUV rolled along the dual lane roadway and Mercer was inside. The man who she believed ordered the abduction and enslavement of countless young women was approaching them.

Inside the car they waited, until finally, the subject sped past them. They were shadowed beneath an overpass at the airport's exit and, after a few moments, Nick pulled out onto the same roadway.

He radioed the others. "I got him. Heading westbound onto SR 195 now."

They trailed him for several more minutes. "Where is he going?" Kate asked.

"Don't know yet. We're heading into the suburbs. He's probably already arranged the meeting and won't want to waste any more time. If he stays the night, I'd be surprised as hell," Nick replied. "We just need to be patient."

"We'll wait to see if he meets with Corbett and/or Kovac," Jameson began. "Firstly, to draw them out and secondly, to establish a connection between them. According to the communications between Corbett and Druseburg, no one really seems to know for sure if Mercer is the man in charge. The name was tossed around, but Corbett's main point of contact comes from a man only known to him as the Arranger. Apparently, rumblings from others in the operation suggest that it is Mercer who calls the shots. And, thanks to Inspector Montrose at Interpol, his name raised a red flag. What we really need to see is them in action."

"You mean we have to wait for them to actually kidnap someone?" Kate asked.

"No. We just need to see them together. I'd like to bag all three of them in one fell swoop." Nick looked at Kate through the rear view. "That's the ultimate goal."

"He's pulling into that parking lot," Jameson said. "Hang back."

"Suspect has pulled into the parking lot of the strip mall located on Stratford and N. 42nd," Nick relayed to the team.

Another car pulled alongside the black Cadillac and although it was difficult to see, it appeared each had rolled down their windows to converse.

"Shit. We need ears on them, damn it," Nick said.

» » »

Jim Corbett waited for Mercer to roll down his window. As it slowly descended, the man inside didn't look thrilled to be there. Then again, neither was Corbett. He'd suspected that this was the man in charge, but it remained unclear what would happen to him for having this knowledge.

Corbett had the requisite number of assets. They were in Kovac's hands and he hoped there wouldn't be any more fuck-ups. He had to assure Mercer that he had things under control.

"Do you have them?" Mercer asked from inside the car, his face masked in shadow.

Corbett surveyed the parking lot, noticing the odd car coming or going. It wasn't a particularly busy row of shops, partly the reason for the rendezvous location. Still, he wanted to be sure there were no eyes fixed on them. "I do. Just as you asked."

"And who is handling the cargo at this moment?"

"Same person we discussed earlier. I've got everything under control, sir."

"I'm sure you do. I've already had to take care of one problem you let fall out of your hands. Don't make me handle another."

"That won't happen." Corbett was growing tired of offering assurances to the Arranger and now to the head of this organization, and wanted to get the hell out of the parking lot. He knew the man was referring to Druseburg's death, but failed to believe that it had been a result of his mishandling of the situation. Martin Druseburg may have been loaded, but his money made him careless. That carelessness allowed his girl to take her own life with the drugs he used to make his time with her more pleasurable. The guy was a borderline addict himself and Corbett knew that, but still, he'd taken it upon himself to clean up the mess. And that was what he was doing until Mercer decided to take over. It was the only reason the man was here right now.

The more he thought about it, the more pissed off he became. Unloading the cargo was Corbett's only priority and they were wasting time.

"All right. I have a colleague who will take them off your hands. I'm just here to ensure a successful transition. I don't want to lose faith in you." Mercer rolled up the window.

"Of course, thank you sir." Corbett raised his own window and retrieved his phone. "We're on our way. They'd better be ready. The handoff is tonight."

» » »

"He just called Kovac." Vasquez radioed Nick with the information that'd come through on the Stingray simulating a nearby cell tower that had picked up the call.

"We'll follow, but do you have a location on Kovac? We can send our guys out ahead of them."

"425 N.W. Harbor St.," the agent replied.

"We're on our way."

TWENTY

Dusk was settling as the teams continued to follow James Corbett and Richard Mercer. A call had been made to Detective Garrett updating him on the situation, but the details would be handled by the feds. This was not a time for heavy-handedness.

The headlights of Nick's SUV went dark and he rolled to a stop, a safe distance from the meeting. The rest of the team arrived in the same manner and Nick radioed them. "I want everyone to stay where they are. We don't know if the victims are here or are being held in another location. I do not want to jump the gun."

"Ten-four. We'll wait until we get visual confirmation," one of the agents replied.

"What if the victims aren't here?" Kate asked.

"Then we follow them. Whatever's going to go down will happen tonight. Mercer will want this finished as quickly as possible," Jameson replied.

The men under surveillance stepped out from their respective vehicles, which were parked in front of a home. The agents waited and watched as the men went inside. A team had arrived minutes ahead and were equipped with surveillance gear. Parked cars lined the street nose to bumper and made it easier for the FBI van to blend with the surroundings. Nick's car was only a few feet ahead, but still about thirty yards from the home.

"You guys picking up anything yet?" Nick radioed the surveillance team.

"We've got audio."

"Put it on this channel. I need to know what they're saying."

A moment later, the voices of the men inside the home sounded over a static-filled line. "Damn it. We've got a lot of disturbance here," Nick said.

They listened as Corbett spoke of this latest delivery.

"Look, I got what you asked for, but with this heat, we have to wait until shit cools down before the next order. You can see here, the websites are functioning and we're operating below the FBI's radar. I won't make the same mistakes. These sites are being bounced all over the world and there's no way in hell they're going to track me down. I stay out of sight and Kovac's been handling most of the acquisitions. Problem is, word is getting around too that the streets are getting dangerous. So we need to find a better way. Maybe head over to the Carolinas or Florida. We can organize a shipment from Cuba."

"I am aware of your colleague's unfortunate situation and the number of bodies that seem to be stacking up against the both of you. Quite frankly, I see that you two are the problem here, drawing the unwanted attention, not Druseburg. And, I've already got people working those areas." The voice had an English accent. That was Mercer.

"The problems have been taken care of and we are on track again, sir. My priority is to get these assets dispersed as quickly as possible. I just wanted you to see that the operation is effective. I am getting daily inquires via these websites."

Kate turned away with disgust. Listening to them speak as though the women were nothing more than products to be sold made her want to jump out of the car and beat the hell out of them right now.

She caught Nick's glance in the rear view. He seemed to sense what she'd been thinking. "You okay back there?"

"Fine."

"Be patient. It'll happen."

The radio sounded again. "The warehouses at the pier. Kovac will have them there in thirty minutes."

"They're getting ready to move," Jameson said.

» » »

Nicola was home with her mother and brother. A patrolman had been stationed outside the house for the past few days, since Vito's body was found. Detective Garrett arranged it in order to keep watch on the family and the officer now sat in his car across the street from their small home. The call had come in that something was going down with Kovac and Corbett, and the officer was on high alert.

The family knew he was there and were instructed not to leave the house until further notice.

Nicola still didn't feel safe, even with the knowledge that a policeman waited outside their home. Her mother's nerves were on end and her brother simply sat on the couch, his eyes fixed to the television. He hadn't spoken much since Vito died, believing he was the one responsible for his brother's death. If he'd just kept his mouth shut, none of this would be happening right now.

The dinner her mom made still sat, now cold, on her plate. Nicola hadn't much of an appetite. She was afraid and so long as the man who killed her brother was still out there, she would stay afraid.

She decided her appetite was gone for good and pushed up from the tattered wooden table that was covered in a blue cloth her mother had sewn together. Above the kitchen sink was a small window with bars. Bars covered all of their windows. That was what all of the houses in her neighborhood were like.

Nicola took her plate to the sink and emptied the remnants into the disposal. The curtains were drawn closed, and she raised a hand to pull one of the panels back just enough to peek through. The unmarked police car was still there. She knew what it looked like. Dark blue, four-door sedan, a Ford or something like that. She wasn't well versed in American cars, or any car, for that matter.

She narrowed her eyes to gain focus in the dusky evening sky and tried to see inside the car. Maybe the officer was getting hungry and she could bring him some food, or maybe something to drink. It appeared that he was still inside. She was sure the head-shaped shadow was him. It was just so hard to see.

Nicola dropped the curtain and opened the refrigerator. A few cans of RC Cola rested on the wire shelves and she grabbed one of them. In the small pantry were some bags of chips she usually packed in her school lunches and she took one of those too.

On her way to the living room, Gregor looked up at her. "Where's Mama?" she asked.

He shrugged his shoulders and returned his gaze to the flashing images on the screen.

"Mama?" Nicola stood in the hall, then she spotted the bathroom light on and the door closed.

She walked to the front door and unlocked the deadbolt.

"Gdje ideš?" *"Where are you going?"* Gregor asked.

She rolled her eyes, wishing he would use English more often. "Outside." She raised the soda and bag of chips. "He might be hungry."

The humidity had risen when the sun set and now the warm air felt sticky. Summer here was not very pleasant and she much preferred summers at home.

Nicola made her way to the end of the drive and looked both ways before crossing the street, just as her mother taught her. It seemed like her flip-flops were the only sound and the neighborhood was unusually quiet.

The car's windows were still rolled up and tinted, so it was difficult to see inside, but she still saw his head. He must not have noticed her, though, because he hadn't turned in her direction.

Nicola stood at the driver's side door and rapped gently on the window. "Hello?"

The officer didn't move. She turned her head left and then right. No one was around. Nicola reached for the door handle and pulled.

The can dropped to the street and split open, a forced spray of soda spinning on the ground. The bag of chips slipped from her fingers as Nicola looked at the man. His head was secured to the headrest by a rope; a rope that was used to strangle him. His face was purple and his eyes were bloodshot and bulging.

Nicola screamed and started running back to the house. As she reached the steps of the porch, a man lurched out of the shrubs and snatched her. Her feet flailed in the air as she punched his arms and screamed as loud as she could.

The man slammed his hand over her mouth. "Shut up! Shut the fuck up or I'll kill your entire fucking family."

Her legs stopped moving and no more screams arose, but she still gripped his arm and tried to pry it from her waist.

His pant leg caught on the split stair tread that Vito had promised to fix. After stumbling over the damaged step, he regained his balance and continued to walk towards the front door. The door was still ajar and he pushed it open.

Gregor must've heard Nicola's screams because he stood just feet from the door, a knife raised in his hand. "Let her go."

With a burly frame, the man stood not more than five and half feet tall, and he grinned at Gregor's demand. "Put the knife down or I put a bullet in your sister."

A gun was jabbed into Nicola's side and she winced in pain. Tears streamed down her face as she looked at Gregor. "Don't let him hurt me."

"Boy, you'd better put that knife down. You think I don't know your mother's here too? Do you think you can save them both?" He pulled the gun from her hip so that Gregor understood this was not a situation that he could win.

"Did you kill my brother?" Gregor still gripped the knife hard, his white knuckles outlined his trembling hand.

The man lowered Nicola to the ground, but did not loosen his hold. "Son, you have no idea that you and your brother stepped into a heaping pile of shit. Now, he already paid the price. Don't make me collect from you too. Put down the fucking knife."

Gregor and Nicola locked their eyes, understanding what it was he had to do. He cast a brief glance sideways towards the kitchen.

"She in there? Your mama?" The man waited, but no reply came. "Come on now. I ain't got all night. Let's just get this over with, you hear?"

Nicola understood what was about to happen. She knew just as well as Gregor that none of them were getting out of there alive.

» » »

The call came in on Kovac's phone. He was at the pier inside a warehouse, waiting for Corbett and Mercer to arrive. Three young women were bound by plastic ties and sat on the floor against the exposed brick wall. They all wore battered faces, the punishment for trying to scream or run away.

"I've got them. What do you want me to do?"

"Mercer might be interested in the girl. Bring her. Kill her brother and mother." Kovac shoved his cell back into his pocket and opened the metal door in order to spot the expected guests. Still nothing. He was beginning to wonder when the hell they were going to show up. The girls were growing restless again, but he didn't want to push more heroin. Couldn't risk an overdose. His only other option was to gag them or knock them unconscious. Neither option was desirable at this moment. It would make them more difficult to transport.

» » »

"What the hell's he doing?" Nick asked, a rhetorical question that remained unanswered. Instead, Dwight and Kate cast a watchful eye towards the wandering Stan Kovac.

He propped himself against the exterior of the building with a lit cigarette hanging from his mouth.

Nick reached for his phone, which vibrated against his waist. "Scarborough." His eyes never left Kovac. "What? When? Are any units there yet?"

Kate became increasingly interested in Nick's conversation and so did Dwight. They had no idea who he was talking to, but it seemed each began to suspect it was Detective Garrett and that it wasn't good news.

"We can go in now, but we won't get Corbett or Mercer, you know that. I need both of them here to finish the deal. We're too close," Nick continued. "Just get the family out of there, goddammit."

Kate turned to Jameson. With wide eyes, she looked at him and, in that moment, they both knew what was happening. She began to shake her head. Her chest heaved as the thought of bolting from the car ripped through her body. It was Nicola and she was in danger.

"Shit!" Nick slammed his palm against the steering wheel. He turned to the wall where only a moment ago, Kovac stood, but no longer. He'd retreated back inside.

"Is it Nicola? Is she dead?" With a trembling voice, Kate tried to get the words out in something that resembled an audible tone.

"The patrolman isn't responding to radio calls. Garrett thinks something might have happened to him. Units are already on their way to the house, but we don't know anything yet."

"Oh, God, we have to get over there. We have to help her," Kate replied.

"We need to stay here, Kate," Dwight began. "Garrett's got people heading there now. She'll be fine. You got to let them do their job. We can't let Mercer get away."

Kate knew he was right – they were both right – but that didn't change the fact that her heart raced and her mind flashed images of Nicola, dead. "Please, just let me go there. I can ride with one of the other agents."

Vehicles appeared in the distance, but with headlights shining towards the agents, it was difficult to discern what type. It had to be Mercer and Corbett. The larger van was likely intended for use as a transport.

"They're here," Nick radioed the team. "Wait for the go from me."

"Ten-four."

"We wait for the exchange. Once the women are in the van, we go. We can't take any chances the victims end up in any crossfire." Nick relayed the message to the team once again.

The risk was too great to charge into the building. The victims could easily be targeted. Nick was sure this was the safest bet.

» » »

The door snapped from its hinges with ease as the officers kicked it in, guns drawn and walked inside the home.

Detective Garrett stood outside of the opened patrol car door. His officer was dead. He'd been too late. "We need an ambulance at 135 E. 45th Street. Officer down. I repeat, officer down."

Two other units raced along the roadway towards the house, lights flashing and sirens blaring. Neighbors began to peek out their windows and step out onto their front porches with a sense of déjà vu. It was only weeks ago when a similar scene transpired.

"Where the hell were you people earlier?" Garrett growled under his breath.

Inside the house, the two officers demanded any occupants reveal themselves. One person lay on the floor, a pool of blood still flowing from beneath him. The officer pressed his fingers against the carotid artery to check for a pulse. "This one's gone." He said. Returning to his feet, he continued with his partner.

"Richmond Police. You need to come out." The officer stood at the edge of the hall, gun pointing in the direction of the darkened corridor. He looked to his partner and shook his head. A pointed finger suggested they move forward with caution and the two officers stepped along the carpeted floor.

Each room was cleared until they reached the bathroom. A barely audible whimper sounded from beneath the door. The light was on and the first officer looked to his partner before announcing their presence. "Richmond Police." He turned his head and whispered, "Someone's inside." Returning to the closed door, he announced again, "Are you armed?"

Another faint groan and the officer pushed the door open, ensuring the barrel of his gun would be the first thing the person would see. "Do you have any weapons? Are you armed?"

"Help." It was a female voice, but her face wasn't yet visible.

He continued to push the door open and revealed the victim lying on the floor. "Jesus." Lowering his gun, the officer moved towards the woman. "We need an ambulance now."

The other patrolman turned on his heel and ran through the home and back out the front door. "We have an injured victim inside. GSW in the chest," he said to Detective Garrett.

"Christ. Ambulance is on its way."

"What about Hicks?"

"He's gone." Garrett pushed his hand through his hair, disgusted by the scene.

"There's another GS victim in the living room, but no pulse. What the hell happened here, detective?"

"They came for them and we weren't ready." Garrett turned around to see the ambulance barreling down the roadway. "I underestimated their capabilities."

Garrett and the officer entered the home and made their way to the bathroom. The other officer had placed a towel under the woman's head and was applying pressure to the wound.

"She's lost a lot of blood, but good news is that the bullet struck just beneath her shoulder and exited. Getting her treated quickly; I think she'll be fine."

"My daughter," she moaned.

"What'd she say?" Garrett leaned over.

"Something about her daughter."

"Ma'am, did they take your daughter?" Garrett looked over to the officer. "Did you find a young female victim?"

He shook his head. "Just the male in the living room."

"That's Gregor Bjuric."

The woman on the floor again tried to speak. "She's gone."

"God's sake." Garrett marched out of the bathroom and back outside of the home. He ripped his cell from his pocket. "They got her, Scarborough. They got the girl."

TWENTY-ONE

The black Escalade rolled to a stop just feet from the building's entrance on the pier. The headlights switched off and all eyes were fixed on the now parked car. No one had yet emerged from inside.

The other car pulled up alongside Mercer's. The two cars remained parked; still, no one seemed ready to step out.

The last to arrive was the van that stopped several feet behind the other two. The sound of its engine quickly died and its lights dimmed. Corbett was the first to get out. He stood at the front of his car and waited, glancing towards the door of the building and shifting his gaze to the surroundings.

Mercer stepped out from the rear passenger seat of his Escalade, a cell phone fixed to his ear. "My colleague will be waiting for the shipment," Mercer said, ending the call. "Shall we complete our transfer?"

Corbett nodded and began to walk towards the building. Mercer followed him inside.

Three unmarked FBI cars and a surveillance van were positioned around the perimeter of the pier and warehouse at a safe distance. Agents Scarborough and Jameson waited with Kate inside the SUV. Her head still reeled from the thought of Nicola and she needed to know if the girl was safe.

"On my mark," Nick relayed to the team.

With the men inside, they waited. Kate's heart wanted to beat out of her chest. It took everything she had not to run inside by herself and demand to know if Nicola was okay.

"Wait. What the hell is that? Who's coming?" Nick asked, pointing ahead at the approaching car.

A moment later, the door to the warehouse opened and the first to appear was James Corbett. His arm was linked with one of the girls as he propped her up, the effects of the drugs still weighing heavily on her.

Kovac followed with another young woman.

Kate looked at the faces of these girls. They had to have been in their late teens or early twenties. Seeing the marks on their faces and incoherent movements made her pulse rise even more. "We've got to go get them now."

"Wait." The firm command from Nick was issued. "Who the hell is that?"

The unknown vehicle continued to approach and was nearing the other two cars.

"Anyone else have eyes on this vehicle?" Nick lowered the radio, waiting for a response.

"We see it. Don't know who it is. I thought all the players were already here," the agent in the second car answered.

The mysterious car stopped just feet away from the van that Corbett and Kovac were now moving towards. They appeared unfazed, as though this arrival was completely expected.

A stocky, muscular man stepped out of the car, tossing his cigarette to the ground. He moved towards Corbett, who now shoved the girl inside the van. The two began exchanging words.

"What the hell are they saying?" Nick's eyes searched the area as if that alone would allow him to listen in on the conversation. "Goddammit. What the hell's happening? Who the hell is that?" He engaged the radio. "Can anyone ID this son of a bitch?"

Mercer stepped outside the building, but he was not transporting any of the girls. It seemed that was left to his subordinates. He moved towards the unknown subject. A moment later, Corbett retreated back inside to get the final asset to the van.

"They're coming back out," Dwight said. "How many they got in there?"

"Don't know, but we'll know pretty damn quick if they close the van doors," Nick replied. "Everyone in position." Nick pressed on the radio once again.

"We're going in?" Jameson asked.

"There's too many, we need to be on the ground for assistance," Nick replied.

Kovac stood at the back of the van, while Corbett started to move towards the men.

"This is it. Move!" Nick pushed open his door and leapt out of the SUV. "Stay here!" he shouted to Kate.

Dwight flung his door open and then dashed to the side of the building behind Nick.

She couldn't just stay there while everyone else was risking their lives. If Nick believed she would stay put, then he truly didn't know her at all. Maybe it was the sense of safety the Kevlar vest strapped to her offered, but the adrenaline that coursed through her veins begged her to leap out and help those girls and her team. She rushed out moments behind Dwight and headed towards them.

The first team was situated in the front and was also now in position. The final team was stationed on the east side of the building and all waited for the go.

"Move, move, move!" Nick drew his weapon and ran to the end of the building. He turned to see Kate trailing behind.

"Damn it! Get back in the car!" But it was too late; their presence had become known. "FBI. Don't move!"

The men pulled their weapons and ran for cover behind the opened car doors. The rest of the team quickly appeared, flanking Scarborough, Jameson, and now Kate.

This wasn't a drill, these were not paid actors, and the threat to their lives was very real. Kate's gun was drawn. She did not shake, she did not waver. Her aim was dead onto Corbett and she would pull the trigger and take him down if she had to.

The agents scattered to various locations that offered cover while bullets sliced through the air. Some striking the van, some bouncing off the lampposts, clanging in their ears. Others sounded as they slammed into the water off the edge of the pier, leaving behind mini bursts of spray in their wake.

"Kate, find cover," Nick shouted as he continued evading bullets.

Another agent appeared from the right and fired on Mercer, but missed.

The unknown man pulled open the back door of his car and yanked out a small girl.

"Nicola!" Kate shouted.

"Get back!" Nick lurched in front of her.

The man pointed his gun at the girl.

"Hold your fire. Hold your fire." Nick raised a hand and the bullets stopped.

"Let us go, or she dies," the man said.

Corbett and Kovac were near his vehicle now, still shielded behind the opened driver door.

From the shadows just beyond the parked cars, Dwight appeared. He'd traversed the perimeter and made his way behind the suspects. Nick spotted him out of the corner of his eye.

Kate saw him too, but her focus was sharp and she'd stepped out from behind Nick's protective cover and was ready to take down James Corbett if something happened to Nicola.

"Let the girl go," Nick said. "Then we'll talk about those girls you've got inside that van."

"Yes, I'm sure you just want to talk, Mr. F-B-I," Mercer's voice sounded from behind the vehicle.

"I suggest you accept my proposal. This won't end well for any of you," Nick replied.

"Then it won't end well for the girl," Mercer said.

Nick shifted his gaze just slightly to the right, hardly discernable, except the man who held Nicola noticed. The subtle change in his expression meant Nick knew he saw it too. A slow blink of his eyes was all Jameson needed. *Take the shot.*

The man's eyes widened, understanding that a signal had just been given, and he began to turn, but the shrill sound of gunfire pierced his ear and the bullet pierced his head. Nicola screamed as the man dropped to the ground, and she stumbled back.

This was her chance. Kate ran towards Nicola to keep her from being snatched up by the other men. She had only milliseconds before the bullets flew again. The girl called out for her and Kate ran as fast as she could. Shouts in the distance were coming from the other agents and she heard Nick telling her to stop. Dwight wasn't far away, but it seemed he had his own problem right now.

Kovac began to fire again in fierce retaliation and his aim was on Dwight. A bullet struck the agent and, although he wore a vest, the force still knocked him down.

Kate grabbed Nicola and ran for cover behind the large concrete base of a light post. Corbett was taking shots at anyone within his reach, but was failing. Kate was only a few yards away from him. She could take the shot. "Don't move," she told Nicola as she began to emerge from behind the protective cover.

"No, please don't! You'll get killed!" Nicola cried out.

Kate turned to the girl, placing a finger over her lips and shaking her head. She recalled the words of her instructor and took aim. Corbett was sideways and taking the shot from this angle would be tough. She began to apply even, steady pressure to the trigger. The kickback was what she had to watch out for. The round fired off, leaving a trail of smoke. She had time to blink and then Corbett fell.

"All right, all right!" Mercer shouted as he watched his man fall. He raised his hands above the car door in surrender.

Nicola jumped into Kate's arms, her eyes filled with tears, cold from fear and trembling.

"It's okay, sweetheart, you're safe now." While she felt confident that was true, the residual effects of the adrenaline and fear that pumped inside her brought about a dizzying sensation, as though she might fold.

Nick had his sights on Kovac, who appeared to concede in defeat. "Drop your weapon."

The rest of the team converged and began to secure the area and one of the agents relieved Kovac of his gun, placing him under arrest.

Nick approached Mercer, whose hands were still raised. "You're under arrest for sex-trafficking and kidnapping and that's just for starters." He pulled Mercer's arms down behind his back and cuffed him. "Let's go take a look at your cargo and see your handiwork."

Jameson, still laboring to breathe from the bullet's impact to his vest, managed to hand off the injured Corbett to one of the other agents and approached Kate. "She all right?"

"Yes. Are you?" Kate reached out to steady him.

"I just need a minute."

Kate could see in his eyes that Dwight had been disappointed she'd ignored Nick's demand to stay in the car. How much hot water this might put her in would be up to Nick, most likely. As the Agent-in-Charge, she disobeyed his direct order. "She said that man killed Gregor, and shot her mother, but he took her away and she doesn't know if her mother is still alive. We should get her to the hospital."

Dwight looked towards Scarborough and Mercer standing in front of the van. "We've got an ambulance coming now for Corbett. I'm going to need to help processing the scene. Why don't you take her and I'll check in with you when we're finished here? Have another agent take you both."

He wasn't going to reprimand her, at least for now. Or maybe he was leaving it up to Nick. She'd taken Corbett out of commission and that meant she'd protected the team. That had to stand for something.

Kate directed Nicola to one of the agents' cars. "Come on; I'm going to take you to see your mom." Kate had no idea if her mother was still alive or not. A quick call to Detective Garrett would confirm the mother's location.

"It's Agent Reid. I've got Nicola Bjuric. She's safe."

"I just got the radio call about what happened down there. Everyone all right?" Garrett asked.

"Our guys are fine. The man who took Nicola is dead. Corbett's injured and we've got Kovac and Mercer in custody."

"Son of a bitch. I don't know how her mother's doing, but her brother is dead. Head down to Miramond hospital. She's there. I'll meet you down there as soon as I can."

Agent Scarborough pulled open the van doors and inside, three young women bordered on consciousness. "It's okay, we're here to help," he said.

One of them looked to Mercer with uncertainty and fear.

"He's not going to hurt you and neither is anyone else."

» » »

Kate arrived at the hospital with Nicola and only the security guard at the check in desk was present. It hadn't occurred to her the late hour, but on checking the time, she understood why he was the only one on duty.

"I'm Agent Reid. I need to see Gloria Bjuric. This is her daughter." Kate showed her credentials that indicated she was a new agent in training, but this didn't seem to concern the security guard. Perhaps it was the look on Nicola's face that convinced him to let them through.

He punched in the name into his computer. "She's out of surgery and is in room 234. Second floor and to the right of the elevators."

Kate nodded. "Thank you."

Nicola pushed open the door to her mother's room and rushed to her side. "Mama." She threw her arms around the frail, injured woman who had, in the span of just a few weeks, lost two of her three children and had survived a bullet to the shoulder.

Kate stepped out of the room and called Nick on her cell. "We're here. Her mother's out of surgery and seems to be doing all right. What's happening over there? How is Agent Jameson doing?"

"He's fine. Local PD is here helping, and we're working on getting these girls to the hospital to get checked out." He paused for a moment. "We've got Mercer. That's the good news. We should be able to get a handle on this thing and shut it down. Are you okay?"

Kate knew he was referring to the fact that it had been her that fired on Corbett, injuring his arm. All that target practice and it turned out a real life target was much harder than paper. She wondered, though, if he would lecture her for disregarding his order. "I'm not sure yet. I can't process everything right now."

"It'll take some time to get over the shock of it, but you did what you needed to do and you saved lives, including mine. We'll talk later about why you didn't stay in the car."

"I'd better get back in there to make sure Nicola's okay. I can't imagine what her and her mother must be feeling right about now. You heading down here soon or should I meet you back at the station?"

"I'll head back to the station with Mercer. We'll book him into federal custody. Meet me there when you can."

Kate placed her phone back into her pocket and stepped inside the hospital room once again.

Nicola turned to her. "Thank you, Agent Reid. You saved my life. My mother wants to thank you too."

Kate moved towards the still trembling young girl. "I'm so sorry about your brothers, Nicola."

The girl looked to her mother again. "She says we're going to go back home. That there's nothing left for us here. No future."

The family had already lost so much, Kate understood why her mother felt this way. Hadn't she left because everything had been taken from her?

» » »

It was four in the morning and any person in their right mind would have been exhausted, but Kate couldn't stop replaying that moment in her mind when she pulled the trigger. The feel of the gun in her hands, the smell of the smoke as the bullet fired. The sight of him falling to the ground. She'd disabled him with a single shot. The only thing she regretted was not killing him.

"Hey," Nick said.

She looked up from the chair in the lobby of the Richmond police station. "Hey, what's going on?"

"The victims are being checked out now. Detective Garrett is with Kovac and Jameson is talking to Mercer. I'm going to have to get in there in a minute, but I just wanted to see how you were doing."

"I missed curfew," she replied with a shrug of her shoulders.

"I think they'll understand. Why don't you go check into a hotel and get some rest? You must be exhausted."

"No. I'm fine."

"I'll be finished here in about an hour and then we can drive back to Quantico. Can you hold out?"

"Yes. What's going to happen to Mercer?"

"Hopefully, we'll get enough information to shut this operation down. I've got a message in to Montrose in London."

"Good. I hope we put that son of a bitch away for the rest of his life, and everyone else who's involved in this." The moment she pulled the trigger was the moment that Kate figured out who she really was. All the second-guessing, all the uncertainty of whether or not she had what it would take had all vanished. Kate knew exactly who she was now.

TWENTY-TWO

Fatigue finally caught up with her, and Kate had had enough time to shower before class by the time they'd reached base. But now, she listened as intently as she could, having promised Hawes there would be no more distractions, and she was fading fast.

"Kate? Kate, the lecture's over," Will said.

"Oh." She looked to the front of the class and noticed the instructor packing up his things.

"Are you okay? I heard about what happened last night. I'm surprised you're here."

"I'm fine."

"You say that a lot, don't you?" Will led her from behind the row of desks. "Come on, why don't I get you a cup of coffee?"

"Yeah, okay. I could probably use one of those."

The three minutes to the coffee shop was walked in silence. She didn't know what to say to Will or to anyone.

"Go and sit down. I'll bring you a coffee."

Kate did as he asked without specifying her preference for cream and sugar. That didn't really matter right now.

"Here." Will set the cup in front of her with a few packets of sweetener and cream. "I wasn't sure how you took it, so I just got a little of everything."

"Thanks, Will." She sipped on the hot beverage only just now realizing she hadn't eaten anything since about four o'clock yesterday afternoon.

"Well, you won't have any trouble graduating now; not that I was really concerned to begin with, but I know you had your own doubts."

"Why do you say that?" Kate replied.

"Really? You helped bring down a human trafficking ring. You don't think you'll get some recognition for that? Not to mention your last tactical test that you passed with flying colors. No, Kate. I don't think you'll have any problems finishing. And then you'll be off working with Agent Scarborough in the D.C. office."

In the grand scheme of things, her role was fairly insignificant and she could hardly take credit for bringing the operation down. At least, that's how she saw it.

Kate looked at him for a moment and realized what this was about. Not that she'd been given an opportunity to work on an important investigation, but that it was with Nick and that she was going to be working with him. He still had feelings for her. "You'll be working in Louisville, which is where you wanted to go. So I guess we'll both get what we wanted."

"I guess so." Will turned toward the window and sipped again on his coffee.

"I can see you're bothered by something. What is it?" She was going to have to get this out into the open once and for all. Too much had happened and the thought of pretending it didn't exist seemed juvenile.

"What do you mean? I thought after last night, the least I could do would be to buy you a cup of coffee. Look, Kate, I've taken more lives than I care to remember. It's not easy. I know that man you shot is still alive, but regardless, even shooting someone isn't something you get used to. I just thought you might want to talk. I'm trying to be a friend here, that's all."

She felt ashamed for thinking he was displaying some sort of jealous tendencies. Of course he was being a friend. He'd been a friend to her since day one. And this was how she would repay him? Implying that he just couldn't get over her? She looked away, embarrassed by her arrogance and began to absentmindedly stir her coffee. "I know you're trying to help. And you're right; it's not something I think I would ever get used to. How do you do it, Will?"

"Do what? You mean live with it?"

She nodded.

"What other choice is there? I live with it or I die with it. *It* never goes away. *It* changes you daily. Talking to others who've been through similar situations helps, of course. I have some very good friends from my time in the military that I keep in close contact with. And then there are my new friends here, at the Academy, like you." Will paused for a moment. "You know, most of us know what you've been through based on what we read in the papers or heard on the vine, but until I watched you speak about it during that presentation with Agent Scarborough, I never really understood what happened. And then of course…" Will trailed off and gave her the look she'd seen in others so many times before.

She already knew what he wanted to say and although she'd gotten to the point where she could speak about it, the desire to was not there. Especially not now when her emotions were so raw. Kate was growing tired of wearing her heart on her sleeve and letting the vultures, the evil in this world, tear away at it, piece by piece. So maybe it was time to put it way, for good. "It's okay, Will. You don't have to tiptoe around me. Like you say, you have to live with it because there is no other choice." Kate peered out the window and watched a young woman, not unlike herself, walk by. She turned back to Will. "I suppose I could consider the silver lining."

"What's that?"

Kate smiled. "There's nothing left for anyone to take from me anymore. That makes me invincible, right?"

Will seemed to study Kate for a time and was beginning to feel awkward. "I suppose it does."

"Right." Kate crumpled the napkin she'd been twisting between her hands. "I'd better get going." She pushed her chair back.

"Where're you headed? Home?"

"Not yet. I've got to run by the field office and help Agent Jameson with some paperwork." As she stood up to leave, Kate looked to Will again. "Thanks for the coffee. I'll see you tomorrow?" She smiled and continued on her way out of the coffee shop. As she walked past the window, she noticed Will watching her. She raised a hand with a final goodbye and headed back to her room.

» » »

The dormitory was already growing quieter on this late Friday afternoon. Her class, along with two others, had already progressed far enough into the program that they were allowed to travel home on the weekends. Now, only the newbies remained, or those who didn't have another home to stay.

The weekender bag sat opened on her bed and Kate pulled the elastic band from her hair and let it drop to her shoulders. She opened her dresser drawer and began tossing items inside the bag. Didn't matter what, just a few things. She would be back here for half the day tomorrow anyway, but after last night, she wanted nothing more than to sleep in her own bed, surrounded by her own things. Here, in the dorm room she now shared with no one, was only a reminder of those who had failed the program, either due to physical ineptitude or from pressures at home. Kate wasn't going to be one of the failures.

The bag zipped with ease as only a few items were inside. She tossed it over her shoulder and looked at the empty bed next to hers where her roommate had been. Kate knew her to have been an intelligent woman with a background in law enforcement, but she let the pressures of her husband and family get to her and, in the end, it cost her the dream of becoming an agent.

Kate had no such pressures, not anymore. It was solely on her shoulders, her success or failure in the program. There would be no one to blame, no one's shoulder to cry on if she did not succeed. It was better that way.

On her arrival to the WFO, Kate parked in the garage and stepped out to strap her belt back onto her waist. It was a strange thing to get used to, wearing a weapon at all times. But it was beginning to feel a part of her, like wearing a ring, and being without it made her feel as though she'd forgotten something.

Kate reached for the necklace and felt for the engagement ring she still wore around her neck. It too had already become a part of her.

The doors to the elevator parted on the fourth floor where she would find Agent Jameson at one of the workstations and Scarborough, who would probably be in his office. There were no set hours here and so she expected to find a fair few agents still working and as she stepped out into the office, she was not wrong on that count.

In only a matter of weeks, Kate would find herself among these people. The best and brightest the Bureau had to offer, as far as she was concerned. She'd thrown herself into her work before and would do the same now.

"Agent Jameson," Kate started as she approached him with a raised hand.

"Kate, glad to see you. What are you doing here? I figured you'd be heading for home right about now."

"Agent Scarborough asked me to stop by and assist with the reports from last night. I guess there's some paperwork I need to fill out as well." Kate pulled up a chair next to Jameson.

"Right, of course. Let me get a few things wrapped up here and I'll get you logged in and we can file the reports together."

"Okay, sure. Um, what should I do in the meantime?" She looked around as if searching for someone.

"Agent Scarborough's in his office. Maybe just check in with him first?"

"Okay." Kate rose from the brief moment in the chair and began heading towards Nick's office.

"Hey, Kate," Jameson said.

"Yeah?" She stopped and turned on her heel.

"You okay?"

A thin, white-lipped smile briefly showed on her face. "I'm fine. Thanks for asking, Dwight." She didn't often call him that, although he frequently insisted. But this felt like an occasion to address him in a more personal manner. He'd been there last night too and probably knew exactly how she was feeling.

Kate continued on towards Scarborough's office and knocked on the frame of his opened door. "Agent Scarborough?"

Nick looked away from his computer screen. "Hi Kate, please come in." He gestured for her to have a seat. "You look a little tired."

"I feel a little tired. I just stopped and talked to Agent Jameson. He said he's got a few things to finish up and then he'd help me with the reports."

Nick continued to hold her gaze and Kate was growing weary of those around her constantly analyzing her. It was beginning to make her feel less worthy of wearing the badge as if somehow, she was simply too delicate to handle what happened to her last night. Still, she tried not to be offended. "So, is there anything I can do in the meantime?" she continued, discounting his sympathetic stare.

This seemed to shake him out of it as he began to look at his desk in search of something. "Uh, yeah, actually." He retrieved a flash drive from the edge of his desk. "These are the forensics photos from last night. Can you get these uploaded into the case file for me?"

"I can do that." Kate reached for the small stick. "Which workstation should I use?"

"I think Agent Vasquez is still here. Why don't you track her down and she can get you set up?"

"Sounds good. Thanks." Kate stood up to leave.

"Hey," Nick said before she could step out of his office.

Kate, with her back already turned, closed her eyes, fearing he was going to have a talk with her that she really had no desire to hear. "Yes?" She turned back to him.

"Corbett's attorney wants to work a plea deal with the federal prosecutor."

This sparked her interest. "So, he testifies against Mercer and Corbett goes free?" Sometimes the justice system and, in particular, plea-bargaining, allowed too many criminals to manipulate the system. Kate believed this was what Corbett was trying to do now and after what happened to Nicola's family, she was feeling nauseated by the idea.

"Not free, likely a reduced charge, but he's agreed to tell us where the remaining runners are and where they plan to take their next victims. Just because we have these men in custody, doesn't mean this is over, Kate. We believe there are still several operatives out there kidnapping and selling these women to the highest bidder. Mercer won't talk for obvious reasons, but if we can get Corbett to cut a deal, we stand a better chance of finding those women before they end up like Madlena."

Kate began to walk back toward Nick and rested her hands on the back of the guest chair. "Is this the way it always works? They scratch our backs and we scratch theirs? Does anybody ever see the justice that's coming to them?"

"You want the truth? Somewhere in the range of 90 percent of federal cases go through plea-bargaining. It's just the way it is. Right or wrong. But in this case, I'd say since it's likely to save lives, then we do what we need to do."

She understood his reasoning, but despised it just the same. "Okay, so what do we do from here then?"

"Both Kovac and Mercer are currently being transported here for federal holding. Corbett's still in the hospital. Once they arrive, I'll be meeting with the prosecutor and Corbett's attorney to get the terms of the deal. Kovac won't get a deal; we don't need him. We've got him on murder charges and with the trafficking on top of that, he won't see the light of day for a very long time. Once we know where the drops are going to be, we'll coordinate with the agencies involved and get our guys in place to assist."

"Is there anything I can do to help?"

"Yes. Start with uploading those photos and get with Jameson. I'll contact you on my return and fill you in.

However, I'm not sure how much more you'll be able to do. My suggestion would be to stay here, work with Vasquez and Jameson on the coordination efforts. The field teams will handle their end of things."

"You don't want me back out there, do you?" This was her punishment for disobeying his order. She wasn't going back out in the field most likely until she graduated.

"This has got nothing to do with what happened last night. I brought you in on an operation, it went bad, and it certainly wasn't because of you. You stopped Corbett from firing on us and that was your job." Nick inhaled a deep breath. "I'll take my lumps for having you out there when I shouldn't have. ASAC Campbell wasn't happy that you were there at all. It wasn't protocol."

Kate regretted her earlier irritation with Nick. "I'll do what I can to help here, then."

"Good." Nick returned to his monitor and began typing, signaling the meeting was over.

» » »

As the hours grew later, Kate realized nothing would be happening tonight. Nick hadn't returned from meeting with Corbett's lawyer and the likelihood of coordinating multiple law enforcement jurisdictions in the span of a couple of hours was slim and none. The problem with that was if any drops were scheduled for tonight, they wouldn't be stopped and more women would fall prey to the coyotes. That was what she remembered them being called back in San Diego. Because of the proximity to Mexico, human trafficking was all too prevalent and so were drop houses. A slightly different scenario than this, but Katie likened the criminals to the same as the coyotes.

"Thank you for helping me get my reports finished," Kate said.

"Hey, no problem at all. That's why I'm here," Dwight replied. "You ready to get home?" He glanced at the time on his phone. "It's getting late."

"What's going to happen to Nicola and her mother?" Kate's preoccupation with the girl finally revealed itself.

"I'm not sure exactly. I haven't talked to Agent Scarborough to find out. Why do you ask?"

"I was just wondering if they were going to be deported. Nicola told me her mother wanted to take her home, back to Croatia, but will they suffer any repercussions because they were here illegally?"

"So it's not the fact that you took down one of the bad guys that's bothering you, is it? It's the girl." Dwight seemed to understand and had been the only one to notice her behavior.

"I don't know, maybe it's both." Kate felt resigned to the idea. Perhaps it was exhaustion, but there was something else too. "I know we've never talked about this before, not really, but you were there when Marshall decided to go to Shalot's place and search for evidence."

"Yes." He appeared reluctant to answer.

"But he didn't tell you where he was going?"

Dwight shook his head. "I was tending to the woman who'd injured herself."

She looked at him and wondered if Dwight was telling her the truth, or was he shielding her from something. "Why would he do that? Marshall was highly experienced. Why do you think he would go alone like that? Especially given what had just happened with that woman." Kate didn't like to recall the names of those involved the day Marshall died. It would be like an admission of Marshall's culpability for taking matters into his own hands. She didn't want to remember it that way.

"Kate, you don't want to relive that right now, do you?"

"I want to know, Dwight. Please, tell me why he would do such a thing?"

He hesitated and looked away for a moment, appearing to gather his words. "He was afraid—for you, Kate. He was afraid Shalot was going to come for you and I truly don't believe he thought Shalot would return to the apartment before he'd had a chance to find what he was looking for."

"It just worked out that way." She finished the thought for him.

"Yes."

Kate stood up. "Thank you, Dwight. I suppose there's not much more for me here tonight. I'm going to head home. I've got to be back on campus at eight a.m."

"Of course. I'm sure Agent Scarborough will be in touch when he returns. Good night, Kate."

"Good night."

TWENTY-THREE

The SUV flashed its lights when Nick pressed the remote and unlocked the doors. Stepping inside, he immediately turned the engine and flipped on the air conditioner. The night air was sticky as hell and he was already sweating just from the walk to his car.

It didn't help that he'd been overheated too from the marathon negotiating session with Corbett's lawyer and the federal prosecutor. He knew the unnecessarily long wait cost him the ability to set up the operation for tonight. And according to Corbett, he wasn't aware of any drops scheduled until tomorrow anyway, but Corbett couldn't be trusted. He could have made sure some of his buddies would be made aware of the situation so they had the time to make the necessary adjustments. Whatever the reason, Nick was pissed about the delay and was taking it out on the gas pedal and spinning the tires as he roared onto the streets.

Georgia was waiting for him at her apartment. She was closer to the field office and had texted him earlier that she'd arrived home. Nick wanted to see her; needed to see her. He'd already faced so much flack for letting Kate come along last night. It was only because of what happened. If it had gone to plan, ASAC Campbell wouldn't have said a goddam thing about it. Now he was dealing with this son of a bitch who knew if he gave up the right amount of information, he'd be off in a matter of a few years instead of a few decades, if at all.

They'd gotten what they'd wanted in the end. Corbett gave up one of the operatives working in Alexandria, not far from the man's former residence. He began to think about what Kate said. The plea-bargaining chip. She was right about it benefiting the bad guys, but he had to protect the victims here. That was what was important. They'd already involved Inspector Montrose and informed him of the arrest of Richard Mercer. Now Montrose would have the authority to search the man's residence, place of business, everything. That would surely reveal even more members of the trafficking ring.

Nick still didn't know how big this was, although he suspected it was larger than anything he'd worked on before. He was used to national investigations, but international was something new.

Georgia's place was just ahead. He'd started to cool down both physically and mentally. Once inside her parking garage, Nick turned off the engine and closed his eyes for a moment. He didn't want any of what he'd been through today spilling over and burdening Georgia. The woman had enough on her plate. Nick reached for his cell, which rested in the center console and double checked for any messages. One last check before putting the day behind him.

He considered for a moment that he should reach out to Kate. He had told her he'd be in contact after the meeting, but it was so late. She was probably asleep after having had none the night before. No point in disturbing her. She'd been through enough in the past twenty-four hours and it could wait until tomorrow.

Nick stepped outside, back into the sauna-like air, and locked his car, tossing his suit jacket over his shoulder. Her apartment was near the top of the building and he stepped inside the air-conditioned elevator, pressing the button to the tenth floor.

The cool, dry hallway towards her unit set his mind even more at ease. Perhaps it had just been the heat. That was what he wanted to believe. A gentle knock on her door and only a moment later, there she was. Just as beautiful as always. He loved it when she wore her hair down. "Hi." He stepped inside and pulled her close, kissing her lips.

"Hi, come on in." She closed the door behind him. "I was beginning to think you weren't coming."

"I know it's late. It's been a hell of a past few hours, I'll tell you that." Nick placed his jacket over the back of the dining chair and pulled off his tie. "You got anything to drink?"

Georgia had already returned with two cocktails in her hand. "Here you are."

"You read my mind."

Nick was hesitant to discuss work. It would only serve to agitate him and, right now, the smooth flow of bourbon down his throat was the best thing to happen to him all day. He parked himself on the corner of the sofa sectional and kicked off his shoes, crossing his long legs, which stretched the better part of the length of the couch.

Georgia sashayed toward him, setting her drink on the coffee table. She began to climb over him, her body pressing against his. She unbuttoned his shirt, pulled it from the waist of his pants, and pushed it off his chest, exposing his still too-warm skin.

Nick smiled as the cool air rested on his skin. He raised her chin with his index finger and kissed her again. This time, with more passion than before. That had only been a warm-up.

The kisses lingered and the heat rose between them. Nick slid her blouse from her shoulders and kissed her delicate, pale skin. She pulled aside her thick, red hair, exposing a long, slender neck and his lips moved slowly towards it.

Nick's eyes clicked open at the vibration in his pocket. He considered ignoring it for a moment, but he couldn't do it.

Georgia must have felt the jarring vibration too because she immediately stiffened. "Please don't get that," she whispered.

He shoved his hand into his pants pocket and pulled out the phone to see the caller ID. The identity of the person who was so rudely interrupting this moment was immediately visible to both of them.

"I gotta take this, babe. I'm sorry. I told her I would call her when I was finished with the meeting and I didn't. She's probably just checking in." Nick waited for Georgia to lift off of him. "I'll only be a minute, I swear."

He pushed off the couch and walked towards the sliding glass door. "Kate, hey." He stepped outside, closing the door behind him. "No, no. It's fine. You know you can call me anytime." He waited for her to continue. "We got our information, but nothing's going down until tomorrow night." Another pause. Nick directed his eyes to the Washington Monument while she spoke. "I'd say go ahead and do what you need to do at the base, then come on down to the field office. I'm sure we can use you. Great. See you tomorrow. Good night, Kate."

Nick pulled open the door again and noticed Georgia buttoning her blouse. He also noticed that she didn't look very happy. "I'm so sorry. I should've just called her on my way home like I told her I would. She was just checking in." He raised the phone into her line of sight. "I'm setting this over here." Nick walked to the credenza against the adjacent wall and set his phone down. "No more calls tonight."

He walked back over to her and sat down on the couch. "Please don't be upset. If you were on a case right now, you'd have done the same thing. Bad timing, yes, but please don't let it ruin the moment."

She seemed to examine his eyes, searching for something. "What?" he whispered. "What is it?" Nick placed his hand on her knee.

"Nothing." Georgia revealed a rueful grin. "Let's just pick up where we left off."

» » »

Monitors flashed, agents with headsets were double checking locations and viewing GPS maps and Kate walked into the WFO as they readied for the final takedown of the remaining operatives. She spotted Dwight talking to Agent Vasquez and headed towards the two. "Is there anything I can do to help?"

"We can use all the hands we can get." Dwight patted her on the back. "I'll leave you with Vasquez and she'll fill you in. I'll let her handle assigning any tasks that she needs. I've got to go see Agent Scarborough."

"Okay," Kate replied. "I guess I'm all yours, Agent Vasquez."

"So right now, we're getting the teams in place. We've got three locations, according to Agent Scarborough, that will be used to hand off the victims to their end users. We're coordinating with Richmond PD, Virginia State Troopers, and surrounding state police. They've received the information on the suspects; however, we don't know how much cargo they're bringing."

"So when is this all supposed to happen?" Kate asked.

"A matter of hours, from what I understand. We've already got field teams heading to the drop locations to set up."

"Great. What do you need from me?"

"Nothing right now. Give me an hour and I'll have you positioned to assist me with coordinates and making sure we've got eyes and ears on our guys in the field. We're working on getting the surveillance up and running. In the meantime, just sit tight. Maybe give Agent Scarborough a heads up and let him know I've got you covered."

"I'll do that. Thank you, Agent Vasquez." Kate turned away and headed towards Nick's office. In the hallway, she ran into Dwight again.

"Vasquez get you hooked up?"

"She did. I was just going to let Agent Scarborough know that I was here and that I'd be working with her."

"I just left his office. Better catch him while you can. We're both heading out with one of the teams soon."

"Okay, hey, be safe out there tonight."

"Always." Dwight smiled and continued down the hall.

"You got a minute?" Kate peeked into Nick's office.

"Sure, come in." Nick leaned back in his chair for a moment, appearing as though he needed a break as he rubbed his eyes. "Thanks for coming down. I know we could use the help."

"I want to be here. Thank you for letting me help." Kate pulled up a seat. "Agent Jameson said you and he are going into the field too?"

"We're going to take the rest of them down."

He seemed different, like he was speaking to her as a colleague. She was being treated as an equal, not as if she was someone he needed to help. Maybe it was because she wouldn't be in any danger this time. Whatever the reason, it felt good to be a part of the team. And it gave her a renewed sense of purpose.

"Agent Vasquez has got me tasked with a few things to assist her. So, I think I'm all set. Anyway, I won't take up any more of your time. I just wanted to let you know that I was here."

"How'd the training go today?" Nick asked. "I suppose you're getting down to the wire now."

"It was mostly online stuff today, but yes, it's getting close now. I can't thank you enough for helping me get through this. And I don't just mean the Academy."

Nick leaned over his desk, his firm triceps bulging slightly beneath his white button-down shirt. "You did the work, Kate, not me. And I don't just mean the Academy." He leaned back again and turned to his computer. "I'd better get back to work. I'm leaving in a few minutes."

Kate stood up to leave. "Thank you, Agent Scarborough." She wanted to tell him to be safe, that she was worried he might get hurt. But what good would it do except to set his mind to the dangers that he faced? He was already well aware of them and didn't need her pointing them out. "I'll see you when you get back."

» » »

The time had come and all the pieces were in place. According to James Corbett, there were three drops happening tonight inside of a two-hour window. Local authorities stood at the ready. Roadblocks were in place and Agents Scarborough and Jameson were in the field running the teams. Tensions were high inside the communications room where GPS monitors tracked the agents' locations and audio connections were being tested.

Kate stood behind Agent Vasquez who was monitoring one of the stations. ASAC Campbell was running the show from the comm. room. Kate half-expected him to insist she not be involved, but she quickly realized that he had far more important concerns than whether or not a NAT was hanging around. She became acutely aware of her insignificance. In all honesty, it felt good not being the one to whom the focus had shifted. She was truly part of the team here and not a victim.

"You might as well take a seat," Vasquez began. "We're going to be here a while."

Kate pulled out the chair next to the agent and sat down, not noticing that Georgia had come into the room. It wasn't until she heard her speaking to another agent that she realized her presence. An immediate understanding occurred to Kate as to why Georgia was there. It would have been no different if it had been Marshall. She would have been there too.

Kate pushed back her chair and walked towards Georgia. "Agent Myers," she greeted her with a handshake. "How are you?"

"Fine, thanks. Just thought I'd see how things were going in here."

Kate knew it was more than that, much more. Georgia was worried for Nick and Kate couldn't blame her for that. "So far so good, I hear."

Georgia pressed her lips together and nodded.

"They've got eyes on an approaching vehicle." One of the agents turned to ASAC Campbell.

"We're on," he replied.

"I'd better get back." Kate walked back to Vasquez and waited for instruction.

There were no visuals on the teams. No body cameras being worn by the agents, only audio from the headsets. It made for an odd sense of blindness inside the room, at least as far as Kate was concerned. In her training, she'd learned about the FBI's use of drones. Their occasional uses were narrow and infrequent, often only incorporated in terrorism or hostage situations. It was difficult to understand in this moment why drones could not be implemented in this current situation. Lives were at stake and having the ability to visually monitor the situation would seem to be invaluable. But there were rules and regulations to which they must adhere. Kate felt increasing conflicted by this, especially now when her friends were out there.

The sound of people running bellowed inside the room over the audio system. This was it. It was happening now. Kate's back pulled stiff; her breath nearly stopped altogether.

Still, noises surrounded them inside the room and no one there could do anything more than what they were already doing, which was simply listening to the teams. ASAC Campbell was monitoring the locations of his agents, ensuring he at least knew where they were. One of the other agents was on his headset speaking to state troopers, making them aware of the movements. They were ready and waiting at the roadblocks.

A voice sounded, calling out orders. Kate knew it was Nick. She turned to Georgia, who didn't appear nearly as nervous as Kate had. But then, Georgia had been through this sort of thing many times before and probably worse. She was the one who had discovered Branson's group.

Nick began shouting again, this time for Jameson to take his position. The suspects were aware of the raid and gunfire quickly erupted. It was happening so fast, Kate could hardly understand what the agents were saying. Footsteps, yelling, and now loud popping, but Kate had no idea who the voices were coming from. She felt so helpless. At least when she was there the other night, she'd been able to help and knew what was going on. Now it just felt like she was riding a roller coaster in the dark. The voices were hardly discernable; good guys or bad guys, they all sounded virtually the same buried beneath the screams of the victims, the shouting, and the gunshots.

"What's happening out there?" Kate's anxiety couldn't be disguised.

"They're in control," Vasquez replied as she monitored the screens.

Who is in control? Us or them? she thought to herself.

Chaos seemed to reign, but those inside the room, the agents monitoring and coordinating, they appeared to be the ones in control.

"What's happening out there, people?" ASAC Campbell stepped towards the video screens to view the locations of his team.

Pop! Pop! Pop! More gunfire sounded.

Kate had almost forgotten to breathe. Her heart was racing and her mind started to replay the events from the other night. As she sat unmoved in the chair next to Vasquez, her hands could almost feel the heat of the gun as the bullet left the chamber and struck Corbett. It had been so chaotic and time seemed to stop when in reality, it had passed with break-neck speed. She swallowed the lump in the throat and rubbed her palms against her pants. Sweat clung to her neck and her stomach began to roll.

Georgia stared at the little dots on the screens, but made no sound. Kate looked to her, knowing that she must feel the same, but in no way did she show it.

The gunfire stopped. Jameson's voice sounded over the speakers. "He's down! He's down!"

Kate whipped her head to Georgia, who remained unmoved, but whose eyes darted between the screens.

"We got 'em! Suspects down. Move in to secure the victims."

It was Nick, and Kate's heart started again.

"We've got five victims inside the vehicle and need medical assistance ASAP."

Vasquez immediately contacted the waiting police and called for an ambulance. "Help is on the way, Agent Scarborough."

"Are our people accounted for?" ASAC Campbell asked.

"Yes. Safe and accounted for, sir," Jameson replied. "We got four suspects. They're all down, but the victims are safe and so is the team."

A collective sigh of relief spread throughout the room and a few claps sounded. Smiles quickly appeared on the faces of the agents.

"What about the other drops? Are the teams in place?" Nick asked.

"Yes. They're listening and are aware of what's happened. They're ready for the take down. Good work, agents." Campbell replied.

Nick began ordering the other team members to secure the scene and the sound of ambulances sounded in the distance. It wasn't over, but Kate was grateful Nick and Dwight were out of danger.

"We got 'em, Kate. We got 'em." The tension in Nick's voice was gone as his words carried inside the comm. room.

A few voices could be heard in the background, but their words were inaudible, until Nick spoke again. "We'll clean up this mess and head back to base. Scarborough out."

ASAC Campbell approached Kate. "You two make a pretty good team, Agent Reid. I'll be glad to have you working for this office."

Kate turned to Georgia. "Agents Scarborough and Jameson deserve the credit here, sir and so does the rest of the team."

"Don't sell yourself short, Kate," Georgia began. "You helped bring in Corbett. ASAC Campbell is right. You two will make a great team."

TWENTY-FOUR

It was over. Corbett's information led to the arrest of seven men and the rescue of almost fifteen women. Mercer was still in federal custody and would face multiple charges of human trafficking. Although no evidence suggested Mercer was involved in trafficking inside of Europe, Inspector Montrose was coordinating efforts with the FBI to continue the investigation on his end because it was believed the ring extended far into Eastern Europe.

James Corbett was also still in federal custody and would get his plea deal. Stan Kovac would be in lock up until his trial, and the Bjuric family, what remained of them, would be going back to Croatia.

Kate insisted she travel back to Richmond with Nick because she wanted to say goodbye to Nicola. There was still a whole lot of bureaucratic red tape to sort through because this case involved several jurisdictions, and so the trip back was necessary in any event.

They didn't speak much in the car. Kate wondered if Nick was still processing the events from last week. She wouldn't blame him for it. He'd put his life in danger twice in that week alone. And she began to question his theory that most agents who work in BAU are analysts or hang in the background while the field agents take the glory, although she supposed he was the exception. His work crossed over because he was assigned to the WFO as a BAU operative and coordinator. He did a little bit of everything.

Nick pulled into the parking lot of the police station and Kate noticed Detective Garrett near the entrance.

"Welcome back," Garrett said. "Glad to see you came through without a scratch."

"I wouldn't say that," Nick replied.

Kate spotted Nicola immediately as the young girl sat next to her mother in the lobby. The two were being deported, but as it was considered voluntary, and bearing in mind all that had happened, Immigration would not flag their passports and they would be allowed to return to the United States— someday. But Kate figured that day would likely never come and she wondered what life would be like for Nicola in Croatia. Poor, unskilled, her mother would struggle once again to find work, just as she did in this country.

Nicola noticed Kate and immediately ran towards her, arms extended. The smile on the girl's face was contagious and Kate greeted her with the same warmth and open arms.

She squeezed the girl and was filled with a sense of joy she'd not felt in a very long time. Nicola was a survivor and she'd been through a terrible thing. Kate understood all too well what it was like to lose someone you loved.

"I don't want to leave here," Nicola cried.

Kate only had to bend a little to meet the girl's eyes. "I know, Nicola, but it's for the best. There's nothing here for you, not right now. Maybe when you're grown…"

"When I'm a grown-up, I'm going to be an FBI agent like you."

Kate's eyes started to burn and she smiled at Nicola. "There is no doubt in my mind that you will be whatever you want to be." She looked up at Nick, who had just approached the two of them.

"I bet you'd make an awesome agent, Nicola." He smiled at Kate, the first smile she'd seen on him in days. "Just look at your name. Same as mine." He winked at her. "We'd better get started, Kate."

Kate pressed up on her toes and returned to standing. She pulled out a business card from her days in San Diego and reached for a pen from the lobby desk. "Here." She began scribbling on the back of it. "This is my email address and my phone number. You can contact me whenever you want to, you hear me?" She handed Nicola the card.

The girl nodded. "Yes." She smiled a final time and returned to her mother's side.

"I'll be right behind you," Kate said to Nick and began to approach the mother. "You have an amazing daughter. I wish you both a safe journey home."

"Thank you, Agent Reid," the woman replied. "I will do whatever it takes to make sure my Nicola has a good life."

"I have no doubt, ma'am."

» » »

The class assembled in the main training room for a briefing on the day before the final exams. Kate began to scan the room and noticed that nearly one-quarter of the agents who'd started with her were now gone. She recalled the speech one of the Supervisory Special Agents delivered at the beginning of the training. That many of the people in the room would not be there by the end and he was right.

Kate doubted how it was that she made it this far. Had Nick not stepped in, she believed she could have been one of the twenty-five percent. But she had worked damn hard too and needed to remember her part in achieving the goal. The grueling physical tests, the tactical training; all of it was something she had doubts about in the beginning, but by the end, had mastered. It wasn't over, though. The final exams were tomorrow and Friday. She still had to pass and had been hitting the books particularly hard since the case was over. She'd had to regain her focus on the training.

Will had been there to help and she was indebted to him. His friendship, although she'd nearly set it to ruin, had been invaluable. Now he sat next to her, waiting for this final speech from the instructor.

"Those of you who are still here should be proud of your accomplishments. You've put in the hours, you've practiced, and you've learned. But this isn't over yet." The instructor started to pace the front of the room. The large screen behind him was on and showed the FBI emblem on a light blue background.

"The next two days will probably be the worst. Your physical and mental strength will once again be put to the test. However, I'm looking at the best of the best and so this should not be a problem for any of you."

Kate was ready. This was what she wanted. If a shred of doubt remained in her mind, it had vanished when she saw Nicola for the last time. It had been weeks since then, but her memory hadn't faded; in fact, it propelled her to work even harder.

She was missing Nick, though. He'd been busy wrapping up the investigation and she'd hardly seen him more than a few times in almost a month. And when she had managed a quick lunch with him, he seemed preoccupied. Maybe it was better that way; she needed to do this last part on her own.

"If you pass," SSA Hawes continued, "then I'll see you all at graduation. You're dismissed."

Almost at once, the remaining NATs took to their feet and shuffled out of the training room. Kate made her way from the aisle with Will trailing behind.

"You heading back to the dorm?" he asked.

Kate looked at her watch. "I think I'll grab some dinner first at the cafeteria. You hungry?"

"Always."

"Great. Let's go eat."

It appeared as though most everyone had the same idea, as the cafeteria was packed. It was doubtful any of the remaining members in her class would be doing anything else tonight except for studying and getting rest, which was exactly what Kate was planning on doing.

"It's been a pretty incredible five months." Will shoved a section of a large cheeseburger into his mouth.

"You could say that." Kate paused for a moment. "I really wasn't sure I'd even make it to this point and I know you've played a part in my success. Thank you for that, Will."

"Please." His mouth still half-full of food. "You did the hard stuff. I was just a shoulder."

Kate looked down at her food. "But it was more than that, wasn't it?" They hadn't once spoken about that night, but Kate felt compelled to explain her behavior because she didn't want to finish this and say goodbye to him without at least acknowledging that while she hadn't been ready for it, she didn't hold him responsible for her actions.

He put his burger down and held her gaze. "Kate, I'm not going to lie to you and say that it didn't sting a little because it did. I like you. What can I say? But I understand that it is too soon. I get that. That doesn't mean we can't continue on as friends and who knows—maybe someday—when you're ready... but in the meantime, I will always be your friend and when we're finished here and we go our separate ways, I want you to know that I'm only a phone call away. Hell, I'll only be an hour's flight away too." He smiled. "The last thing I want you to have are regrets about me."

"I would never…"

Will raised his hand. "I'm just saying. Don't be too hard on yourself. You needed someone. We all need someone. Give yourself a break, is all."

"Thanks." Kate worked to keep the tears at bay because she had regretted it and it would be something she would have to find a way toward forgiveness. But hearing him let her off the hook, well, maybe she needed that.

» » »

"There you are." Georgia walked into Nick's office. "I've been looking for you for the past twenty minutes."

As she approached, Nick pressed a button on his keyboard and his monitor flashed to its screen saver. "I must've just missed you then, because I've been here for the last fifteen minutes. What's up?"

Georgia walked around his desk and kissed his lips, glancing for just a moment at his computer screen. "I just wanted to know if you felt up to grabbing dinner soon."

"What? No work?"

"Nope. I've got a few consults heading my way, but nothing yet, so I thought it'd be nice to get out of here early tonight."

"Sure. I could eat." He turned back to his monitor. "I've got a few emails to shoot out first. Can you give me, say, thirty minutes?"

"I can do that. I'll see you in thirty."

As she walked out of his office, Jameson approached. "Agent Myers, nice to see you." He watched her begin to head down the corridor. "Heading home?"

"Not just yet. Waiting for that guy to finish up so we can go eat. Care to join us?"

"Maybe another time. I'm swamped right now," he replied.

"Okay. Goodnight then."

"Good night." Dwight continued in to Nick's office. "How'd it go?" He pulled out the chair and waited for Nick to reply.

"Not great."

"Goddamn it, Nick. What the hell are you going to do?"

"Wait, I guess. Nothing else I can do."

"Look, you know I got your back, right?" Dwight said.

"I do."

"Whatever that asshole says happened, you did what you needed to do, and any of us would have done the same. They'll see that and this will all blow over."

"I sure as hell hope you're right, man."

"Did you tell Georgia?"

"No." Nick turned away and shook his head. "Not until I know for sure what the higher-ups plan on doing. No point in worrying her."

"Sure. I guess not. And what about Kate? She's taking her exams tomorrow, right? Does she know?"

"Definitely not. She's got enough on her plate without worrying about me."

"This could affect her, though, you know that. Shit goes down the wrong way and they might not keep her here. Might ship her off someplace else."

"I don't think so. All the assignments are out."

"Maybe so, but if they end up laying the blame on you for what happened out there, there's no telling what else they'll do."

"I'm not going to worry about that for now and neither should you. Like you said, I got plenty of people on my side, including you, who saw exactly what went down. I didn't do anything wrong. They just need to make sure they got all their ducks in a row. That's all this is."

Dwight nodded his head. "Okay, man. You're right. I'll let you get back to it. I've got a few things to wrap up myself before heading out. I'd better call Kate and wish her luck." He stood up. "You should do the same."

» » »

Her legs were burning, but Kate pushed on. Only a quarter mile more to go, but she had no idea of how much time she'd had left. *You've done this before. Move, goddammit!*

The track was still wet from the early rains, but there would be no accommodations for the weather. Some parts of the track had puddled water and she worked to avoid them, which was throwing her off her time. She was more concerned with slipping and falling than running.

The finish line was moving in closer now and she could see it. A few of the other female trainees were ahead of her, but she had no idea how many were behind because Kate refused to look back. Only a few more feet now. Her arms and legs pumped hard; she would not fail this test. *Come on. Come on.*

Kate crossed the line and she almost stumbled over her own feet as she came to a stop. Dropping her hands to her knees, she hunched over and pulled in as much air as her lungs would take.

It seemed only moments when the man with the stopwatch approached her. "Time, 11 min., 30 sec. You passed, Reid."

Kate returned to full height and looked up to the sky, laughing. She'd done it. She'd passed the physical test. It had been a grueling day, but it was over and she made it.

Her exam results were due to be ready by the end of today, including the academics portion. But she would have enough time to get back to her room and get cleaned up.

Kate began walking back to the field where the other trainees who'd already run still waited. Will was among them. She threw her arms around him. "I passed."

He picked her up and twirled her around. "Yes!" He laughed. "Was there ever any doubt?" Will lowered her back to the ground and the other trainees clapped for her, even Hewitt.

And with each classmate that approached, all had made it and all congratulated each other.

This is my family now. Kate clapped along with the others, who were now more like brothers and sisters. They'd all been through hell and made it out the other side. But she tried hard not to be too confident. They still had to get the rest of their results.

» » »

It was late afternoon and the trainees waited inside the main classroom to meet with the instructor and it was Kate's turn.

"Reid, come on in," SSA Hawes said, holding the door open to his office. "Have a seat."

This was probably not the first time he'd seen an apprehensive student, but Kate was downright terrified.

"So, NAT Reid, you had some struggles early on, but I've been particularly pleased as to how you've handled them. I've watched you grow a great deal and I know it's because you've worked very hard to overcome a very troubling time in your past."

"Thank you, sir." Kate tried to hide her trembling hands and legs. In fact, her entire body was shaking.

"And with the work you did for SSA Scarborough, you've shown exceptional ability. He has given you an outstanding recommendation."

Kate smiled and took a breath to steady herself.

"I suppose you'd like me to get to the point?"

A brief, awkward chuckle escaped her. "Yes," She cleared her throat. "Yes, sir, please."

"Okay. Well, I won't keep you in suspense any longer." Hawes stood up. "Congratulations, Agent Reid. Welcome to the Bureau." He extended his hand.

Kate launched to her feet. A broad, irrepressible smile masked her face. "Thank you, sir. Thank you." She returned his handshake.

He held the door open for her and it was all she could do not to scream the second she walked through it. Instead, she clenched her fists and pumped them just a little bit.

Kate arrived into the room where those who had already received their passing results waited. Will was already there and he began to smile and nod his head. As soon as she entered the room, classmates approached her, hugging, slapping her on the back, and shaking her hand.

Will waited for her in the back row. "Congratulations, Agent Reid." He held out his hand.

"Congratulations, Agent Caison." She reached for his hand and pulled him forward into a hug. "We did it."

» » »

Kate arrived at the local bar near the edge of the base. Those who passed, which were all but three, were meeting there to celebrate. The graduation ceremony was on Monday and she'd phoned her parents to give them the news. She hadn't been back to see them since moving to Virginia, but she'd gotten much better at calling and staying in touch with them. Both had been supportive of her decision, even if her mother was more than a little hesitant.

Kate spotted a few of her classmates, who immediately waved her over. "Agent Reid!" one of them shouted. He'd clearly already started on the festivities. She greeted them and sat down. Kate ordered a beer.

It wasn't long before the rest of the group showed up and joined the party. In fact, Kate hadn't realized almost two hours had already passed. She was feeling pretty tipsy.

Out of the corner of her eye, she spotted Nick walking towards her. A little unsteady, she rose to her feet. "Agent Scarborough! Come and have a drink!"

Nick smiled. "Well, it looks like you all are having a good time."

The others in the group called out his name and raised their glasses to him.

"Have a drink with us, Agent Scarborough!" Will said.

"Oh no. I'd better not. Still got work to do. Just wanted to have a quick word with Agent Reid."

Nick was answered with drunken boos, but he laughed it off.

Kate tried to stand firm, but Nick had to grab her arm. "You all right?"

"Oh yeah. I'm fine." Her rosy cheeks betrayed her.

"Uh-huh. Listen, I can't stay long. I just wanted to congratulate you in person. You did a hell of a job, Kate, and I couldn't be more proud of how far you've come. Marshall would be proud too."

The smile faded from her face at the mention of his name. "I hope so. Thank you for everything Nick. I wouldn't be here without you." Kate wrapped her arms around him and held him tightly. She had come a long way and it felt good. She felt good for the first time since Marshall died. "You guys are my family now." Kate kissed his cheek.

Nick gently pulled her away. "Okay, okay, let's not get all mushy here. You're a federal agent now. We don't do that sort of thing."

Kate laughed as she wiped a tear from her cheek. "Oh yeah, that's right. You're coming to the ceremony, right?"

"Are you kidding? Of course I am. You go on back to your celebrating. You've earned it. I'll see you at the ceremony on Monday. Will your folks be there?"

"They're coming in tomorrow afternoon. It'll be the first time they'll have seen my place."

"Good. See you Monday." Nick started to leave, but not before announcing his departure with a wave. "Remember, you all are representing the Bureau now." He looked to the bartender. "Hey, don't let these guys go too overboard!"

The group booed him again. "I'm just kidding. Good night, everyone, and congratulations."

Kate sat back down and watched Nick leave the bar, the wide smile still plastered on her face. She turned towards Will and noticed he'd been looking at her. "What?"

He grinned. "Nothing. Come on; how about another beer?" He raised the pitcher to her glass and poured.

» » »

The auditorium was filled with friends and family of the graduating class. Kate waited in the wings with the others, dressed in a suit. She'd spent the weekend with her parents, showing them around the base and taking them out to eat. There was never a time she could recall seeing as much pride in their eyes. So much had happened between the three of them and although their relationship had been on the mend for some time, especially when she'd stayed with them after Marshall died, this was different. She felt their pride and their love. Now, they waited in the seats with the other family members, ready to watch her receive her credentials.

Kate peeked around the curtain and finally spotted Nick. Dwight and Georgia were sitting next to him. She was glad they were there. They'd all been there for her.

The lights dimmed and the Director of the Academy stepped up to the podium and began to speak.

"You ready to do this?" Will whispered in Kate's ear.

"You're damn right I am."

In only moments, the names would be announced and she would walk across that stage and her entire life would have transformed once again. She was getting a second chance at a new life, just as those women she'd helped to rescue would get. Conflicting feelings arose; pride and sorrow, happiness and fear, they all swirled in her head, creating a cocktail of emotion. But she was ready for this next chapter in her life to begin. She prayed it would see her through what remained of the pain and the memories, but had vowed not to expose them; not to let anyone use them against her. She had nothing else to lose.

The director began calling out the names.

The veteran agents waited for their friend's name to be called. Agent Jameson, Agent Scarborough, and Agent Myers had helped to see her through one of the most difficult periods in Kate's life and they were here for her now.

"Looks like your protégé did all right for herself," Georgia said to Nick.

"I guess she did."

"Agent Katherine Reid."

Kate walked out across the stage and stood next to the director who handed her the badge and a certificate. "Congratulations, Agent Reid."

"Thank you, sir." Kate continued to the other side of the stage, but not before glancing into the darkened auditorium to smile. She couldn't see her parents or her friends, but she knew they were there.

A few hoots and hollers erupted as they had for the other graduates and Nick put his fingers to his mouth and whistled.

The rest of the names were called and, by the end, the director introduced the newest members of the Bureau. "Congratulations, agents, and welcome to the Federal Bureau of Investigation."

The auditorium exploded in applause. Nick took to his feet with the other two following. "She did it." Nick looked to Georgia.

Dwight grabbed Nick's shoulder. "Come on; let's go see her."

The newly minted agents were walking down the steps to find their families. Kate found her parents and they embraced her.

"We're so proud of you, sweetheart," Deborah said.

John could hardly keep from tearing up.

"It's okay, Dad. I know you're proud too."

"You're darn right, I am."

Kate continued to talk to her parents until she spotted Nick. "I'll be right back." She began walking towards him.

His arms opened and he pulled her close. "Congratulations, Kate."

"Thank you, Nick. For everything." Kate turned to Dwight and tossed her arms around him, too.

Kate was soon pulled away by her parents, but a few minutes later, returned to the agents who had made the rounds to some of the other graduates.

"Nick." It had been the second time Dwight called his name.

He was still talking to Kate and Georgia and again hadn't heard him.

"Agent Scarborough." Dwight called again, louder this time.

"What?" Nick was irritated by the disruption, but on turning back, he realized why Dwight had been calling on him.

"SSA Nicholas Scarborough?"

"Yes?"

"I'm afraid you need to come with me." A man in a dark suit with a deadly stare reached for Nick's arm.

Nick quickly realized what was happening and he glanced at Dwight.

"What's going on?" Georgia asked.

"Nothing. It's fine. I'll catch up with you guys later," he said, just as cool as ever.

This wasn't right. "Where are you taking him? Nick, what's going on?" Kate asked.

Neither Nick nor the man who had a grip on him would answer. Instead, he looked to Nick again. "Sir? We need to go now."

"What the hell is going on?" Kate's nerves spiked on end and her pulse elevated.

"Nothing. Everything's fine. I just have some business to take care of. I'll see you all later, okay?" Nick placed his hand on Georgia's cheek and leaned in, lightly kissing her lips. "I'm sorry."

"Wait. What's happening here? Where are you going?" she asked.

Nick only looked at her and smiled. "I'll be fine." He turned to Kate a final time. "Congratulations, Kate." He began to follow the man out of the auditorium, neither appearing to want to cause a scene.

Kate looked at Dwight. "Do you know what the hell is happening here?"

He watched the man lead Nick out, rubbing his hand over his short, spiked hair. He turned to the women, who looked to him for answers. "Some things went down that night during the operation."

"What things? Dwight, you better tell me where they're taking him," Georgia demanded.

"We thought—Nick thought it would blow over. Jesus Christ."

Dwight was clearly shaken and Kate had never seen him like this before. It made her feel all the more nervous and afraid. She watched him struggle to find the words. "Please.

You have to tell us what's going on, Dwight. What happened out there?"

He looked at them; their inquiring faces now demanding answers. "During the chaos, bullets were flying and—shit, I don't know—but one of the suspects who went down." He stopped and took a deep breath. "They think Nick might've...he's in trouble."

THE END

ABOUT THE AUTHOR

Robin Mahle lives with her husband and two children in Arizona. She found her passion for writing, which later became her second career, after spending 20 years in the construction industry.

Having always been a lover of books, Robin attributes her creativity to the wonderful overseas adventures she has shared with her husband of 15 years. Traveling throughout Europe and having lived in England opened her mind and with that came a steady stream of story ideas inspired by her author-idols in the mystery/suspense genre.

If you enjoyed Ms. Mahle's work, please share your experience by leaving a review with your online retailer!

OTHER WORKS

Inherent Clarity
Law of Five (Redwood Violet 3)
Landslide
Beyond the Clearing
Redwood Violet (Book 1)
All the Shiny Things (Redwood Violet 2)

For more information about Robin Mahle or to see additional books already released, please visit her at:
http://Robinmahle.com or on Amazon

Also, you can keep up on all the latest news by signing up for her newsletter:
http://bit.ly/RobinMahleNewsletter

61907035R10171

Made in the USA
Lexington, KY
24 March 2017